The Foolish Duke

E.B. Featherston

Print: 979-8-9884230-1-0
Ebook: 979-8-9884230-0-3

Note from the Author

As I sit here typing out this 'note from the author' for my very first novel, I cannot help but think of everything that has led me to this point. I have always loved writing, whether it was for school, keeping a journal, or just for the fun of it.

That being said, my love of writing was nearly crushed before it ever had the chance to grow. I had the misfortune of having a writing teacher—who shall remain nameless—in the first grade, who sent me home crying on multiple occasions.

At risk of showing my age...back in elementary school, as many people my age will recall, schools provided this crappy, super thin lined paper to write on. And I, being a heavy-handed writer, never failed to go through the paper, or write so hard that any attempt to erase something would create a hole. My teacher would become irate every time I asked for a new sheet of paper. She would constantly threaten to call my parents—which she did—to tell them I would never have a career as a writer.

Fast forward a few years—college, to be precise—and I am working at a retail store in our local mall, when who would walk in? You guessed it, my dreaded writing teacher. I have changed little facially since elementary school and knew that she would instantly know who I was if she saw me. I am ashamed to admit that I hid like a coward in the back room and asked my boss to let me know when she left.

During my childhood, there were a few things that I wanted to be when I grew up, including a marine biologist, a music teacher, a chef and a writer. My marine biology dreams never came to fruition because of my horrible home sickness. So, being a huge marching band nerd, I started off my college career as a music education major. I played clarinet for thirteen years, but I quickly burned out and decided on a different path.

From there, I took my passion for cooking and graduated from culinary school. I catered for a while with my aunt's catering business, then became a chef on an operational vintage train that served fine dining as it traveled through some of the horse farms in Kentucky. Sadly, I lost my job when they closed their doors.

My husband is a thirteen-year retired Navy Veteran, and we spent much of our time moving between Virginia and New Jersey. I was constantly on the hunt for things to occupy myself, as my husband was away for extended periods, and I was often alone.

On one such occasion, I had just finished reading a regency romance novel when the urge to write took hold. That night, I picked up a pen and began writing.

Between moving wherever the military told us, my husband retiring from the Navy, jobs, and kids, my book writing got put on the back burner for a while—though it never strayed very far from my mind. One day I mentioned to my husband and my mother how badly I wanted to publish my book, and they simply looked at me and said, "then do it."

So, I end as I began. As a little girl who cried because of a writing teacher who said I would never make it as a writer, to a woman who has now cried because she proved her writing teacher wrong. And made her dream of publishing a novel a reality.

To my family and friends,
without you, none of this
would have been possible.

Prologue

Derrington Chase
March 1811

Fast as lightning, they flew—horse and master—through the dark of night, over the hills that spread before them like the vast sea, running as though the hounds of hell were nipping at their heels.

Hell, an apt word, for that is where he was headed.

Cresting the hill, Royce pulled Titan to a stop as his ancestral home came into view, unprepared for what the message he received a few days ago might mean. He had pushed Titan harder than he should have, but the horse seemed to understand the urgency and never balked at the pace he had set.

Even with the sturdy beast obeying his every command, Royce prayed he would make it in time. He would never forgive himself if he did not.

Lightning streaked across the sky, casting an ominous halo over the usually peaceful façade as fat raindrops slashed down from the dark, churning clouds, stinging his face. With a click of his tongue, Royce urged Titan forward, mud spattering his clothing with each beat of the horse's hooves.

A young man came running from the stables as they approached, and Royce tossed the reins to him as he rapidly slid from the saddle. Scrivens, a tall and rather slender man—who had been with the family for years, as had his father before him—was already standing with the door opened to allow Royce entrance.

"I wish I could say good evening, my lord, but under the circumstances, may I just say we are all thankful you are here," Scrivens said somberly, offering a weak smile.

"Thank you, Scrivens. Where is my father?" Royce tried to remain outwardly calm, though his thoughts were racing.

"He is in the Green Room, my lord."

Royce bounded up the stairs two at a time and made his way down the hall, leaving a trail of water behind him. But dripped water was the least of his concerns as he made his way toward the Green Room. The enormous clock at the end of the hall chimed the hour, lending a dark resonance to the heavy silence that had seemed to settle over the estate.

Shaking his head to wipe the sense of foreboding the chiming evoked, Royce raised his hand to knock on the door, but hesitated. Glancing over his shoulder, he looked into the Ducal bedchamber to see the bed neatly made and empty. The sadness he had not allowed himself to feel now threatened to consume him, realizing that soon that room might belong to someone else.

Taking a deep breath, Royce turned back and knocked on the door. He waited for a reply, and when none came, he gently turned the knob, letting himself into the room. Immediately, the stench of sickness assailed his nostrils, accompanied by the cloying heat emanating from the fireplace.

"Royce." A soft voice called to him.

Wilhelmina Derrington, the Duchess of Exeter, was sitting in a chair, leaning forward over the side of the bed. Her head resting upon the soft covers as she held onto the hand of the man she loved. It was painful for Royce to stand there, unsure of what he could do to lessen his mother's heartbreak as small dark circles appeared on the covers with each tear she let fall.

"How is he?" Royce whispered.

"Not good, I am afraid. The doctors have seen him, but there is nothing else they can do. His heart is sick, Royce. He does not have much time left with us." She sniffled softly, sitting up to dab her eyes with her handkerchief. "They gave him some laudanum to help ease the pain."

Royce noticed a whisper of gray had become visible in his mother's brown hair as he kneeled alongside her chair and pulled her into a loving embrace. No doubt caused by the years of dealing with the stubborn family she had raised and the man who now lay motionless in the bed.

His father was an imposing figure in his day; unbreakable, unshakeable, and had eyes that could take a man's measure with amazing accuracy. Even the most hard-nosed man thought twice before crossing him for fear of what might lie beneath his calm and collected exterior.

He had a deep-seated affection for his family while still maintaining a clear sense of his responsibilities. For many years he grappled with the hardships his father before him had brought upon the Derrington family—leaving them nearly destitute. He had worked tirelessly since assuming the title, taking care of all tenants under his care, investing wisely, and ensuring that all partners involved with those investments could be trusted. Trust, understanding, and the ability to compromise had been the foundation he had rebuilt his dukedom on.

"If you cannot prove that you are worthy of your position, a title is merely a title, Royce. You need to show those under you that you hear what they say and do your best to help them. When investing, be sure you know who you are dealing with, and do not back down until you feel you have reached the best compromise for all involved. You can be tough, but fair."

Royce remembered riding atop his father's broad shoulders while they played in the garden. His siblings always played the soldiers, while he and his father played the pirates.

"Looks like it be us against many!" His father would bellow, waving the wooden sword he swiped from one soldier. "One last kiss before I go into battle." Royce's mother would laugh as his father pulled her in for a kiss.

In his boyish eyes, his father was above reproach, honorable, and just, but the man Royce saw lying in the bed did not resemble the man he held in his memory. His father lay there barely breathing, and his face—which usually laid claim to prominent features—was now ashen and gaunt.

"Have you rested?" Royce whispered to his mother, his voice filled with concern.

"I have been by your father's side since he collapsed." She looked at Royce, her heartbreak showing in her eyes.

"Great gods, Mother. It has been three days. You must rest," he gently reprimanded her.

"I belong by your father's side, and I will not abandon him when he needs me most," she chided.

"Where are my brothers and sisters?"

"Margaret was keeping me company for a while, but I could tell she was getting restless. I sent her down the hall to help the governess keep Samuel and the twins occupied," his mother said as more tears streamed down her face. "I have sent for Grayson and Desmond, but they have yet to arrive."

Royce's eyes slowly swept across the room. The walls were light green damask, faded by the years of generous sunlight that poured through the large doors leading out onto the balcony, now shut off by an immense number of heavy drapes.

A quill and parchment lay forgotten on a desk, next to miniatures of him and each of his siblings. He looked at their smiling faces and over to the large portrait of his mother hanging above the mantle decorated with a jumble of items. Among them was a small, oddly shaped gray lump. Royce smiled as he recalled how that dull, colorless lump had become something proudly displayed on the mantelpiece.

Digging in the dirt was probably not a commonplace thing for the future heir to a dukedom, but his father had insisted that he learn every tiny detail of what he would one day oversee.

So, on a warm day, when Royce had been about five, he helped their estate gardener pull various weeds and vines out of the flowerbeds. His mother and father watched on from where they sat in the shade of a large tree. A small three-year-old

Grayson toddled around as a plump rosy-cheeked baby Desmond bounced on their mother's knee.

The gardener watched in amusement as Royce pulled and pulled on a vine that would not release its hold on the ground. Feeling very discouraged by his lack of progress, he began searching for something that might help him, and spotted a small shovel. He lifted it up and plunged it down in the soft, wet soil, striking something hard.

Royce was so curious about what he might have discovered that he began to dig. He eventually uncovered a rock which seemed to act as an anchor for the roots of the vine that were coiled around it. Determined to show his father what he could do, he planted his feet firmly on either side of the hole—his tongue sticking out in concentration—and pulled with all the might his little body could muster. With one last tug, the rock and vine broke loose, causing Royce to land on his backside with a hard thump.

Realizing he had succeeded, a smile broke across his face, and he ran to show his father, waving the rock wildly. His mother had praised him for a job well done, and here that rock sat these many years later, still gracing the mantel as though it were the greatest treasure in all the world. His eyes continued to trace down the fireplace, and he spotted a book that lay forgotten on a small table.

Every evening before going to bed, Royce and his siblings would come together around the chairs that had been placed a comfortable distance from the fire, excited about the next adventure in the book their mother had been reading.

This was the room that his mother had given birth not only to him, but to his brothers and sisters as well. It seemed only fitting that the room, which was once used to bring life into the world, was now being used by those leaving it.

A knock sounded at the door, and Scrivens—always attuned to what was needed—carried a tray laden with a light repast and tea. Royce thanked him and fetched a cup of tea for his mother, gently placing it into her shaking hands when his father stirred. Wilhelmina immediately set the cup on the table by the bed and leaned in closer, placing her hand gently on her husband's arm.

"Reginald, darling, I am here, and so is Royce." she said comfortingly.

"Royce?"

"I am right here," Royce uttered as he walked to the other side of the bed and took his father's hand. He looked down at those all-too-familiar green eyes and smiled. Unwilling to let his father see how scared he was.

"I know that we have not always seen eye to eye, but I have always strived to do the right thing. And no matter how hard I tried, there were things I could never get through that thick skull of yours," his father grumbled.

"Like father, like son," Royce quipped, his voice cracking a bit.

His father's brief rumble of laughter ended in a fit of coughs.

"I am proud of you, my boy. Watch out for this family and become the duke this family needs." Reginald turned his head and reached for Wilhelmina's hand. "I love you, my dear wife. Eventually, we will come together again, but likely not soon. Your presence is still needed here," he uttered hoarsely. "One last kiss before I go into battle?"

"I love you too." Gently, Wilhelmina rose to her feet and kissed her husband's lips, her love for him expressed through her tears and smile.

Royce heard their goodbye in the words left unspoken and bowed his head, watching his father's breaths grow slower and slower, until they ceased. The deep, reverberating bong of the clock echoed through the silence, announcing that his father's time had come to an end. Leaving Royce to start his life as the new Duke of Exeter.

Chapter 1

London, England
March 1812

Another stack of documents was placed with a mighty thud on the desk before him. Contracts, land holdings, tenants to be looked after, and bills to be paid following his father's passing had been consuming so much of Royce's time that he had yet to have a spare moment for himself.

"Will there be anything else, my lord? I-I mean, Your Grace?" the man asked hesitantly.

"Another three of me perhaps, and another five years to sort through everything," Royce grumbled, as he raked his hand through his hair and looked around.

Heaps of papers covered every available space on his desk, not a bit of its rich mahogany color visible. Except for his chair in front of the fireplace, everything in the room was covered with thick piles of papers, ledgers, and various documents. The bookshelves lining the walls were the only things holding the one thing for which they were meant.

Sighing, Royce pushed himself away from the desk and attempted to make his way through what should have been his study.

"Mr. Milby?"

"Yes, Your Grace?" Mr. Milby responded quietly. He was a tall, gangly, and timid man with mousy brown hair and had been sent as a representative of Tarpley and Thompson—his father's solicitors.

"I have been at Derrington Chase for the past year since my father passed, seeing to tenants and the like. I gave ample notice and expected everything to be in order upon my arrival back in London. Could you please explain to me why my father's records are in such disarray? I can barely imagine that he would have tolerated such carelessness." Royce tried to imitate his father's commanding tone.

"I-I have not the faintest idea, my lord...Y-Your G-Grace." Mr. Milby said as he nervously messed with the top hat in his hands.

"Have your employers send you and a few others to come organize this mess. If done quickly and correctly...perhaps I will not take my business elsewhere." Finally reaching the sideboard, Royce poured himself a drink. "Would you care for a drink, Mr. Milby?"

"Oh, no. Thank you, Your G-Grace. That is, if you have no further need of me, I have another meeting I must get to."

"Of course." Royce nodded. "Deliver my message to your employers. I will expect to see you within the week, with help, or I will search for another business that will see the job done correctly."

Mr. Milby bowed repeatedly as he backed toward the door. Being more focused on bowing rather than where he was going, he bumped into a precarious pile of papers and pieces of parchment scattered as the pile fell to the floor with an echoing thwack.

"I-I do apologize, my lord...I-I mean Your Grace."

"Leave them," Royce muttered over the rim of the glass.

"Are you quite sure, Your G-Grace?" Mr. Milby asked hesitantly.

"I said, leave them," Royce said a little more forcefully.

"As you wish. Good day, Your G-Grace." Mr. Milby bowed once more and hastily left the room, seeming relieved at being dismissed from Royce's presence.

Truthfully, Royce could not blame the man. He was in a foul mood and had been since his father had passed. Making his way to his chair, he sat, burrowing down into its comforting softness.

Nursing his drink in one hand, he covered his eyes with the other and sighed. This was a nightmare. It had been a year, and he still was not ready to take on this responsibility, though he doubted anyone ever truly was.

Royce threw back the rest of his drink. Until the solicitors got their act together and sent a few men here to make sense of everything, there was nothing further he could do.

He looked at the stack of papers Mr. Milby had knocked over and decided he should pick them up lest they become damaged. Royce bent down and riffled through the papers, picking up the few that had seen fit to scatter as they fell. He glanced about to make sure he had left nothing behind, when he noticed a letter wedged beneath the settee.

Royce picked up the letter and saw his name written in his father's elegant hand across the front. He wondered why it had been with estate records instead of being given to him directly.

He added this to the ever-growing list of things to discuss with the solicitors when they came back...if they bothered to show at all. Breaking the dark green wax seal embossed with the Exeter crest, Royce sat back down and read.

Dear Son,

If these words reach your eyes, it means I have departed from this life. Please, do not let my death cast a shadow over the time we had together as a family. Instead, let the warm, golden glow of the sun guide you toward a new chapter in your life, as you lay the foundation for the legacy you will one day leave behind.

My solicitors have been somewhat neglectful of their duties to this dukedom, and I acknowledge my responsibility for it. I have not been as vigilant as I ought to have been. These last few months have been...difficult. But I sincerely hope they have everything in reasonable order.

Royce glanced around the room. *If this is what the solicitors deemed as having everything 'in reasonable order',* it is no wonder he had not received this letter until now.

That aside, there is one more thing I have yet to address, and I would like to share it with you now, in hopes that you will grant me this last favor.

It is uncommon and even looked down upon among the Ton to marry for love. Therefore, when I married your mother, I was marrying for all the reasons the Ton deemed acceptable. Then, the day you were born, I realized what it meant to love and be loved in return.

With the best intentions in mind, I approached my closest friend, Mr. Ezra Rowntree, with this request. If you are unwed by the time you are thirty, and Mr. Rowntree's daughter Della has accepted no other suitor, I would like you to offer her your hand in marriage.

I know that my request may seem sudden, but I care for Della as if she were one of my own, and I would like to see her settled as much as her father. Mr. Rowntree is a respectable man, and I am honored to call him my most cherished of friends. This is one last thing I can do to bring the people that mean so much to me together.

Always remember, life is what we make of it. And sometimes...it has a way of reminding us that what we think we want is not always what we need. I am proud of you, my son.

Your father,
Reginald Derrington
Duke of Exeter

Royce nearly choked on his drink. He had turned thirty not two weeks ago. Before that he had spent his time at his family estate, Derrington Chase, establishing himself as the new duke. He stood abruptly and paced in front of the fireplace, raking his hand through his hair.

His mother had insisted on holding a ball to celebrate his return to London and his birthday. It had been the first event he had attended since his father passed and knew the remarks about securing a wife and producing an heir would be rampant. When his mother had mentioned the ball, he decided it was as good a time as any to begin searching for the new Duchess of Exeter.

Informing only his mother of his plans, Royce asked to be introduced to women who she deemed a good match. His only request was that she keep quiet about his intentions so marriage-minded mothers would not accost him at every turn. If those women got even a hint he was searching for a wife, they would surround him like a flock of chickens at feeding time.

The only thing Royce refrained from informing his mother of was a requirement he had imposed on himself. Of the candidates his mother presented to him, he would only consider the ones who were the opposite of what he was usually attracted to. Doing this would ensure his interest in his wife was minimal, which would decrease the likelihood of him falling in love.

At the ball, his mother presented him to several possibilities, and then she introduced him to Miss Putnam. He vaguely remembered her making her debut with his sister and Della.

Miss Putnam was the daughter of Lord Milton; graceful, with golden-blonde tresses, and a calm, but serious bearing. Within moments of being introduced, Royce had decided—without having said more than a few words to her—that she was the one he would ask to be his Duchess.

After calling on her, a few conversations at various balls, carriage rides, and one walk in the park, they came to an understanding. Miss Putnam's only request was to be formally asked to be his wife once the details with her father had been settled. She also agreed that a marriage between them would be one of convenience, nothing more. No messy entanglements, no hearts to be broken.

Her father, Lord Milton was a stocky man with a round belly that showed his fondness for food and drink. His arrogant and over-bearing personality was unappealing, but if Royce hoped to make Miss Putnam his duchess, he would have to learn to deal with the man.

He only wished Lord Milton was more concerned about the happiness and security of his daughter, rather than what doors his daughter's new title would open for him.

Royce settled back into his chair and re-read the letter, but its words remained unaltered as he let it go and watched it float to the floor. With a furrowed brow, he steepled his fingers in front of his mouth and closed his eyes. His father wanted him to propose to Della Rowntree?

He struggled to remember his last conversation with Della or if she had been among the mourners at his father's funeral, but the memories from that day were hazy. He and his best friend, Aden Carmichael, Lord Aynesworth, had been traveling the continent before his father fell ill, enjoying the revelry of being two young men without a care in the world. Unfortunately, that carefree happiness did not last, and his world was turned upside down after receiving a message from his mother, just days after returning.

What was he going to do? Well, he supposed he needed to speak with Mr. Rowntree first.

"Giles!" Royce bellowed while struggling to find his way to the desk, yet the heap of papers he had gathered impeded his progress, causing him to fall to the floor as Giles walked into the room.

"Your Grace? Your Grace, are you in here?"

"Yes..." came Royce's muffled answer as he flopped onto his back.

"Good heavens!" Giles was understandably taken aback by the sight of his employer on the floor, but he quickly regained his composure and pretended nothing unusual was occurring.

"I need to have a message sent to Mr. Rowntree."

"Right away, Your Grace." Without being asked, Giles retrieved a quill and parchment from the desk and handed it to Royce.

Royce nearly laughed at the awkwardness of the situation, but hastily scribbled a note and handed it back.

"Is there anything else I might help you with?"

"No, thank you." Royce's pride prevented him from accepting help just now. "In fact, I think I will just take a nap while I am down here."

"If you are sure."

"I am," Royce said, folding his hands behind his head.

"Very well." Giles nodded, affecting his usual unruffled demeanor. "Enjoy your nap, Your Grace."

The sound of the door clicking shut resonated in the room, marking Giles' departure, and left Royce lying amongst stacks of papers that served as a poignant reminder of a life that ended too soon. He looked around the room as the cold of the hardwood floor bit at him through his shirt and wished it would somehow freeze away his memories of that stormy night.

His mind had barely registered the faint sound of his mother's sobs or the slow, thoughtful movements of the staff as they prepared the room. Yet, the haunting image of Grayson and Desmond's faces filled with despair upon their arrival—after realizing they had missed the chance to speak with their father one last time—would be etched in his memory forever.

Once they had left, Royce remembered standing at the foot of the bed, looking down at his father's still form, willing him to take a breath, to sit up and say everything was right with the world, but he never did.

The heartbreak he witnessed his mother go through made Royce realize that marrying for love was a risk he would never be willing to take. Of course, losing one's partner would never be easy, but a thought occurred to him.

If love was never part of the equation, then perhaps losing them would be a bit more bearable. It may be unfeeling and selfish to think such things, but it would be best for everyone involved if he did not permit such a soul-destroying emotion into his marriage.

A knock on the door startled him, and Royce looked at the clock. He had been lying on the floor for nearly two hours, lost in the memories and his uncertainty.

"Your Grace?" Giles' voice came from the other side of the door. "I have a message for you."

"Enter," Royce said, scrambling over to the desk.

"A response from Mr. Rowntree." Giles handed Royce a letter.

Your Grace,
I will be at my residence for the rest of the day. Please stop by at your convenience.
Mr. Rowntree

"Thank you, Giles. Please have Titan readied."

"Yes, Your Grace. Also, your mother would like a word with you before you leave. She is in the drawing room with your sister."

"Tell her I will be there momentarily," Royce said, shifting some papers around on his desk.

Giles bowed and left the room.

Royce grabbed his coat from where it lay slung over the back of his chair and made his way toward the drawing room, wondering how he was going to handle this situation. Why would Mr. Rowntree not have said something by now if it was a request he desired to see fulfilled? Had he even told Della about the arrangement he had made with the Duke?

If not, surely Mr. Rowntree would recognize the advantage of handling the matter quietly, without Della finding out.

Royce stopped to talk to his mother where she sat sipping her tea with his sister Margaret, or Maggie, as she liked to be called. Della and Maggie had been best friends since birth. Indeed, Della Rowntree had been a part of his family for more than half his life, as their fathers had become good friends.

A mutual acquaintance had introduced his father to Mr. Rowntree, after some valuables were to arrive on a ship but had vanished without a trace. It had been said Mr. Rowntree was adept at locating lost items, capitalizing on the three ships he owned with the East India Trading Company, and the two that traversed the seas to America. And after several months of diligent work, Mr. Rowntree traced the whereabouts of the Duke's valuables and saw them returned safely.

When the Duke's praise of his work reached the ears of the Ton, many of them opened their homes to him and even hired him to find their own personal items that had gone astray. Others simply looked down their noses at the fortune Mr. Rowntree had amassed from his work in trade.

Unlike many people of the Ton, Mr. Rowntree had earned everything he possessed through hard work and dedication. Many of the men and women who considered themselves part of the upper crust of society did not possess such qualities. These people had lived lives of leisure, untouched by the toil and sweat of manual labor. Royce acknowledged that he, too, had lived a privileged life, but he had always shown respect for those who tried to improve their circumstances.

He said goodbye to his mother and Maggie after sharing his plans to meet Lord Aynesworth at White's, a gentleman's club on St. James Street, later in the evening. Knowing that Maggie would have insisted on joining him, he deliberately left out any mention of Mr. Rowntree's residence. This was not just a casual visit, but a visit that had the potential to impact his future marriage.

It was imperative that he resolved this situation before his meeting with Lord Milton and the public announcement of his engagement to Miss Putnam. And he most certainly did not want to think about the chaos that would ensue if anybody were to find out about the agreement.

Giles opened the door as Royce approached and gently closed it behind him, denying him the satisfaction of slamming the door in annoyance. Usually, when he slammed the door, anyone in his general vicinity knew not to approach him for idle chat, giving him a wide berth so they did not cross paths with an irate duke. He was not typically in a sour mood, but lately, that seemed to be the only way he presented himself.

He only wanted to do right by his father and honor the sacrifices he had made to restore the dukedom from the brink of ruin. But it was proving difficult since the solicitors hired by his father had shown themselves to be completely inept.

Swinging up onto Titan's back, Royce set off toward the Rowntree residence and concentrated on the steady rhythm of the stallion's powerful strides, letting it drown out his worries about how the conversation with Mr. Rowntree would unfold.

Chapter 2

"What business could His Grace possibly have with Father?" Della asked nonchalantly from where she sat in the morning room with her Aunt Tilly. "Ow!" she looked down at her hand where a small bead of blood appeared on her finger, having pricked it with a sewing needle.

"I have not the faintest idea, but your father said it was business of a..." Tilly looked around. "Sensitive nature," she whispered.

Aunt Tilly was a plump woman, round as she was tall, with green eyes and black hair tied back at the nape of her neck. She always had such a cheery personality that Della sometimes wondered if perhaps her aunt imbibed a little when no one was looking. Della had been all but five years of age when her mother fell ill, and Tilly had come to stay with them. Not long after, her mother passed away, and Della's father asked Tilly to stay on a more permanent basis to help watch over her.

Tilly's husband, Mr. Timothy Blatchford, had passed away at a young age before they had the chance to have children of their own. When she was still a young girl, Della had been curious why Tilly had not chosen to remarry. She remembered the wistful look on Tilly's face as she recalled her marriage to

Tim. She explained that even though their marriage had been brief, the depth of her love for her husband was not something she ever expected to feel again.

Besides, to marry another man meant risking the comfortable living Tim had left her. She had become far too used to doing what she wanted when she wanted. No other man, in Tilly's eyes, had ever been worth the risk of having those choices taken away from her.

As time passed and Della grew up, they developed their own small and special traditions. Which is how—twenty years later—they sat in the morning room, drinking tea, pretending neither of them was horrible at needle point.

"What could that possibly mean?" Della asked, looking down concernedly at her needlework. Somehow, the dog she had started out with had sprouted an extra tail and was now missing a leg. She set it on the settee, picked up her teacup, and took a sip.

Tilly shrugged. "I would wager it has something to do with the late Duke."

"Oh," was all Della said. Well...whatever business they had to discuss was of no matter. If it did not involve her, she did not feel the need to pry any further. Della looked out the doors that led out onto the terrace, a small sigh escaping her lips.

At five and twenty years old, Della was slightly taller than most women of her acquaintance. And despite not being particularly well-endowed, she had some curves that made her dresses fit decently. But her brown-blonde hair and hazel eyes could not compare to the golden-haired girls who had debuted alongside her. Especially when compared to a woman name Miss Putnam.

Radiant from head to toe, Miss Putnam had been considered a diamond of the first water when she made her debut. With a severe but beautiful countenance, Miss Putnam was quickly the object of every man's desire and was soon engaged, but her fiancé had been killed tragically in a horse racing accident.

As soon as it was appropriate, she had graced the ballrooms with renewed hopes of finding another match.

Della froze when she heard a knock at the front door and looked at Tilly. They swiftly snatched up their needlepoint and started some trivial gossip, so they were not suspected of being nosy.

"Right this way, Your Grace. Mr. Rowntree is waiting for you in his study." Croxton's voice echoed from the hall.

Della heard the tread of footsteps and caught a glimpse of Royce as he followed Croxton past where they sat in the morning room. Once they had passed, she turned to Tilly and was about to say something when a figure appeared in the doorway.

Royce wore an expertly tailored coat with a white cravat and tan breeches tucked into a pair of highly polished black hessians. His dark brown hair was short, curling slightly at its ends. Royce was a duke now, and Della supposed he had to look the part...and he did so...*very well.*

"Your Grace." Della stood, stepping on the hem of her dress, which caused her to curtsy awkwardly.

"Miss Rowntree." Royce smiled as he grasped her hand and bowed, his warm breath whispering over the backs of her fingers. "Lovely to see you. We missed you at the ball."

"I am sorry I could not make it, but Father was under the weather, and Tilly was out of town. I did not think I could enjoy myself while my father was unwell." Della looked down to where his hand still held hers, and for a brief moment, their eyes locked.

She gazed at his handsome face, at the thick eyebrows that perfectly framed his deep, captivating brown eyes...she could have looked into those eyes forever.

"I understand." Royce said softly.

Her heartbeat quickened at the sound of his voice. It was deeper than she recalled, richer, smoother. Only when Royce's hand slid from hers did her heart begin to slow its erratic rhythm. With a polite bow to her aunt, Royce left to accompany Croxton to her father's study.

Della was astounded by the changes a year could bring, how people could transform, and memories could fade. Only a year had passed since she had seen Royce at his father's funeral. But if someone had asked her to describe him, she would have been at a loss for words. She most certainly would not have been able to paint an accurate picture of the man that had just stood before her.

She took a deep breath before settling back onto the settee, her hand nervously playing with the fabric of her dress. It should have come as no surprise that the sight of Royce stirred such emotions in her. For years, she had secretly harbored feelings for him, and she would be lying if she said she had not once dreamed of Royce reciprocating her affections.

As she grew up, Della saw Royce less and less while he attended Eton. It was there he crossed paths with Aden, and they quickly became the best of friends. There had been several holidays and summers that Aden had joined the Derrington family, and Della always looked forward to seeing him.

His laughing and joking nature had been a much-needed distraction from her feelings for Royce, and he had become a good friend to her.

When Royce and Aden were of age, they left for a tour of the continent and spent a great deal of time away. Della had missed them greatly but had become accustomed to their absence. While abroad, the Duchess asked that they make their way back in time for Della and Maggie's debut.

Aden had asked Della for the honor of her first dance and Royce had danced with Maggie. But later that evening, her heart had nearly skipped a beat when Royce had offered to partner with her.

Della was sure the Duchess had put him up to it, but it did not matter. She was not about to pass up the only chance she might ever have to dance with him.

She had never been graceful, and Royce had caught her more than once as she stumbled her way through the steps, but he never mentioned it as he swept her around the room.

He smiled at her, and she at him, but the song was over all too soon, and Royce turned to bestow his smile on another young lady. In that moment, Della had realized Royce would never care for her the way she hoped he would.

He was the heir to a dukedom, forever out of her reach. And since her father held no title, she would never be worthy enough—in the eyes of the Ton—to be his duchess.

After that night, fortune hunters seemed to come from everywhere once they learned of the ridiculous amount her father had settled on her. Della herself had given up hope that there was any man who wanted her and not just her dowry.

As time went on, Royce and Aden continued their travels. Meanwhile, the Duchess and Tilly dragged Maggie and Della here and there, placing them in the paths of any eligible gentleman they deemed a good match. Della danced and talked with them, but none ever held her interest.

Many gossips of the Ton called her too picky for someone with no status, but she did not care. Della had decided the night of her debut—when she realized that she and Royce would be nothing more than friends—that she would not settle for a marriage of convenience with only mild affection. Nor would she marry a man who only wanted to use her dowry to fill his coffers.

She wanted to marry for love, like her parents had, and was more than content to wait until she found what she wanted.

She most looked forward to her weekly tea with Maggie and the Duchess at their London home and hearing the Duchess rant about the infrequency of letters from a particular son. It was the only time Della had gleaned any information about Royce and Aden, aside from the occasional gossip rag.

The Derrington and Rowntree households had become like family. The duke and duchess had been there when Della's mother had passed away, offering comfort in their time of need and, likewise, when the duke had passed. Della had felt a keen loss for the man who had been like a second father to her.

Afterward, the Duchess moved the family to their London residence permanently, stating that Derrington Chase no longer felt like a home without her husband.

Della had wondered when she would cross paths with Royce since she could not attend the ball the Duchess had hosted for him upon his return to London. She thought, perhaps, it might be at their weekly tea, but each time he had been out.

It had come as a surprise when her father announced Royce was paying them a call later, and though she said she would not pry, she had to admit; she *was* curious.

"I think I am going to stroll in the garden for a spell, should anyone need me," Della said. Tilly simply smiled and nodded.

After I stop by the study, Della thought to herself. After all, changing one's route to the garden was no big deal. It was just a fortunate coincidence that the study just *happened* to be on the way.

"Della, are you not going out the terrace doors?" Tilly asked softly.

"I am going to, uh, to get my wrap from my room first," Della quickly said the first excuse that came to her.

"What about the wrap you were just using?" Tilly motioned to the swath of fabric that lay forgotten on the settee.

"That is the wrap that I like to leave in here. I shall go upstairs and get the wrap I use outdoors."

It was a pathetic excuse, but Della did not give Tilly time to reply as she made her way into the hall. She looked around to make sure no one was about; heaven forbid someone caught her eavesdropping.

As she drew closer to the study door, Della felt torn between what she wanted to do and what she should do. She wanted to listen in on the conversation but knew she should probably walk away. Despite her best efforts, her inquisitiveness triumphed over her self-control.

Della grabbed a small, empty glass vase sitting on a nearby table and placed it against the door. Leaning closer, she pressed her ear against the cool, smooth surface , and attempted to listen in on the conversation from the other side.

"That letter should have been the first thing your father's solicitors delivered upon his death." Mr. Rowntree shook his head. "I had wondered why you had yet to approach me on the matter."

"You want me to honor the request?" Royce's voice rumbled darkly as he paced in front of the fireplace, raking his hand through his hair. It was a habit he was trying to break, but it was becoming increasingly difficult when his temper got the better of him.

"I do," Mr. Rowntree said matter-of-factly.

Mr. Ezra Rowntree was a tall, amiable man with blonde hair that had silvered at his temples. His hazel eyes had a gentle kindness to them, but also a glimmer of mischief. And his mannerisms and confident air belied his age to that of a man much younger in years.

"Mr. Rowntree, considering the circumstances, might you change your mind? I mean no offense, but I have no wish to marry Della, and I highly doubt she would want to marry me. Unaware of my father's request, I already have an understanding with Miss Putnam, and I have started to sort out the details with her father, Lord Milton."

"Brandy?" Mr. Rowntree offered as he walked toward Royce. "Did you know your father approached me several months before he passed? He explained his thoughts on the matter of your marriage should he not be here when you wed. I had my doubts, but I could see he was sincere. So, I agreed to the request of a dying man."

"You knew he was dying?" Royce asked, taking the proffered drink.

"I did." Mr. Rowntree nodded as he sat. "He swore me to secrecy and asked me never to tell you or your mother. He did not want you to worry about something that could not be changed."

"The full truth, Mr. Rowntree, if you please," Royce demanded quietly.

"Truthfully?" Mr. Rowntree looked at Royce. "I did not see the harm in agreeing if it helped put my best friend at ease." Mr. Rowntree smiled, though it did not reach his eyes.

"Besides, it is more about what I am trying to do for Della than what I want from you. I worry about her, and I simply want to help her find a bit of direction. She has turned down several offers of marriage for various reasons, all of which I have gracefully accepted. Recently, however, I am wondering if I have been too lenient in allowing her so much freedom."

"Perhaps, but even if I did not have an understanding with Miss Putnam, how would you propose I even approach this idea with Della?" Royce leaned against the fireplace, looking down as he swirled the amber liquid in his glass.

"Call on her, perhaps dance with her at a ball, walk in the square…" Mr. Rowntree listed off many things in rapid succession. Royce began to speak, but Mr. Rowntree held up his hand. "If this does not turn into anything more than a continued friendship, then so be it. Maybe your attentions will help her attract the notice of a gentleman she might find suitable."

"I do not doubt my father did what he thought would be in my best interest, and Della's." Royce sighed as he threw back the rest of his brandy and placed his glass down on the polished surface of the table. "Out of the respect I have for you and my father, I will do as you ask, *with* a few modifications of my own."

Mr. Rowntree remained silent but nodded in agreement.

"First, I will decide when and how I will fulfill what you have asked of me. I will also decide when it begins and ends. Second, I will *not* ask Della to marry me. Though nothing of my understanding with Lord Milton and Miss Putnam has been announced, I cannot, in good conscience, go back on my word to them. I will do what I can—within the bounds of propriety. But even with the attentions of a duke, it is not guaranteed that the men who notice Della will have more than two farthings to rub together," Royce said as he paced.

Memories came flooding back of Della and Maggie standing off to the side of the room. Several men surrounded them, serving as a sign of their successful debut. However, Royce recalled that there had been some men he did not want courting Della or Maggie. Many had gambling debts, were drunks, or had some questionable tastes, so he privately warned them off using the full weight of his title.

"I recall some men that pursued Della after Lord Aynesworth and I danced with her at her debut. If those are the type of men that have asked for her hand, she would be better off remaining unwed. I will speak with Lord Milton today to see if I can delay the proceedings for a short time—though I am not sure what I will tell him. He is not a man I would particularly like to cross, duke or not."

"Is there anything else, Your Grace?" Mr. Rowntree asked.

Royce stopped pacing and thought over his words carefully. "If I were to have asked Della to marry me and she had agreed, you realize it would have been a marriage of convenience and nothing more? So, my third request is this. Regardless of what happens, you will allow Della to make the final decisions regarding her future."

Royce knew that forcing a woman to do anything was an unwise decision. He had enough experience with his mother and Maggie. Both were strong-minded women who knew what they wanted and would not be told what to do. And being best friends with Maggie, Royce was sure Della would prove much the same.

Mr. Rowntree looked consideringly at Royce. "Very well, Your Grace," he said as he stood and walked to the door. "But I also have a request of you."

"And what would that be?" Royce asked, causing Mr. Rowntree to pause with his hand on the doorknob, and a sudden crash came from the other side of the door.

"Please do not mention this conversation to Della," Mr. Rowntree said, not reacting to the noise. "I may be getting older, but that does not mean I want my daughter to hasten my shuffle off the mortal coil." He chuckled at his own joke as he opened the door.

Royce inwardly laughed while maintaining his serious demeanor. "As you wish."

"Good day, Your Grace." Mr. Rowntree bowed his head.

"Good day." Royce stepped out of the study onto a small pile of broken glass; the shattered pieces crunching below his boots. The echoing of footsteps had him looking toward the back of the foyer, where he could have sworn he saw the flutter of a skirt disappear around the corner.

Chapter 3

The soft click of a handle being turned had been her only warning. Without thinking, Della let go of the vase, causing it to fall and break before she ran as quickly as she could.

Realizing she would not make it out the doors leading to the garden before being spotted, she quickly turned the corner toward the kitchens as Royce stepped out of the study. She slid to the floor, taking a deep breath to calm her nerves, and froze when she heard voices talking about the broken glass.

"Della, you idiot!" she quietly reprimanded herself as she placed a hand over her pounding heart, willing it to slow down. Della took a few moments to compose herself, and double-checked that the foyer was empty, before making her way out to the garden.

Despite the muffled conversation, she was able to distinguish enough words to gather the gist of their discussion. Apparently, the late Duke had wanted Royce to ask for her hand, the reasoning behind the request she did not fully understand, only that her father had agreed.

How could their fathers think that such an agreement would benefit her or Royce in any way?

Over time, Della and Royce had practically become strangers to each other, with little knowledge of the person the other had become. To make matters worse, the sight of Royce standing in the morning room doorway reignited the feelings she thought had faded.

Della closed her eyes as a light wind blew across her face, drawing the pungent scent of blooming roses toward her. Their small garden offered a means of escape from the hustle and bustle of London city life. Though she enjoyed all the entertainment London offered, a walk in a garden allowed her the opportunity to collect herself.

She strolled the cobbled path, taking in the beautiful scenery. The garden was a colorful display of rose bushes, and behind them were rows of immaculately trimmed hedges. Ivy wound about the trellises gracing the back of the house, reaching their leafy vines up to the balcony that sat above a wide set of French doors, leading into the morning room where Tilly still sat happily working on her needlepoint.

Della ambled past a simplistic fountain, with a handful of marble benches placed here and there, and over to a blooming cherry blossom tree. The blooms were white tinged with pink and a hint of yellow at their centers.

While all the other plants in the garden had their own beauty, this tree was the one she treasured most. When she was a child, Della and her mother had planted it together. And now, whenever she wanted to be alone with her thoughts, she would come and stand in its calming shade.

Though her mother was not there in body, Della could feel her presence, and that knowledge made her smile. She laughed to herself. If only her mother could have heard the ridiculous conversation that had just taken place.

Della knew that for some, a daughter was just a means to an end. Most matchmaking mamas and papas would happily see their daughter wed solely to improve upon their station—especially to a duke—without considering the unhappiness she might come to know.

But her parents had loved each other. It was always there in the way her mother would steal a glance at her father or how her father would kiss her mother's cheek when he thought no one was looking.

It hurt to think she may never find a man who cared for her that way. And now her father had made an agreement with Royce...to *help* her. The shame she felt in that word sent a wave of embarrassment through her.

Della paced under the tree. She did not know what she was going to do, but one thing was for certain: she would rather remain unwed than marry someone she did not love. Nor did she want to be the reason Royce's plans to move forward with his engagement to Miss Putnam went awry, regardless of her feelings for him.

It is true Miss Putnam appeared too serious and reserved, yet one could hardly find fault with her, given her father was the blustery viscount. Della could not help but laugh as she remembered a time when the man had flown into a fit of rage at a ball, all because of a minor offense. The way he had acted that night and the never-ending stream of words that had poured from his mouth had earned him the title of 'the blustery viscount' from her and Maggie.

Letting out a small sigh, Della lifted the hem of her skirt as she stepped over some flowers and made her way back to the house. Tilly had asked Della to accompany her to a ladies' group that afternoon. Some high-to-do author was making a special appearance, and Tilly thought Della might enjoy hearing what she had to say.

The path she was walking on led her past the black wrought-iron gate leading to the front of the house. She looked out toward the street and saw Royce, deep in conversation with his horse.

Royce collected his hat from Croxton and made it to the bottom of the steps as Titan was being brought over, appearing agitated. The groom informed him that Titan had taken issue with a horse named Demeter. They had gotten into a disagreement over some fresh hay, and Demeter proceeded to bite Titan on the arse.

He made his way to Titan and adjusted the bridle, offering him comforting words from his ordeal. Titan was a sleek-looking horse with an inky black coat and had proven to be the best of companions since his father had given him to Royce on his twenty-ninth birthday.

It had been the last gift he ever received from his father.

"I am sorry, my friend. I promise you, not every female is so ornery. Let us get you home, hmm?" Royce patted the side of Titan's neck before placing his foot in the stirrup.

"I would agree...we are not *all* ornery."

Royce instantly recognized the voice as he let his foot down and looked over his shoulder. Della strode toward him and smiled. The sun's gentle touch had transformed her hair into a stunning shade of golden amber; her lips rose-tinted and full, making Royce feel slightly off balance.

Titan seemed to pick up on Royce's moment of sudden lust and whinnied, startling him out of whatever trance he had been in.

"Of course." Royce nodded his head, regaining his composure. "I did not mean to offend. Only that Titan disagreed with a horse in your stables. Demeter, I believe the groom said."

"Oh, Demeter," Della said, sighing. "I am sorry. Demeter is my horse, and I am afraid your earlier statement *does* apply to her."

"No harm done, though Titan may say otherwise."

"I do apologize, Titan, and I promise that when you see Demeter again, she will be on her best behavior."

Royce watched as Della stroked the side of Titan's face. The traitorous beast leaned into the caress and lowered his head just enough to allow Della to give him a reassuring kiss on the bridge of his nose. With a hint of envy creeping up, Royce took a deep breath to compose himself. *Was he jealous of his horse?*

"I hope the meeting with my father went well, Your Grace," Della said as she continued to stroke Titan's nose.

"Indeed." Royce nervously tapped his riding crop against the side of his leg and looked at Titan, who nudged Della for stopping the affection she was showing him. It had been a long time since Royce had been at such a loss for words. "Please, call me Royce."

"What?"

"Call me Royce, like you used to before titles got in the way."

"But you are a duke now."

"I am, but I am still finding it hard not to look for my father when someone says, Your Grace."

"All right, then you must continue to call me by mine. But,"—Della held a finger up—"only when we are with family and friends or alone. Not that we will ever be alone...that is to say..."

"Della..." Royce said, noticing a light blush creep from her neck up into her cheeks at her use of words.

"I am sorry for the loss of your father," Della interjected. "I never had the opportunity to say anything to you after the funeral was over. People surrounded you and then you were...gone. I have not seen you since."

"You were there?" Royce asked, her comment taking him by surprise.

"I was, but I did not want to be in the way, so I stood in the back by the carriages with my aunt. He was an extraordinary man, your father, and I consider myself very fortunate to have known him."

"I thank you, but you should have stood with us. You were just as important to him as we were." Royce's throat tightened. "You would not have been in the way, Della."

"You have my sympathies all the same," she said softly. "I, too, know what it is like to lose a parent you love dearly, as you well know, but they never truly leave us." Della paused for a moment, seeming hesitant to continue.

"Would it be terrible if I were to ask what the meeting with my father was about?" she asked, quickly changing the subject to something a little less morose. "You do not have to share if you do not wish to. I know it is not my place to inquire about such things, but I am afraid my curiosity has gotten the better of me."

"Oh, nothing of great importance." Royce mentally cringed at the lie. "Just a business matter that needed to be settled."

"Everything is agreed upon, then?" Della asked as a slight sadness seemed to appear in her eyes.

"Just so." Royce answered, not knowing what else to say.

His answer had been evasive, but it was better than having to tell her the truth. He needed to leave before Della asked any more questions.

Royce bowed as he bid Della goodbye and pulled himself into the saddle. Titan danced around, irritated, acting like he was being forced to leave the only person who ever showed him affection.

"Oh!" Royce circled Titan back around. "Maggie and Mother asked me to remind you of your promise to have an extra teatime this week."

"Of course. I had forgotten. Thank you."

"You are most welcome—" Royce tipped his hat—"Della…"

As she watched them go, Della tried to hold back the tears that threatened to fall.

Nothing of great importance.

Though his words were not intentionally hurtful, they still stung. But Della could not be resentful toward Royce. To judge him for his reply when he was unaware of her having eavesdropped on his conversation with her father would be unfair.

Her question had probably left him scrambling for an answer that would satisfy her without revealing too much. Regardless, his words had cut deeply.

Della headed up the steps of the front door and paused when Tilly's cat Hypnos rubbed against her skirts.

"There you are, you little troublemaker," she said in a playful tone as she bent down to scoop the mischievous cat into her arms. "Tilly has been looking everywhere for you since you escaped this morning."

Continuing up the stairs, she felt the gentle vibration of Hypnos' purring beneath her fingertips as she scratched him behind the ear.

Perhaps her father and—though she loathed to admit it—the Ton were correct. Maybe she was too picky. Had she been anyone else, she likely would have leaped at the opportunity to become Royce's duchess, whether he was engaged or not.

But Della was not another woman. She did not see the need to chase after a man—who would soon belong to someone else—hoping he might change his mind. Besides, a title did not recommend a man's character, nor was there any assurance the man who held the title was not a loathsome person in secrecy.

When she was younger, Della used to imagine what being married to Royce might be like. The stories she read had made her hope for a fairy tale ending where the prince and princess lived happily ever after.

While a small part of her still clung to the idea of a fairy tale marriage, she understood that real life was much more complicated.

If she were to marry Royce, she would put in every effort to ensure their union was a happy one. And knowing him, he would do the same, trying to ensure a promising start to their marriage. But after a few years of being stuck in a marriage he did not want, married to a wife he did not choose, what then? Would he take a mistress? Would she take a lover?

Her father had always been supportive of her choices, but as each season passed, she noticed the subtle hint of worry on his face whenever he spoke to her about securing her future. Perhaps that is why he had accepted the agreement with the late duke.

But to marry Royce solely for that reason was about as far from a fairytale marriage as you could get...and she could not bear the thought of him eventually despising her because of it.

Chapter 4

A few days later, and clad in her favorite soft blue walking dress, Della walked to the Derrington's home for their extra weekly tea.

Many would frown upon her walking without someone to accompany her though the park, but Della was tired of all the strictures placed upon a woman. It was broad daylight, and she simply could not see the harm in her decision to walk unescorted in such a busy place.

As she walked along the path, a barouche rolled by slowly, its hood pulled back, revealing three young children sitting on one side and two adults on the other.

Two of the children were engaged in a heated argument, their voices growing louder and louder. Meanwhile, the third child, no doubt the youngest of the three, sat helplessly between them, desperately covering his ears to block out the yelling match he had become an unwilling participant of.

"Shut it, will you?!" the little boy finally blurted out. The two girls immediately went silent and looked down at the small boy with an expression that showed they had forgotten he was there.

"Well, Hortense started it, really. I told her we should feed the ducks and then have the picnic," the girl shouted.

"And I was merely suggesting to Ophelia that it made more sense to picnic first and then feed the ducks because we could give them whatever we had left over," Hortense huffed, crossing her arms.

And just like that, the two girls launched back into their debate, neither willing to back down. The little boy, finally having had enough, stood, switched seats, and wiggled himself between his parents...right as his father leaned over and kissed his mother on the cheek. With a groan, the little boy slapped his hands over his eyes.

Della had to laugh. She envied them. Though the little boy may not think so now, he did not know how lucky he was to have a family who obviously loved each other. When she was young, Della always envisioned getting married and having children. But with the way things seemed to be going, she might be destined for a life better suited to a spinster

After her introduction to society, many suitors had expressed an interest in her, some even going so far as to approach her father for her hand, but she could never bring herself to accept any of them.

She was certain that had she revealed her single condition for accepting their proposal, her suitors would have fled without a second thought. They would proclaim her foolish to reject sensible offers for such a trivial emotion that had no business in a marriage. If love was so insignificant, why did her heart suffer when someone she cared for was no longer with her?

What was it about the word *love* that made men seem to tremble in fear? She had once told Lord Berwick that she would not settle for anything less in a marriage while they had been dancing. After the dance had ended, he quickly returned her to her aunt's side, bowed, and dashed back across the dance floor.

His sudden departure had mortified Della, but the man inquired what she valued most from a marriage, and she had responded honestly. Men pretended like they had everything under control, yet when the word love was uttered, they acted as if war had been declared. And they said women were the one with the more *delicate* sensibilities?

Della walked through the gate and up the steps of the sweeping staircase that led to the front door of the Derrington's London home; letting her hands float lightly over the silken petals of the flowers cascading down the railings. What was wrong with having the desire to love and be loved in return? Landing on the top step, she pushed that thought aside and knocked on the door.

"Miss Rowntree." Giles bowed.

"Della!"

Della looked up to see Victoria and Cornelia, the youngest Derrington's, scramble down the steps, tripping over each other in their haste to greet her. She readied herself for impact as they came together and wrapped their arms around her.

Though twins, they looked nothing alike. Victoria had pale skin with a high color in her cheeks, light brown hair, and mischievous eyes bluer than a cloudless sky. Cornelia was a slightly less dramatic copy of Maggie, with skin like porcelain, black hair, and golden-brown eyes. Both were going to be many a man's downfall when they were older.

"Hello, poppets." Della smiled as two sets of expectant eyes peered up at her, and she bent down to hug them. "Look at what I brought for you." Della reached into her reticule and pulled out a small tin of peppermints. "Now, do not tell your mother about these. It will be our little secret."

"Mum's the word."

Della heard the familiar voice and glanced over Victoria's shoulder at the masculine figure heading toward them. "Your Grace," she smiled as she stood and gave a small curtsy.

"Royce," he corrected.

"Royce," Della repeated hesitantly. "I-I just came for tea with Maggie and your mother, as you kindly reminded me the other day."

Victoria and Cornelia looked back and forth between Della and their brother. Although they were only eight years old, they had an astonishing capacity for noticing details. Della was worried that anything she said or did would be remembered and used against her, so she did her best to remain vigilant about how she behaved when in their presence.

"Why do you not just ask Della to marry you?" Victoria asked her brother.

"Yes, why do you not marry Della, Royce?" Cornelia asked, backing up her sister's question. "She brings us the most wonderful gifts, and if you marry her, she can bring us gifts all the time!"

Trying to conceal her smile, Della put her hand in front of her mouth as Royce stood there, seemingly unable to come up with an answer. When the governess's voice called for the girls, the awkwardness of the moment was broken, and Royce seemed to relax, thankful that he did not have to reply.

"Coming, Miss Cora!" they said in unison. Both girls turned their big, all too-knowing eyes on their brother. "Can we keep them please, oh please? We promise we will not spoil our supper."

Della silently laughed at Royce's apparent reluctance to give in to their pleading. Having regained his composure, he bent down on one knee.

"I will tell you what," he said, simultaneously tapping them on the nose. "If you both promise not to cause trouble and behave for your governess, I will say nothing to Mother."

The girls' eyes lit up, and Della could see the admiration they had for their brother. They wrapped their arms around his neck, and Royce smiled. Victoria and Cornelia cheered and sprinted to where their governess waited to take them out for their afternoon stroll.

"Maggie and Mother are in the morning room, I believe." Royce straightened his coat as he stood and motioned for Della to go ahead of him. Upon entering the room, Royce uttered his apologies—stating he needed to pay a surprise visit to his solicitors—and left.

"Men!" Maggie exclaimed. "Always in a rush to be somewhere else."

Maggie Derrington was a passionate beauty, to say the least. With her doe-like brown eyes, dark brown hair, and fair complexion, the daughter of a duke and now the sister of a duke, she had men practically falling at her feet.

"Well, Della, dear," the Duchess said, ignoring her melodramatic daughter. "How are you?"

Della opened her mouth to speak when Giles announced Mrs. Imogen Derrington. Imogen bustled into the room with her purple skirts rustling from side to side, and her orange wrap pulled tightly around her slender frame. Della's gaze drifted upward, past her pinched expression, to the matching orange turban that sat atop her head, embellished with a white plume feather.

She was married to Archibald Derrington, the late Duke's brother. Between them, they had Maggie's five cousins; Ace, Edwin, James, Pearl, and Anna—who all seemed to have developed their father's far kinder and more jovial personality.

Imogen was a gossip of the worst sort, having an unbelievably lousy habit of taking things out of context. She also had a way of looking down her nose at you—making her appear almost cross-eyed—should you show even the slightest bit of impropriety.

"Ah, there you are, Wilhelmina! I cannot believe it! I just cannot believe it! Do you know the horrid rumors circulating around the Ton about Royce?!"

"Calm down, Imogen," the Duchess said calmly. "Sit, have some tea, and tell me what is wrong." As she prepared the tea, Imogen talked about the latest scandal involving her nephew.

"It is said that Royce and Miss Putnam's announcement of their engagement was postponed because Royce intends to cry off!" Imogen exclaimed.

"The ridiculousness of the statement caused Della to scoff inwardly. She may not have heard parts of her father and Royce's conversation, but she was almost certain Royce still had every intention of marrying Miss Putnam."

One thing Della *was* sure of was that listening to Imogen go on and on was giving her a headache. From a young age, Della was taught to always keep her voice controlled and level, that it should never rise to an unbecoming volume. However, Imogen's voice was beginning to resemble a squawking bird.

The colors of her dress and turban, along with the plumed feather swaying in time with her lively head motions, only painted a more vivid picture in Della's mind. To suppress the giggle that was threatening to escape, she quickly took a sip of her tea.

"Della?"

Della jumped a little and peered over the edge of her teacup to see the Duchess, Imogen, and Maggie staring at her, waiting for a response.

Gently, she set her cup down on the table. "I am sorry, Your Grace. Did you ask me something?"

The Duchess' lips quirked up into a small, knowing smile. Showing that perhaps she, too, would rather have been doing anything than listening to Imogen's ranting.

"I asked if you would like some more tea, dear."

"No, thank you, Your Grace," Della replied.

After tea, Maggie asked Della to walk in the garden. Arm in arm, they strolled as Maggie gave her honest opinion about the gossip Imogen had relayed to them.

Della, of course, knew the reason for the uproar, though she certainly could not tell Maggie that. No matter how badly she might want to. She knew what Maggie was like and did not want her to complicate matters by interfering, regardless of how good her intentions might be.

"I am curious about what made my brother change his mind," Maggie mused out loud.

"About what?" Della feigned ignorance.

"About his understanding with Miss Putnam, of course. Were you even listening to what my aunt was saying?"

Della shook her head. "Not really. I was...distracted."

"According to Imogen, Royce has asked Lord Milton if they could wait before announcing his and Miss Putnam's engagement. Whatever it is, it must be incredibly important for him to even ask for such a favor. Mother will, undoubtedly, be furious that she had to find out from Imogen and not directly from Royce. Especially since he was here when you arrived and could have told her then." Maggie laughed. "I do hope I am present when Mother gives him a piece of her mind."

"You cannot always believe the gossip that circulates, Maggie, even if there might be some truth behind what is being said. And we both know the Duchess will do her best to stop the rumor before it gets out of hand. Though with people like Imogen spreading the rumor, she has her work cut out for her. But if Royce has changed his mind, there is not much your mother can do about his decision; he is a duke, after all."

"Are we talking about the same woman?" Maggie asked incredulously. "She was elated that Royce had finally decided to find a wife."

Della shrugged. "Miss Putnam is a good choice, even if she is a bit too serious. And I am sure this rumor will not simplify matters for her, considering everything she has endured from her first engagement.

"You speak far kinder of her than I would. Do you not remember how horribly she treated us during our first season?"

"People can change," Della said thoughtfully.

"I suppose...but do you know what I wish? I wish *you* were the one marrying Royce."

"First your sisters and now you? Do not be ridiculous! Royce has no designs on me whatsoever."

"Oh, it is not so ridiculous," Maggie said as they made a turn back to the house. "Just think of the look on the blustery viscount's face if you stole the duke away from his greedy social climbing hands."

"I would rather not. Especially if that look is directed at me. Besides, I do not have the good fortune of having an older brother to come to my rescue."

"That is true, but you could have a *husband*, who is a duke, to watch out for you." Maggie winked teasingly.

"Where did you get such a notion?" Della rolled her eyes when a thought occurred to her. "I am curious about one thing."

"Only one thing?" Maggie inquired, seeming genuinely confused why Della's list was so short.

"Who started the rumor?"

Maggie seemed to think the question over for a moment. "Perhaps the servants overheard the conversation. They see *all* and to risk them overhearing is to risk information getting out. If this gossip has circulated enough that Lord Milton has heard the Ton knows, heads will start rolling. He will not suffer this embarrassment lightly, nor be made a fool of. I fear the repercussions for Royce if he has changed his mind. But he is a man *with* a title, and the repercussions for them are rarely as bad as what a woman suffers in the same situation."

"But we do not truly know what Royce has decided. So far, we have only received gossip from Imogen, and we both know she is not the most reliable of sources. Unfortunately, no matter how the rumor started, the Ton will act as though there will be no engagement at all. The Ton at large cares naught for the truth. They merely pick a small bit of it and spin it around to make for a more interesting story."

Maggie nodded in agreement. "It will be interesting to hear what Royce has to say on the matter. If he is even willing to tell us anything."

They strolled to the foyer and Della bid farewell, promising to attend a ladies' luncheon the Duchess would host soon.

She tied the ribbon of her hat beneath her chin and made her way down the front steps. Maggie had caught her completely off guard during their conversation about Royce. Victoria and Cornelia had as well, but she was positive their suggestion had only come about because of the tin of peppermints she had brought to them and their hope of receiving more in the future.

Della was unsure of what do to about this mess her father—though he was not fully to blame—had created. Perhaps it would be easier to pretend the agreement did not exist. It is not as if anything had really changed. Royce was still going to marry Miss Putnam, and she was still determined to marry for love. She absentmindedly walked through the gate and turned toward home.

"Oomph." Della bumped into something solid and unyielding, like a brick wall, as two hands shot out and pulled her so close the brim of her hat folded down over her face.

She did not move, desiring to disappear and hide from the embarrassment for not watching where she was going. Still, an apology was probably in order.

Della tilted her head back—the brim of her hat flipping back into place—to see who she had run into.

Chapter 5

The solicitors had tried to placate him—after he paid them an unexpected visit—with meaningless words and guaranteed that everything would be in order by the end of the week. Despite their assurances, Royce had little faith in their ability to follow through on what they promised.

As he arrived at the stable with Titan, his mother and Imogen walked out from the garden to greet him. They mentioned the rumors that had started to circulate, and expressed their concerns about the potential consequences of such rumors. Royce assured them he and Miss Putnam still had an understanding, and there was no need to worry.

Once they were content that all was as it should be, they ventured back into the garden. Royce walked toward the front gate in the opposite direction, seeking quiet to clear his mind and gather his thoughts.

But try as he might, he could not think of anyone who would have known about the postponement besides Lord Milton. And it was with one-hundred percent certainty that Royce could say Lord Milton would not have started the rumor himself.

His meeting with Lord Milton had not gone well, but it had not been as bad as he had perhaps expected it to be. And when asked for an explanation, Royce had told him that pressing estate business would keep him from giving the engagement all the attention it deserved.

Begrudgingly, Lord Milton had agreed, and Royce had let out a small sigh of relief. But now this rumor threatened to undo everything. How was he supposed to balance this and his agreement with Mr. Rowntree at the same time?

He turned the corner and was taken by surprise as a woman bumped into him, causing him to swiftly reach out and steady her before she lost her balance. Royce looked down as the brim of the women's bonnet popped back into place and saw Della's beautiful eyes staring up at him.

"I am sorry, Your Grace. I was just on my way home and was not paying attention to where I was going." Della wiggled, trying to free herself from Royce's grasp.

Royce released her, clearing his throat as he took a step back. "The fault is not entirely yours. I was not watching either." He took a moment to look around and realized Della was by herself. "Who escorted you here?"

"I walked here on my own. Surely you noticed that when I arrived earlier?"

"I had assumed your lady's maid escorted you and had already gone down to the kitchens."

"Well, as you can see, I seem to have managed just fine on my own." Della smiled.

"Allow me to escort you back home."

"There really is no need," Della said irritably. "I am fully capable of walking myself home. It is just a few streets over and through the park."

She attempted to step around him.

"Entertain me then," Royce said, as he stepped back in front of her.

"Men..." Della said with an exasperated sigh. "Always looking to play the part of the conquering hero."

Though Della was disappointed with her father for asking Royce to fulfill the late Duke's request, her disappointment in Royce was greater. She knew what his marriage plans entailed, and those plans did not include her.

So why had he not trusted her enough to mention anything? Della thought herself to be a reasonable and level-headed person. Perhaps he feared how she might react?

Della glanced up in contemplation at Royce's profile, cocking her head to the side; he was so handsome.

"Something on your mind?" Royce asked.

Della averted her eyes and blushed at being caught staring so openly at Royce. "I was just thinking about when we were children. Do you remember Maggie and I chasing you, Grayson, Desmond, and Aden, for having stuck a toad in Maggie's face?"

A small smile spread across Royce's face as he seemed to recall that day. "I remember you coming to Maggie's rescue and reprimanding us."

"She is my best friend. Of course I came to her rescue."

They both laughed at the memory.

"You would have made an excellent governess. Mother and father laughed when they heard about how you scolded us. I miss those days," he sighed and continued. "The days of doing things because we wanted to, not because we had to."

Suddenly, Royce looked tired, like the world's weight was on his shoulders.

They fell into a companionable silence until they reached the entrance of her home. Della stopped to smell a rose that had bloomed on the bushes lining the balustrades that bordered the steps. She remembered pretending to be a character from one of her favorite stories when she was a little girl, La Belle et la Bête. A story of a beautiful girl, whom they called Beauty, and the Beast that imprisoned her because her father stole a rose.

"Are your father or aunt aware that you insist on walking without an escort or your lady's maid?" Royce asked as he knocked on the door.

Della looked down at the ground guiltily.

"I thought as much," he said when she did not reply. "Please allow me to do the honor of escorting you, with Maggie, of course, if you have somewhere you would like to go. It would give me peace of mind knowing you are safe and give us a chance to talk. We have done very little talking these past few years."

"Indeed, we have talked little until recently," Della said. "And I appreciate the offer, Your Grace, but—"

"Royce" he corrected.

Della looked around. "Royce…" she said quickly, hoping no one had overheard her call a duke by his given name.

"Please send a message when you need me, and I will clear my schedule."

Royce bowed over her hand and bid her farewell as Croxton opened the door.

Della watched Royce's retreating form, and her heart ached for him, for the boy he used to be, and for the boy he wished he could still be. But like everyone must, they had to grow up at some point. Each with their own role they had to play in the world.

Her only hope was that when Royce eventually married Miss Putnam, she would rise to the challenge of easing some of his burdens.

Later that evening, after turning down several offers for entertainment, Royce paced in front of the fireplace in his study.

Thanks to his surprise visit, the solicitors finally seemed to take his threats of seeking a different business seriously and sent people almost immediately. The study was not finished, but with the progress they had made, it had become somewhat usable.

"I do not understand what has you in such an uproar," Aden said, twisting a gold signet ring on his finger. "You got out of asking Della to marry you and agreed to be, what exactly? Bait?

A guide to help her draw the attention of someone she might find agreeable to marry?"

"More or less."

"That should be easy enough. And...you managed to avoid the parson's mousetrap with Miss Putnam for a short time. All while still being able to enjoy the company of both women." Aden waggled his eyebrows.

"Do not be crass."

Aden Carmichael was the first son and only child of the Earl of Jersey, and had been Royce's closest friend since they had met at Eton. He had been labeled as the Ton's very own Adonis—the Greek god of beauty and desire—with hair so blond it took on a silvery glow and piercing blue eyes.

So handsome as to be considered pretty, one had to be wary of how long they stared at him lest they become smitten themselves.

"I recall a young lordling who used to think along those same lines." Aden shrugged. Possessing his looks and that devil-may-care attitude, it was no wonder matchmaking mamas with impressionable daughters steered clear of his path.

"Some of us had to grow up," Royce grumbled as he paced around his study.

Aden ignored Royce's jab. Setting his glass on the table as he leaned forward, Aden rested his elbows on his knees and clasped his hands. "If you are asking for my opinion..."

"I do not think I was," Royce replied sarcastically.

"Oh, you were, otherwise you would not have told me about this at all."

Royce could not deny what Aden said was true. He was looking for advice to help him get through this situation as quickly and as painlessly as possible.

"If you are asking my opinion," Aden repeated. "There might be a solution to your problems."

"And what, pray tell, would that be, exactly?"

Aden got down on one knee before Royce and placed a hand over his heart. "You must marry me instead."

It was silent for a split second before both men burst into laughter.

"You flatter me, but I would sooner be married to a horse's arse than married to you."

"And thus, he fell, as words of rejection speared him through his heart. Argrrgh..." Aden collapsed to the floor in a pretend but very convincing fit of agony.

"So, what is your solution?" Royce asked, helping his friend up from the floor.

"Look." Aden busied himself brushing out the wrinkles from his coat. "You want to marry Miss Putnam, and fulfill what you promised to Mr. Rowntree, correct?"

"Of course I do!" Royce said defensively, acting as though Aden were mad to think otherwise.

"And marrying for love is out of the question?"

"It is. Miss Putnam and I agreed this would be a marriage of convenience."

Aden considered Royce for a moment before continuing. "Then your solution is simple."

"Simple?" Royce looked at Aden as though he had sprouted two heads.

"Allow *me* to ask Della for her hand."

The moment of silence that hung between Royce and Aden was palpable. He must have misunderstood. Aden wanted to ask Della to *marry* him. Royce stood there; his brow furrowed as he contemplated the potential of such a proposition.

"You would ask Della to marry you?" Royce asked, breaking the silence. "*You*, who chases everything wearing a skirt?"

"I would." Aden nodded. "Listen, neither of us wants to see Della hurt. I think she and I would scratch along well, considering that I have known her almost as long as you have. It would save me the trouble of having to grace many a ballroom to find a wife who could hold a reasonably intelligent conversation. She is smart, witty, and lovely, inside and out."

Royce could not disagree with how Aden described Della. She was all those things and more. The sudden admission caused his eyes to widen, and he opened his mouth to respond, only to close it without uttering a word.

He could tell Aden meant what he said about offering for Della and pictured what their life would look like. Aden would wake up every morning with Della in his arms and kiss her every night before they went to bed.

Their older children would frolic in the gardens while they played with their youngest on a blanket beneath a shady tree.

Taking a deep breath, Royce shook his head to erase a future that did not involve him. "There is no allowing. I cannot stop you from asking Della, but I do not know if she would accept."

"The only way to find out, my friend, is to ask her," Aden said, as he placed his hat on his head and gave it a light tap. "Well, I am off. I have a meeting at the club I would hate to miss." Aden winked at Royce, and with a wave of his hand, he swept into an exaggerated bow and quit the room.

Royce made his way over to the sideboard, wondering where the sudden desire to punch something had come from. Finding his drink of choice, he tossed the top over his shoulder and drank straight from the bottle; welcoming the slow burn as it slid down his throat.

He could not think of a logical explanation for the intense irritation he felt at the thought of Aden seeking Della's hand. Aden was his best friend, and probably the best person to offer for Della out of the men who circulated amongst the Ton. And if Della said yes, there would be nothing to say against the union. But this feeling of uncertainty would not subside.

Sure, Aden had had his share of women, but if he were to marry Della, he would be faithful to her or risk the displeasure of the Rowntree and Derrington families. Royce set the bottle down and leaned against the wall.

Should Della accept the proposal, he would no longer be obliged to pay her attention, having already ensured her a suitable match. But there was no guarantee she *would* accept.

If she did not, Royce would still be honor-bound to do what he promised.

But if Aden's solution was so simple and straightforward, why did it leave such a bitter taste in his mouth?

Royce raked his hand through his hair.

Perhaps it was because he utterly disliked the idea of trying to manage someone's life without their knowledge. He should tell Della, she deserved to know the truth. And since no one else knew about this agreement, aside from Mr. Rowntree, it would be up to him to tell her.

With Aden gone, and his family and servants asleep, Royce grabbed the bottle, and stormed up the stairs, hoping some rest would help bring some clarity to this entire situation.

Chapter 6

There was a knock, and then some more knocking. Sprawled on his stomach, Royce opened his eyes; the room was too bright, and his head ached. Exhausted, he grunted as he lifted his head and glanced in the door's direction. That seemed to be where the noise was coming from...or had it been part of his dream?

A slight smile tugged at the corners of Royce's mouth. His dream had been so vivid and explicit that he could still see the image of a woman, naked and radiant, lying on his bed.

She had been on top of him, below him, and in every position imaginable. Royce remembered his gaze roaming over her form as his fingertips caressed every dip and curve, tracing a line up her neck and tucking a stray wave of amber-colored hair behind her ear.

But then he remembered the way her hazel eyes looked up at him lovingly, and his smile quickly fell from his face. Royce ran through the dream in his head several times and could not recall picturing anyone but Della. Bloody hell. The banging resumed, and he dropped his face into his pillow.

"Royce...Royce! If you are in there, answer me, or I will have Mother come up here. And heaven save you if I must do so. I will give you to the count of three to open this door. One...Two..."

Royce drew the blankets up, having divested himself of everything the night before. He found sleeping in the nude to be invigorating and only used a robe when he needed to leave his room for something in the middle of the night.

"For God's sake, come in and stop banging on the door, will you?" Royce yelled.

The door burst open as Maggie flew into the room with her hands fisted on her hips. "You look horrible."

"Thank you," Royce mumbled into his pillow.

"Giles!"

Royce winced as Maggie's call echoed through his head.

"Yes, my lady?" Giles said, slipping into the room.

"See that His Grace is given coffee and some sustenance, please. Then he is to be shaven, dressed, and report downstairs within the hour."

"Yes, my lady." Giles bowed and left to do Maggie's bidding.

"And here I thought I was the master of this house," Royce said in response to Maggie's high-handedness.

"Not when the master of the house looks as though he was robbed or perhaps drank a bit too much. But, seeing as everything seems to still be here, and the owner looks like he got trampled by a horse, I will go with the latter."

"Must you shout?" Royce groaned as he sat up. "Hand me my robe, will you?"

Maggie crossed over to where the robe hung on the bottom post of the bed, picked it up, and threw it at Royce.

Royce sat there on the bed with his robe hanging over his head. "You know you should not be in here. It is not proper," he said as he pulled his robe on and threw a pillow at Maggie.

"You are to escort us around today," Maggie said, catching the pillow and throwing it back at him. "We have several places to visit before the Bellamy's ball tonight. Della sent word, and she said we were to inform you should we desire to go out."

"Correction—" Royce held up a finger—"I told Della to send a messenger if *she* wanted to go somewhere and did not have an escort. Last time I checked, you were not a messenger, nor did I give you permission to read my correspondence."

"I did not read it. Mother did," Maggie said with far too much enthusiasm.

"I will have to have a word with mother. She should not be reading my correspondence without my knowledge. But it comes as no surprise that she sent you to deliver the message."

"I was not sent. I volunteered."

"Of course you did." Royce rolled his eyes.

"Why did you offer to escort Della, and when did you talk to her?"

"I spoke to her after we literally bumped into each other as she walked home from tea with you and Mother. Did you know she came without an escort yesterday?"

"She always does." Maggie waved a dismissive hand. "And you did not answer my question."

"Not even her lady's maid?"

"It is not like she must go far, and Mother knows. You talk as though she has committed an egregious act. There really is no point—"

"The *point*," Royce was quick to interject, "is that neither of you should go anywhere alone. It is very irresponsible of her aunt and father if they do not notice that she does so. And even more irresponsible that our mother knows and does nothing about it."

"Why are you suddenly so protective? Della is not your responsibility, dear brother." Maggie tapped her toe in an irritated fashion. "Why did you offer to escort her around?" she repeated.

"I figured she needed some form of protection, seeing as how she must endure your company so often." Royce sarcastically answered Maggie's question without giving her the truth.

Maggie stuck her tongue out at Royce when Giles appeared in the doorway, holding a towel and a basin of water. Royce let out a silent sigh of relief. Thank heavens for Giles' arrival.

"I will see you downstairs within the hour!" Maggie reminded him, ending their conversation as she swept from the room.

Giles moved swiftly and efficiently around, pulling everything together that he would need for the day. Royce thought for a moment. Escorting Della, his mother, and Maggie could work in his favor—and he had promised he would.

Many gentlemen would be in and out of shops this time of day, and until Aden decided if he was serious about offering for Della, Royce had to continue as if nothing had changed. He sighed. At least it was a starting point until he figured out his next move.

Royce got up and made his way into the dressing room to ready himself for what was sure to be an interesting day.

Della sat alone in the dining room, eating breakfast. Her father had left earlier for a meeting about a business he had planned to acquire. And Tilly, feeling under the weather, elected to have breakfast in her room. Not having much of an appetite herself, Della absentmindedly moved the food around the plate.

"We are here!"

Della nearly jumped out of her seat, her fork clanking against her plate as Maggie came charging into the room. Croxton hurried after her, looking crossly at Maggie for denying him the opportunity to announce her arrival.

"Thank you, Croxton." Della looked at the man with sympathy.

Croxton bowed and left the room, but not before throwing a quick exasperated look in Maggie's direction.

"What?" Maggie asked when Della looked at her with her eyebrow raised.

"Have a care for poor Croxton. Could you maybe, just once, let him announce you before you come bursting into the room?" Della asked, taking the last sip of her morning chocolate.

"Bah, he should be used to it by now." Maggie waved her hand dismissively.

"Be that as it may," Della laughed. "Just so we do not have to hire someone new, allow him to announce you...just once."

"Fine," Maggie said exasperatedly, plopping down in the seat. "But I make no promises on anything past that."

"I guess that is all one could ask for," Della said bemusedly. "Thank you."

"You say *thank you* as though I have no care for other people. I care about them greatly, but I am a busy woman. I simply do not have the time to wait for an announcement of my arrival every time I come here." Maggie slumped back into her chair. "Well, let us go!" She abruptly stood, as if remembering why she was there. "I have already informed Royce that he is to accompany us today as you asked me to do."

"But I did not ask you to tell him that. I sent *him* a message."

"You did...but then mother read it and I told him."

"How did your mother know there was nothing in that message that was to remain private?" Della asked.

Maggie shrugged. "I think since it came from you, she figured it would be safe to read it."

Even though she trusted Maggie and the Duchess implicitly, Della could not help but feel a twinge of unease knowing her letters to Royce were being read before they reached him.

"Let us go. Royce and the rest of the family are waiting for us. We have so much to do and so little time before the Bellamy's ball tonight!"

Just about that time, Della looked out the window to see Royce go around to the stables. Puzzled, she headed to the front door and before she could finish tying the ribbon on her bonnet, Maggie linked arms with her and practically dragged her outside.

Della looked into the carriage and saw not only the Duchess, but Samuel, and the twins—accompanied by their governess. She had not expected this small trip to turn into an excursion for the Derrington family. Especially since she only needed to pick up a book she had ordered.

"Della," the Duchess called out. "The carriage is full up, I am afraid." She gave Della an apologetic look. "Would you mind riding with Maggie and Royce alongside the carriage?"

"It would be no problem at all, Your Grace."

"Thank you, dear. Royce has already gone around to have your horse readied."

Della's eyes went wide, remembering the last interaction Titan and Demeter had been involved in. She looked where Titan stood innocently munching on some grass. Poor horse, he was in for a surprise.

The clacking of hooves made Titan's ears perk up, and he shifted restlessly. At the first sight of Demeter, he whinnied and pulled on the leads, nearly lifting the groom from the ground. Demeter was pulled up next to Titan, who eyed Royce with a look of betrayal and snorted his discontent.

"Your horse has a clear lack of respect for boundaries. I tried to be kind and retrieved a fresh carrot the groom had waiting for her. But apparently the only thing she cared about was finding the opportunity to sink her teeth into something else."

Royce grumbled, turning to show the smeared dirt and hay stuck to the back of his coattails. He stepped closer to Della as everyone in the carriage laughed at his obvious displeasure.

Della's breath hitched, his nearness filling her with nervous excitement as Royce gently lifted her up onto the saddle, and slowly released his grip, allowing his hand to leisurely move down to rest on her knee.

"If everyone is ready, we must hurry. We need to get to Madame Delphine's before she closes," the Duchess said.

Royce acknowledged his mother with a nod, his fingers delicately caressing the fabric of Della's dress before he shifted and turned to look at Titan. Placing his foot in the stirrup, he gracefully swung his leg over the saddle to sit astride.

Della could only imagine the freedom men must feel completely unburdened by multiple layers of clothing or the need to ride side-saddle.

"Ladies first," Royce said, motioning Della and Maggie to go ahead of him.

Della had to laugh at Royce's blatant dislike of Demeter, but she could not really blame him. If the shoe had been on the other foot, she was sure her reaction would have been much the same.

As they made their way to Bond Street, Della felt the weight of Royce's eyes on her back and could only speculate what he was thinking when he looked at her.

Royce followed from a safe distance, his eyes remaining vigilant of the four-legged temperamental beast in front of him. His mind, however, remained focused on its rider. He had helped Della many times before, but, for some reason, the feel of her body beneath his hands left him feeling unsteady.

Maybe he should have taken Aden up on his offer the other night. It had been far too long if he could not recall the last time he had lain with a woman. That could be the only plausible explanation for why he had let his hand linger on Della longer than he should have.

A short time later, they arrived at the Inn. Royce dismounted and hurried to help everyone alight from the carriage, then proceeded to where Della and Maggie waited. He helped Maggie first, then turned to Della, keeping a firm eye on the annoying equine that stood beside him.

"Does she have something against *all* men, or just the Derrington men?" Royce asked as Demeter snorted at him, her pinned back ears a telltale sign of her evil intentions.

"Demeter, we must be on our best behavior. You will make me break my promise to Titan, and it really is unladylike to act in such a manner." Della reprimanded the horse as Royce helped her slide from the saddle. "She really is a big sweetheart once she gets to know you," Della cooed while rubbing Demeter's nose affectionately.

Oh, she was a big something, all right, but Royce held his tongue.

Leaving the care of horses to the lad outside the Inn, Royce placed a hand at the small of Della's back, guiding her to where their group had gathered.

Everyone needed to go in different directions. Maggie and his mother to the milliners for a few things, then to Madame Delphine's to pick up Maggie's dress. The twins would accompany them with the aid of Mrs. Cora.

Della only needed to dip into the bookshop to pick up a book she had ordered and then wanted to walk in the park. When Royce offered to accompany her, he noticed the look his mother and Maggie had exchanged. Hoping they were not jumping to conclusions, Royce hastily asked Samuel if he would care to join them on their walk.

With Samuel's emphatic yes, they all went their separate ways, agreeing to meet at the Inn for luncheon in one hour.

"Shall we?" Royce offered.

Royce greeted the occasional acquaintance as they strolled down the street and considered the various gentlemen they encountered. He noted the way they looked at Della, and how effortlessly she would smile at them as they passed, but acknowledge no sign of their interest.

Upon entering the bookshop, a young man named Thomas greeted them. Della gave him her name, and he ran to the back to retrieve her order, while Samuel wandered off to look around. Soon, Thomas came back, his face flushing an intense shade of scarlet as Della smiled and thanked him for his help.

He could not blame the boy for his reaction. If a woman like Della had smiled at him in that manner when he was younger, he likely would have responded in a similar fashion. Della thanked Thomas once more before they departed the shop with Della clutching her book to her chest as though it was the most precious thing in all the world.

Royce drew in a deep breath as they exited onto the street. The scent of chocolate and freshly baked bread permeated the air...he knew exactly where the intoxicating smell was coming from. Looking further down down the street, he read the aged wooden sign swinging lightly in the breeze: Mrs. Babbage's Sweet Shop.

When he suggested they might indulge in a treat, Samuel's eyes lit up, and he gave a small cheer before racing ahead of them. The tinkling of a bell sounded as he opened the door and went inside. Royce and Della had almost made it to the door themselves when Royce glimpsed Miss Putnam and Lord Milton standing by their carriage.

Lord Milton would not react favorably if he were to see Royce walking down the street with someone other than his daughter, even if there was no wrongdoing involved. When he had gone to Miss Putnam's house to address the rumors, she had not been at home.

And when he inquired when she might return, he was informed that she was at the local orphanage for her weekly visit. Her return was unknown as the demands on her time at the orphanage varied from week to week. Since then, the opportunity to speak with her had not yet presented itself.

His eyes frantically scanned the area, desperately looking for something he could hide behind to prevent being spotted.

Noticing a dimly lit alleyway to their right, Royce immediately took Della's hand and pulled her into the shadows with him.

"What are you—"

"Shhh." Royce held a finger to Della's lips, effectively silencing anything else she might have said that would have garnered the Putnam's notice.

He quickly glanced over his shoulder and saw their retreating figures heading off in the opposite direction. Royce felt his tension ease and released a sigh of relief, but a tap on his arm brought his attention back to Della and she pointed to her mouth.

"I am sorry," Royce murmured softly, his gaze fixating on where his finger rested. He felt the warmth of her breath against his finger as he lazily slid it down and hooked it beneath her chin, tilting her face upward.

Gently, he drew his thumb across her rose-tinted lips and grew more intrigued by the thought of kissing her. How it would feel to coax a moan from her mouth, to have her beneath him in his bed, just as he had pictured in his dream.

The subtle scent of lavender coming from Della danced with the faint smell of chocolate, creating a sweet fragrance he found impossible to resist. The feel of her skin akin to velvet—soft and smooth—as he leaned in and gently ran the tip of his nose along her cheek and down the delicate curve of her neck.

Royce snaked his hand around her waist and let out a deep growl of satisfaction. He could feel the book Della had just purchased pressing against his chest, its paper wrapping crinkling between them, as he backed her up against the nearest wall.

His clouded mind whispered reminders of his obligation to find a suitable partner—that was not him—for Della. But with every breath, it became harder to heed those words. Suddenly, they were surrounded by the resounding echoes of footsteps, effectively pulling him back from his thoughts, and reminding him of where they were.

Royce let his hands fall and quickly stepped away as Della's grip loosened, causing the book to slip from her hands. Her eyes were wide with confusion and surprise as she stood there looking back at him. He understood that look.

What had come over him?

He had become so lost in the moment that he had nearly kissed her amidst the repulsive and squalid atmosphere of the alleyway. As a duke, he was expected to carry himself with grace and dignity, to lead by example with his actions. But in this moment, he had thrown caution to the wind, behaving as recklessly as a drunkard in search of a hasty rendezvous.

"Care to explain what that was about?" Della asked, straightening up.

Royce's eyes greedily followed her every move as she ran her hands over herself, ensuring everything was still in place.

"There was a rat," Royce said, silently berating himself.

"A *rat*?" Della looked at him as though he had gone crazy. "Is it gone?"

"I believe so." He nodded, knowing that she could have easily scolded him for what had just transpired, and was grateful for her willingness to go along with his feeble and slightly embarrassing excuse.

"Come," he said, bending over to pick the book up. "Samuel will wonder where we are."

Quickly walking the remaining distance, Royce ushered Della through the bakery door and promptly closed it behind them.

Chapter 7

Effecting a smile as she entered the shop, Della looked at her surroundings. The well-worn tables, chairs, and floor showed this to be a highly frequented establishment. And judging by what she smelled, she could understand why.

"Where did you two go? I came into the shop and thought you were right behind me." Samuel asked when he saw them finally come through the door.

"Your brother got spooked," Della said casually, joining Samuel to inspect the array of sweets on display.

"By what?" Samuel's eyebrows shot up in disbelief, seeming shocked that something could ever frighten his brother.

"A rat," Della replied.

"It was an enormous rat, and I barely managed to save you from its grasp!" Royce boasted, as if he alone had rescued them from the clutches of certain death. "You should thank me!"

"My apologies. Thank you for saving my life." Della lifted her heels off the ground, leaned forward, and gave Royce a swift peck on the cheek.

She immediately recognized her mistake, but it was too late to take it back. Why had she not just expressed her gratitude with a simple *thank you*?

With a quick smile at Royce, Della averted her gaze, her eyes widening in disbelief at her own actions.

"Yes, well..." Royce cleared his throat. "You are most welcome."

Samuel seemed to find their interaction amusing, almost as if he were watching a lighthearted theatrical performance, and laughed.

"Yer Grace! I was no' 'specting you today," a kindly-looking woman said as she came through the doors leading from the kitchen, her eyes lighting up with a smile. "But I know exactly wha' you came in 'ere for."

With a wag of her finger, she vanished behind the counter, only to reappear moments later with a small pastry topped with chocolate.

"May I?" Royce looked at her as she nodded. Royce took a bite, his eyes rolling heavenward. "Please tell François that he has outdone himself with this batch, and I would also like to purchase whatever you may have left. I will take three with me and have the rest sent to her Grace's residence."

Mrs. Babbage smiled and hurried off to the back room. A short while later, she came back with three individually wrapped parcels.

"'Ere you are, Your Grace. François gives his thanks and is packaging the rest of 'em for you as we speak. I will have Mr. Babbage deliver them as soon as he returns."

After they finished paying, Della, Royce, and Samuel ventured toward the square, eventually coming across a bench that was unoccupied.

"Have you ever had a petite duchesse?" Royce asked, taking a seat, and offering a parcel to Della and Samuel.

Della shook her head as she untied the string and unfolded the piece of cloth to reveal the pastry within. Lifting it to her mouth, she took a bite and almost moaned out loud.

The pastry was light with a soft crunch, the custard rich and sweet, and the chocolate...Della did not have the words. Now she understood the look she had seen overtake Royce's face when he had eaten one back in the shop.

"So, what do you think?" Royce looked at Della hopefully.

"It is divine! I have had several pastries from various bakers, but I must say, this is probably one of the best I have ever had." Della smiled before taking another bite.

"Mrs. Babbage is famous for them, though François is the mastermind behind the door. I have been eating them for as long as I can remember. I once begged my mother to bribe François to become our cook, but she is devoted to Mrs. Ivers and said it would ruin Mrs. Babbage's business.

"Well, I could not have that—where was I to sneak off to while trying to avoid my studies? I visited her shop more regularly than I care to admit before leaving for Eton and during the summers we came home. I have a particular weakness for sweet things." Royce's serious expression transformed into a smile.

Della quickly looked away and focused on the people milling about the square, feeling a nervous tension beginning to pool in the bottom of her stomach.

She did not understand what Royce had seen when he pulled her into that dark alley, but she was sure it had been no rat he was hiding from.

"I see my friends right over there! Might I go over and say hello?" Samuel excitedly pointed to a group of boys playing.

"As long as you stay where I can see you." Royce nodded.

Samuel stuffed the rest of the pastry into his mouth before running off to greet his friends. Royce and Della laughed at Samuel's exuberance as they turned to face each other.

"You have some chocolate…just there," Royce said, pointing at the corner of her mouth.

Though un-ladylike, Della stuck out her tongue to lick the stray chocolate. "Did I get it?"

She held her face up for inspection as Royce gently placed his finger under her chin, moving her head slightly to the right. With a gentle touch, he brushed away the remaining chocolate from the corner of her mouth.

"Perfect." Royce said softly.

"Your Grace!" a voice yelled from somewhere behind Della.

Royce quickly stood, knocking the empty wrapping of their pastries to the ground.

"Lord Milton, Miss Putnam." Royce nodded.

"I told Father I saw you earlier, but you were gone when I turned around to show him. He said that you stopped by to talk with us the other day while I was visiting the orphanage." Miss Putnam looked at Royce, a question in her eyes. "We were about to depart when I spotted you and decided to come over."

Lord Milton remained quiet.

Della did not know what the conversation between him and Lord Milton had entailed, just like Royce did not know that she knew why this exchange felt so awkward and tense. Noticing Royce's obvious discomfort, Della took pity on him.

"Hello, My Lord, Miss Putnam," Della curtsied.

Lord Milton did not acknowledge that Della had spoken. He simply narrowed his eyes at Royce without uttering a word.

"Miss Rowntree." Miss Putnam pursed her lips as she eyes Della up and down. "Whatever are you doing here, *alone*, with His Grace?"

That was an impertinent question, Della thought to herself.

She had never gotten along with Miss Putnam, though the exact reason for their discord was something Della never fully understood. They had never been friends, nor had they been enemies. They had just been two young girls who had made their debut together and gone their separate ways.

"But we are not alone. My younger brother is just over there." Royce stepped aside and pointed at Samuel, who was still running around with his friends.

"Oh, of course. Please forgive my presumption." Miss Putnam gave Royce an overly sweet smile.

"I came with the Duchess and Lady Derrington. I picked up a book I purchased, and they needed to pick up Lady Derrington's dress for the Bellamy's ball this evening at Madame Delphine's. They also had another errand to run, so I walked a few doors down to Mrs. Babbage's, where I bumped into His Grace and his younger brother. They were simply honoring me with their presence while I waited," Della said in defense of both her and Royce.

"How thoughtful." Miss Putnam turned toward Royce, dismissing anything else Della might have to say. "I was wondering, Your Grace," she said, stepping closer to him. "Since Miss Rowntree must get back to your sister, would now be a good time for the discussion you wanted to have?"

"Well-met, brother!" a booming voice echoed along the green.

They all turned to see Desmond and Grayson, Royce's other brothers, making their way to where they were standing. Royce's posture seemed to relax at their well-timed interruption.

"Good day, everyone." Desmond's kind and cheery countenance greeted them. "My Lord, Miss Putnam, Miss Rowntree." Nodding his head as he said each name.

With his quieter demeanor, Grayson did the same, then glanced back as Miss Putnam. Della noticed Miss Putnam smile and quickly look away, attempting to hide her blush.

"We happened upon Mother and Maggie as they were leaving a shop," Desmond said, lending truth to what Della had told Miss Putnam. "She informed us that Miss Rowntree had gone to the park and asked us to seek her out. We are to meet at the Inn for luncheon. Might we go? I am famished."

"Is filling your stomach all you ever think about?" Grayson laughed, clapping Desmond on the back.

"Is there anything more satisfying than a full stomach?" Desmond joked.

"Will you join us?" Grayson asked Royce.

"What about me?" came a childish voice.

"Where did you come from, little brother?" Desmond chuckled, ruffling Samuel's hair.

"I have been here the whole time!" Samuel exclaimed, swatting at Desmond's hand.

Della glanced at Miss Putnam and Lord Milton discreetly. Neither of them seemed happy at having been interrupted while conversing with Royce, even if it was his brothers doing the interrupting. As her eyes fell on Della, Miss Putnam's lips turned down in a displeased frown, devoid of the feigned sweetness she had used on Royce.

"Will you be attending the Bellamy's ball tonight?" Royce asked, pulling the attention back to him and breaking the contemptuous stare Miss Putnam had been leveling at Della.

"Father and I will both be there." Miss Putnam smiled.

"Might we converse then?" Royce inquired.

"Of course, Your Grace." Miss Putnam nodded, glancing at her father.

Della could feel a nervousness coming from Miss Putnam. No doubt Lord Milton was putting pressure on her to secure her engagement to Royce. And it was obvious she wanted to talk to him now, but with the duke's family present, Miss Putnam was not going to deny his request to speak later that evening.

The Putnams said their goodbyes and made their way to the entrance of the square where their carriage sat waiting.

"Is it just me, or did that seem like a terribly awkward conversation?" Desmond asked, breaking the silence.

"It was," Royce admitted.

"Well," Grayson said, clapping his hands together. "Should we see to feeding our poor brother before he wastes away?"

At that moment, Desmond's stomach took the opportunity to growl in agreement. Everyone laughed and headed to meet up with the rest of the group at the Inn.

Della walked slowly behind the four brothers, listening to their laughter as they joked around, and wondered what it would be like to have a family as large as theirs.

Her eyes locked onto Royce as he burst into laughter at Samuel's comment, before he turned his head to look back at her and smiled. She had always felt like she was on the periphery, looking into the close-knit world of the Derringtons, despite them always treating her like part of the family.

She had to confess to feeling envious whenever she left their company. Their household always remained lively and vibrant until late in the evening, while she went back to her loving but comparatively quiet home.

She only hoped that when she finally started a family of her own, it would burst at the seams with the sounds of joy and laughter.

"I must thank you," Royce said, slowing down to match pace with her.

"For what, Your Grace?"

"For coming to my rescue back there with Lord Milton and Miss Putnam. Though I suppose you do not know what you were rescuing me from."

"I do, actually."

"You do?" Royce quickly turned to look at her.

"Yes. I have heard a few rumors, though I know not everything can be believed. Your aunt Imogen told your mother a few things she overheard the other day at tea."

"Yes, they approached me about it as well."

"Is Miss Putnam the reason you pulled me into that alley earlier?" Della asked, smiling at a gentleman that passed by.

"About that—"

"Please, do not insult my intelligence by saying it was a rat again." Della immediately regretted the harsh tone of her words.

"Fine, it was not a rat...it was a mouse."

Although she tried to resist, she could not help but break into a smile at Royce's attempt to lighten the mood.

"I will admit, it was not one of my prouder moments. If it is all the same to you, it is something I would just rather forget," he said, as if it was something that could be easily done.

Della fixed her eyes on the ground as they walked. Royce was still completely unaware of her knowledge of the situation and therefore could not be held accountable for how his responses affected her. But despite her best efforts to shield herself from the impact of his words, the pain remained the same.

"Consider it forgotten," Della said softly.

But she had no wish to forget his soft caress, how it felt to have his body pressed against hers...or how heart-achingly close he had come to kissing her.

"Here we are," Grayson said, coming to an abrupt stop in front of the Four Crowns Inn. "Shall we go in?"

Royce peered through the window where the rest of his family sat at a table, having procured a private room, and smiled. He liked how close his family was. How his mother always included his youngest siblings on their outings, despite their behavior, which was a bit unruly at times.

His mother had never been one to hold fast to the what the Ton deemed acceptable. She taught her children that rules were not always rigid and, if done properly, they could be adapted to fit any circumstance.

Her commitment to those words was unwavering, and today, she showed it by having the governess join the family for a meal in view of anyone who passed by.

Upon entering the room, Royce made his way to an empty chair and pulled it out for Della before taking a seat next to her at the end of the table. His mother looked at him, then at Della, and back at him, a soft smile playing about her mouth.

He did not like that look—that was her plotting something she ought not to be plotting look, and he silently shook his head at her.

The cooks at the Inn had prepared an amazing assortment for them, complete with cold roasted duck, cheeses, loaves of bread, and a selection of cakes and tarts. Everyone helped themselves and enjoyed the lively conversation.

Everyone, but Della.

"Is anything amiss?" Royce whispered so that only Della could hear.

"Oh...no." Della shook her head, seeming preoccupied with the slice of bread in her hand as she tore it into tiny pieces and let it fall to her plate.

"Penny for your thoughts?"

Della crumbled the last piece of bread between her fingers.

"I think I am just tired. I would like to go back soon and rest before the ball tonight."

"Of course." Royce did not press Della any further as he stood, announcing that it was time for them to leave.

The Duchess followed Samuel and the twins into the carriage, along with Mrs. Cora. Desmond and Grayson bid farewell before heading to meet up with a few friends elsewhere. Royce walked around to help Maggie, then moved to do the same for Della.

"Are you sure you will be all right?" Royce asked.

"Yes." Came Della's brief reply.

Royce, once again, placed his hands on Della's waist and lifted her up into the saddle when he felt a tug at his side.

Distracted by his concern for how Della was acting, he had forgotten to keep an eye on the vexing mare she rode. The intensity of his glare grew as he observed Demeter happily munching on the tails of his coat, and he lightly flicked her snout. Demeter snorted and dropped the offending piece of fabric, stomping her foot in protest.

"Serves you right," Royce whispered harshly before he looked up at Della and saw her smiling slightly. Swinging himself up onto Titan's back, he gathered the reins and turned them toward home.

He had never properly apologized to Della about what had happened in the alley today. Instead, he had asked her to forget the incident had ever happened, and she had agreed without question.

But how could he forget the fact that his heart had been pounding with anticipation at the thought of kissing her? Or how his heart had nearly stopped beating when she played along with his tall tale and given him an unexpected kiss on the cheek in return for *protecting* her from the evil clutches of a fictional rat?

Regardless, with his position as a duke, one would have expected him to possess a stronger resolve in certain situations.

He knew the viscount had a reputation for never backing down from an argument, regardless of how public it might be. So, he had made the quick decision not to give the man an opportunity to create a scene.

But no matter the excuses he kept inventing to justify his actions, his behavior remained inexcusable.

A sense of unease washed over him as he contemplated the upcoming conversation with Miss Putnam at the Bellamy's ball.

He did not know what he would do or what he would say to her. But one thing was certain—he had to find the source of the rumors and put a stop to them before they caused any more damage.

Chapter 8

Lord and Lady Bellamy had spared no expense on food or decorations. Luxurious fabrics cascaded from the marble columns that framed the ballroom, reaching up toward the ceiling. And hanging at the center of the room was a breathtaking crystal chandelier.

The flickering flames of the candles glinted off its many faceted stones, showering the dancers below in a beautiful rainbow of colors.

The dance floor was a spectacle of men and women donning their finest evening attire, executing elegant twists and turns as they danced. Della stood beside a large pot of exotic flowers, swaying to the music. The enchanting atmosphere, combined with the captivating music, made her feel like someone had cast a bewitching charm on her.

Della smiled and glanced at her dance card. She did not have anyone claiming the next dance, so she made her way to the refreshment table. She graciously accepted a drink from a footman, lifted the cup, took a sip. And she cringed as the overwhelming scent of spirits, oranges, and spices assaulted her nostrils.

Rum punch—she should have known. The Bellamy's were famous for serving it at all their events, the recipe having come from some relatives in America. If this was what the Americans were drinking, their gatherings must have been quite...lively.

Returning to her previous location beside the dance floor, Della looked around to make sure no one was paying attention and discreetly emptied her drink into the flowerpot.

"I am sure those flowers needed the fortification as much as I do. However, I believe the concoction they call refreshment may have the opposite effect."

Della let out a squeak as she spun around, looking guiltily up at a familiar face.

"Miss Rowntree." Aden Aynesworth smiled at her, sweeping into an elegant bow. "How lovely you look this evening."

"Thank you." Della curtsied. "You look quite charming yourself. Have you only just arrived?"

"Unfortunately, no. I am afraid I arrived rather early. Royce said he had run into Miss Putnam earlier today and promised to talk with her later this evening. I guess you could say I accompanied him for moral support. Alas, his early arrival was in vain, as Miss Putnam only arrived a short while ago."

Della nodded. "Where is he now?"

"Royce?" Aden turned to look around the room. "He is just there."

Della glanced in the direction that Aden pointed, where she could see Royce engaged in conversation with Lord Ravensdale. Royce looked up as if he had sensed Della and

Aden talking about him and politely excused himself from his conversation before walking toward them.

"Miss Rowntree." With a small bow, Royce brought her hand to his lips and brushed a kiss over her knuckles. "You look lovely this evening."

"Yes, I was saying much the same thing," Aden agreed.

"Thank you, Your Grace." Della beamed.

"Would you do me the honor of a dance?" Royce asked, holding out his hand.

"Excuse me, old friend, but I believe you cut in line. I was about to ask for the honor before you arrived." With a mischievous twinkle in his eyes, Aden held out his hand out to her as well. "Miss Rowntree, would you be so kind as to honor *me* with a dance?"

There Della stood, two very handsome men standing with their hands extended, asking her to dance. She looked up to see several sets of curious eyes staring at her.

And so, she noticed, was Miss Putnam. With narrowed eyes, she directed her gaze at Della while Royce and Aden kept their hands extended.

"In all fairness, Your Grace, Lord Aynesworth was here first." Della smiled at them both.

"Sorry, old chap." Aden took Della's hand and placed it on his arm.

"I am sorry, Your Grace. Perhaps a different dance?"

"Of course," Royce said graciously. "As you may recall, I need to speak with Miss Putnam. Have you seen her this evening?"

"I have. She is standing with her father."

"Thank you." Royce nodded his head and left; his expression unreadable as he prepared for what Della expected would be an uncomfortable conversation.

"I never expected to see you on the dance floor, Lord Aynesworth," Della said as Royce walked away.

"Such formality."

"I beg your pardon?"

"I dislike being called Lord Aynesworth by those I know, and you have known me long enough to call me by my given name, Della."

"Yes, I have known you for a long time, *Lord Aynesworth*. Almost as long as His Grace. However, we are in a public place, amongst the Ton, no less. People would get the wrong idea if I were to call you by your given name or you, mine."

"Noted," he laughed. "It is rather warm in here. Let us make our escape and forget the dance, *Miss Rowntree*." Aden winked at her teasingly.

Knowing she would have to return soon so the next gentleman could claim his dance, Della allowed Aden to guide her into the cool night air.

"May I have this dance?" Royce bowed to Miss Putnam.

"It would be my honor, Your Grace," Miss Putnam said, dipping into an elaborate curtsy.

Royce guided Miss Putnam onto the dance floor as the orchestra struck the first chords. Stepping in time with the music, he could not help but admire Della's beauty as he watched her move across the dance floor with Aden.

Her virescent green dress was adorned with intricate silver details, complemented by her elegantly swept back hair, held in place with a silver comb. And with each step, the dress sparkled in the light, accentuating her graceful figure.

"You seem distracted, Your Grace," Miss Putnam said, drawing Royce's attention back to her.

"Hmm?"

"Shall we have that discussion now?"

"Very well," Royce said, sweeping her into a turn.

"Might we start with what you talked to my father about the other day?" Miss Putnam asked.

Royce took a deep breath before speaking. "I see no reason not to tell you the truth. Indeed, if we are to marry, I would say that being honest about what is on our minds is the best way forward. What exactly has your father told you?"

"He said you asked to postpone, stating that you had business matters with your estate to see to and could not give our engagement the attention it deserves."

"Those were my words exactly." Royce nodded in confirmation.

"But you see, Your Grace, we only have an understanding. I have not said yes, as you have not formally proposed."

Royce came to a stop, causing another couple to bump into them.

"What exactly are you trying to say, Miss Putnam?"

"Only that since rumors have spread about you postponing, I have had several offers from others."

"What others?" Royce growled loud enough that people around him steered clear for fear he would lash out.

"Others, like Lord Haddock, who is currently talking to my father." Miss Putnam glanced over her shoulder.

Royce saw Lord Milton standing by the wall, talking animatedly with Lord Haddock as they argued about something.

Lord Haddock looked dejected, but Lord Milton leaned forward and whispered something in his ear. The man's mood quickly changed as he nodded and shook hands with Lord Milton.

If what Miss Putnam said was true, that handshake did not bode well.

"I see," Royce simply stated, realizing they were still standing in the middle of the floor as couples danced around them. "Might we finish this conversation elsewhere?"

Miss Putnam nodded, allowing Royce to lead her out the same set of doors that Aden and Della had gone through.

He knew Miss Putnam was trying to bait him, to draw his attention to the fact that she was desirable. Informing him that if he did not decide soon, she would choose another. He took a deep, fortifying breath of fresh air, attempting to keep his temper in check.

If she decided she would not wait, then Royce would have to start his search over, or honor his father's last request by marrying Della. Marrying Della would not prove a hardship for him; in fact, he was afraid it would prove far too easy.

Something had felt different between them when he had pulled Della into that dark alley. Something he did not want to acknowledge.

If he married Della, he was afraid the practical marriage he had planned could become a marriage where love could take hold, and he had to avoid that at all costs.

"What shall it be, Your Grace? Is there to be a proposal soon, or shall I continue my search elsewhere?" Miss Putnam looked up at him, schooling her features into a look of annoyance.

"Did you have someone else in mind?"

"And if I do?" she asked.

"I will have you know I do not take kindly to idle threats or ultimatums, Miss Putnam. As you have pointed out, we have only have an understanding. I have not asked you directly to marry me, nor have you said yes. If there is someone else you desire to marry, then do not allow me to stand in your way. I am not a man who would force a woman to do anything she is not also amenable to." Royce attempted to keep his voice level despite his mounting anger at the entire situation.

He found himself growing increasingly suspicious as they descended the stairs to walk along the garden path. The way Miss Putnam was acting and the things she said made him question if she had potentially started the rumors herself.

Before Royce jumped to any conclusions, he needed to determine if his suspicions were correct and understand the reasons for her actions.

And despite his hopes that it was not true, he had to acknowledge the possibility.

"So, there I was, hanging from the rafters in the stable, over an enormous, reeking pile of freshly mucked bedding. My breeches were hanging around my ankles, and I was holding on with every bit of strength I could summon. Of course, Royce was no help at all. He just stood there laughing." Aden chuckled as he recalled the story.

"What did you do?" Della asked, wiping a tear from her eye.

"I could not hold on forever, and eventually, I had to give in to the inevitable and just accept my fate. Mother was furious and had the servants throw cold buckets of water on me before she allowed me in the house."

"What of Royce?"

"Oh, he had an unfortunate event later, involving disappearing clothes while we were at a local watering hole. He had to run, naked as the day he was born, back to the schoolhouse and avoid being seen by the headmaster. His clothes were never found, I am afraid." Aden gave an impish smile.

"I can only imagine that it barely covers the trouble you got into while you were away at Eton. You may have grown up, but I cannot say you have grown out of your mischievousness. I heard what was said about you and Royce while you were away exploring the continent."

"Come now, Della," Aden said, being informal with her since they were alone outside. "I would have thought you—of all people—would know better than to listen to such gossip."

"Oh, do not think that I believe everything I read or hear. I know not all of it can be true...or can it?" Taking advantage of Aden's surprise, she continued. "Just because I am a woman does not mean I do not know how the world works."

"How the world works, hmm?" Aden quirked the corner of his mouth and sat down next to Della. "And how does the world work, exactly?"

"Well, take rumors, for example. They are a tangled web of half-truths and lies. As the rumor spreads, it becomes so far removed from its original source one does not know what to believe. A rumor can make the mighty tumble and the meek rise among mortals to be made gods.

"It is, unfortunately, what makes or breaks people in our society. It can ruin the chances of making a good match; break hearts and destroy lives. Yet, people of the Ton turn a blind eye. If the rumor does not affect them, they are more than happy to gossip behind their fans. It is a rare person who does not add wood to the fire."

"Do you speak from experience?" Aden asked.

"What do you mean, my lord?" Della looked at Aden, confused.

"Have you been affected by such rumors?" he asked with concern.

"We all have at some point, have we not?" Della shrugged her shoulder. "Some more than others."

"Sadly, I cannot deny it," Aden admitted.

They remained silent for a short while before he spoke again.

"Poor sod," Aden mused out loud.

"What was that?" Della asked.

"Oh, I was just thinking about Royce and his current situation with Miss Putnam. You were in the park earlier today when he talked to her, yes?"

Della nodded. "I was. Miss Putnam was the only one who spoke. Lord Milton never said a word. It was an odd conversation, to say the least."

"Yes, I can imagine it was." Aden laughed. "At the risk of sounding like I am starting a rumor, let me just say, I am not. I am, instead, addressing the cause of a rumor. Namely, the one circulating about Royce and Miss Putnam."

"I have heard only a little about it from his aunt when she arrived at my weekly tea with the Duchess and Maggie." Della did her best to sound as ignorant of the matter as she could.

"Her version of events, I am sure, was far more elaborate. But in short, it is being said that Royce is getting cold feet and wants to cry off."

"That is a much shorter story than the one his aunt gave." Della laughed.

"Royce has been trying to figure out who started the rumor, but he seems to be at a loss as to who it could possibly be." Aden's face suddenly became pensive. "You do not suppose..." He shook his head.

"Suppose what?" Della asked.

"You do not suppose that Miss Putnam started the rumor herself, do you? Maybe to garner sympathy or force Royce's hand after he spoke with her father?"

"Surely not. But if that were true, it would not sit well with Royce or Lord Milton. Am I horrible for saying that Miss Putnam is not a pleasant person" Della paused. "Perhaps he should cry off. It is not as if he loves her...Does he?"

"Good heavens, no," Aden scoffed. "That is the exact reason he *wants* to marry Miss Putnam. He is not in love with her, nor she, him."

"That seems like an incredibly lonely life, does it not?" Della looked out over the garden.

"Perhaps to some, but I believe you can love someone without being *in love* with them. And just because two people are not in love with each other does not mean that a marriage between them would not work." Aden turned to look at Della. "What do you think?"

"I suppose that is true, and I am not one to judge how others live their lives. All I can tell you is what I would want if I were to marry."

"And what is that, exactly?" Aden seemed to be genuinely interested in her answer.

"I want to be in love," she said a bit sadly.

"Is that why you have never accepted an offer?"

"You seem positive that I have had any offers at all." Della fidgeted with the fabric of her dress.

"Surely you do not expect me to believe that no man has offered for you."

"I have had a few, but…"

"They do not love you," Aden said, finishing her sentence.

"It is not too much to ask, is it?" Della let out a heavy sigh. "Perhaps that is a silly question."

"I do not think that seeking love is silly at all. I just think it is something that has been bred out of the Ton, and they no longer know what love means. For those who find it…well, they are the rare and fortunate ones." With a tinge of sadness in his smile, Aden extended his hand to Della. "I suppose we had best go back in. Your next partner will be looking for you."

"I think I shall stay out here a bit longer. Could you please inform," Della looked down at the dance card again. "Lord Haddock, I will not be able to claim our dance?"

"Of course," Aden said, bowing his head.

"And one more thing," Della added.

"Yes?"

"Could you see how those flowers have fared?"

Aden laughed as he bowed over Della's hand.

"Thank you for a most stimulating conversation. You have given me much to think about." With a quick bow, Aden went back into the ballroom.

Chapter 9

Della smoothed out her dress, leaving the somewhat hidden alcove off to the side of the terrace where she and Aden had sat. It was a beautiful night as she walked along the path. The light from the moon revealed a lightly treaded area between some bushes, leading to a more secluded area.

She knew she should not be out here alone, but the ballroom was hot and overcrowded. Better to be out here where one can think and breathe.

Wondering where it might lead, Della followed the path for a short time until the sound of voices made her pause. She listened; they were arguing, and the crunching of footsteps sounded as though they were heading straight for her.

Not wanting to be seen should they be out here for a secret meeting—or worse—Della ducked behind the closest tree. She braced herself against the thick bark, her hand coming to rest on some flowers with large protruding thorns.

"Ow..." Della looked at her hand.

Wonderful. Now not only was she bleeding, but she was stuck behind this tree until the other people left.

"I told you I believe that being honest is the best thing moving forward...so be honest with me now," the man said.

"Did you start the rumor that I postponed the announcement because I plan to cry off?"

Good heavens, she must have accidentally stumbled upon Royce and Miss Putnam having their conversation. And by the sound of it, it was not going well.

"So, what if I did?" Miss Putnam's voice dripped with bitterness.

"Miss Putnam, I like to think myself an intelligent man, but I do not understand why you are spreading these rumors. Why give the Ton the ability to harm you? You may think these rumors only affect me, but they affect you as well."

Della could feel the angry tension in the air as neither Royce nor Miss Putnam spoke for a few moments. She only hoped they would finish their conversation soon. It was getting cold, and Tilly was probably looking for her by now.

"Then what are we to do, Your Grace?"

Royce cleared his throat. "I would still like to know that we have an understanding."

"And what of Miss Rowntree?" Miss Putnam asked acerbically.

"What of her?"

"I saw you in the park. Can you honestly say that nothing is going on between you two? While I can tolerate a marriage of convenience, I will not tolerate being your second choice in our marriage."

Thinking herself well hidden, Della attempted to look around the tree to see if she might flee without being seen, when a twig snapped beneath her foot.

Royce's head jerked up, looking in her direction as she ducked back behind the tree. Had he seen her? She prayed he had not. What was she to do? If she attempted to flee now, there was no way she could avoid being spotted.

"It was a temporary lapse in judgement, one that I can assure you will not be repeated. Della is a friend, nothing more."

Della's temper flared. *A temporary lapse in judgement?* What was that supposed to mean?

"Very well, Your Grace." Della heard Miss Putnam say. "Our understanding will remain in place...for now."

"Thank you, Miss Putnam. All I ask is that you cease spreading these rumors. They are doing more harm than good. Does your father know you are the one who started them?"

"He does not, and I ask that it remain that way. He is angry enough as it is." The sound of her voice hinted at a tinge of fear. "Shall we go back to the ballroom?"

"Not together. We have been away for a while. You go back through the door on the terrace, and I shall make my way back later to avoid speculation."

"I bid you good evening, Your Grace."

Della listened, hearing only one set of footsteps leave, which meant...

"Miss Rowntree." Royce called out in an eerily calm tone.

Della closed her eyes and took a deep breath. Perhaps if she remained silent, he would think she had already left.

"Do not think for one moment that I do not know you are still behind that tree. Have you not noticed I am between you and your only way out?"

Della looked around...*damn*.

"I will give you to the count of three...One..."

How dare he count like her governess used to when she was caught filching a sweet from the cupboard. But in this case, she had not been doing anything wrong. She had come upon them by accident and had not the chance to leave before being seen.

"Two..."

For heaven's sake, this was ridiculous.

"Three..."

It was silent for a moment, and Della wondered what Royce would do, when she felt a hand clasp her arm. She screamed as she spun around. *Riiip!* Della cringed as she looked down to see a tear on the bottom of her dress.

"Oh, bother." Della pulled at her dress, attempting to free the hem of her skirt from the thorns.

"Please, allow me." Royce bent down on one knee and carefully pried the angry thorns away from the delicate fabric.

"Do hurry," Della whispered, placing her hand lightly on Royce's shoulder for balance.

"Then stay still," Royce quietly reprimanded her.

Della tried to remain as still as possible, but it was quite hard, panicked as she was for fear that someone would find them together and alone.

"There. Nothing a visit to Madame Delphine could not fix," Royce said as he removed the last thorn.

Her gaze followed the gentle drag of his hands upward over her skirt until they settled on her waist, their eyes meeting.

Della cleared her throat and quickly stepped backward out of Royce's reach, smoothing down her dress as best she could.

"Thank you," Della said softly.

"May I inquire about what you are going out here?" Royce asked as he stood and dusted the dirt off his pants.

"I was not spying, if that is what you are thinking. I came out here to escape from the crowd and was about ready to go back when I heard footsteps, so I hid."

"Where is Aden?" Royce looked around. "If he left you out here alone, I shall have to have a word with him."

"He is not to blame. I told him I wanted to remain out here, and I assured him I would be fine. At least *he* seems to trust that I know my own mind."

"So, you are safe out here...*alone*?"

"I am in a garden at the Bellamy's Ball! What have I to fear out here?" Della held her arms wide, gesturing to their surroundings. "Honestly! Do you think I am so incapable of taking care of myself that I need someone to always watch over me?"

"Someone should."

"I am *not* your responsibility, Your Grace. You are *not* my husband. I am *not* your wife. Nor am I some child in need of reprimanding, and I refuse to be treated as such. Especially not from a man who has an understanding with another woman and thinks me nothing more than a *temporary lapse in judgement!*"

Della stepped around Royce and was about to break into a run when her foot snagged on a tree root, causing her to stumble. Her hands instinctively shot out to break the fall, but before she hit the ground, she felt Royce's arms wrap around her.

The air left Royce's lungs with a great whoosh, his back hitting the ground with a dull thud as Della fell on top of him. Her knee landing hard between his legs, coming perilously close to injuring parts he would prefer to remain intact.

"You were saying?" Royce asked, confused why Della's angry gaze ignited an unexplainable surge of excitement within him. He shook his head and inhaled deeply, attempting to ignore his odd reaction to Della's obvious irritation. "Now, if it is not too much trouble, would you be so kind as to remove your knee from its current location?"

"Oh!" Upon realizing the harm she had narrowly avoided causing, Della's anger seemed to dissipate almost instantly. Trying to distance herself, she placed her hands on his chest to push herself up.

Bright light from the moon shone down through the branches of the trees in distorted rays, casting a dreamlike halo of light around them. The inviting scent from their earlier encounter still clung to her, holding his senses captive. In one swift motion, Royce sat up and repositioned Della onto his lap, pulling her legs comfortably to the side.

Unable to hold back any longer, he gently cupped her face in his hands and planted a tender kiss on her lips, causing an intense longing to well up inside him.

And when he deepened the kiss, Della mirrored his movements, their tongues advancing and retreating, much like his fencing matches.

Royce was so consumed by the feel of Della's heartbeat pulsing against his lips as he trailed a line of soft kisses down the slender column of her neck, that he disregarded the sounds coming from the bushes.

It should have made him instantly aware of how easily someone could stumble upon them in such a compromising position, but his senses had abandoned him.

Della gasped and pulled away, looking at their surroundings. "Did you hear that?"

"I heard nothing," Royce said, ignoring the sound as he attempted to pull Della back to finish what they had started.

Della poked him hard in the chest.

"Ow! What was that for?" Royce idly rubbed the now tender spot.

"That was for trying to kiss me again, and this," she said, smacking him on the chest, "is for kissing me the first time."

Royce looked at Della, the color still high in her cheeks. What reason could he give for kissing her when he could not understand the reason himself? It left him questioning his own actions. Clearing his throat, he removed Della from his lap and stood.

With a gentle yet firm grip, he reached out for Della's hands, effortlessly lifting her up, when she drew in a sharp breath.

"Are you all right?"

"Perfectly." Della straightened her spine and took a step, but collapsed, letting out a small cry.

Royce quickly grabbed Della and swept her into his arms. "You are hurt," he said with concern. "Why did you not mention it before?"

"Thank you for that obvious observation, but *your temporary lapse in judgement* does not need your help—I will be fine. So, if you would kindly put me down, I will see myself back in the ballroom."

Royce cringed as she threw his words back in his face a second time. He understood why Della was angry and he had regretted those words as soon as he had spoken them, knowing she was behind the tree.

He had tried to assure Miss Putnam there was nothing going on between him and Della. But the kiss they just shared may have well tested the veracity of that statement.

"You can hardly stand, let alone walk. Therefore, I will carry you back."

"You most assuredly will not, sir!"

"I cannot keep my title as a gentleman if I were to leave a damsel in distress to fend for herself."

"I am not a damsel, nor am I in distress." Della huffed, crossing her arms. "Put me down!"

"No." Not giving her a chance to argue further, Royce stalked back toward the house with Della in his arms. He could not go straight through the ballroom—that would cause an entirely different set of problems—so he circled around to the front.

Several heads looked in their direction as Royce turned the corner with Della in his arms. She took notice, and he tightened his hold on her as she curled into his chest, attempting to hide her face.

"Royce! What happened?" Aden asked, running over to them as Royce sent a footman to fetch Della's carriage

"I...uh..." Della looked at Royce for help.

"She tripped and sprained her ankle. Would you be so kind as to retrieve Tilly? Tell her Della is waiting in the carriage." Royce looked directly at Aden, ignoring other offers of help.

Aden went to find Tilly and a few moments later, the footman announced that the carriage had arrived. Royce carried Della over and placed her on the seat, being careful not to bump her ankle.

"Wait here. I will go in and help Aden find Tilly."

"I make no promises."

Royce leaned in so only she could hear. "You will stay here, Della, or I will tie you to the seat."

"I would like to see you try," Della whispered angrily, meeting his eyes in a challenge.

Royce rolled his eyes and told the footman he was to stand guard. And under no circumstance was he to let Miss Rowntree leave the carriage.

"Poor dear," Tilly said, patting Della gently on the knee as the carriage rumbled over the cobbled street. "Lord Aynesworth

said you tripped and sprained your ankle, and that His Grace carried you to the carriage," she sighed. "His Grace is ever the gentleman. How fortunate for you he was there to help in your time of need."

"Fortunate indeed." Della smiled at her aunt.

The carriage hit a bump in the road, causing Della to grit her teeth as pain radiated up her leg.

"Are you well?" Tilly asked.

"I am. My ankle is a little tender at the moment."

Tilly nodded. "Do not worry. We will have you home to rest in no time, dear."

Della let her head fall back on the cushioned seat and watched the flickering candles in the lampposts as they went by. Despite her best efforts, she could not make sense of Royce's confusing behavior.

Her thoughts flashed back to the moment Royce had swept her into his arms. She had been furious with him, but she could not deny how safe she had felt. How he had pulled her closer when she tried to hide her face from curious onlookers.

Although she relished the sensation of being held by him, the touch of his lips on hers, and the way her heart skipped a beat when he was close, she did not want his attention solely because of a misplaced sense of obligation.

Maybe she *should* accept an offer from a kind gentleman—if she received another one—who she could share a friendship with. Someone that could bring a smile to her face, even when love was absent.

If she found such a person, Royce would be free from the agreement he had made with her father.

Della angrily swiped at her tears as they fell. She knew it was time to move on...before any more of her heart became irreparably damaged.

Chapter 10

A few days passed, and Della's ankle was much improved, giving her the chance to take a stroll with Maggie around the park on such a beautiful morning. The sun was shining brightly; the birds chirped sweetly, and every manner of person was out and about.

"We are having a family picnic at the ruins the day after tomorrow and Mother would like for you to join us if you feel up for it," Maggie said, looking out over the park.

"I would love to."

"Just so you know, Miss Putnam will be attending as well—Royce insisted."

"Wonderful," Della said sarcastically. She had not spoken to Royce since the incident in the garden.

"Since you were not in the ballroom at the time, I assume you do not know what took place the other night at the Bellamy's Ball?" Maggie looked at Della questioningly. "I was talking with Tilly when Royce and Miss Putnam walked out on the terrace. A short while later, when Lord Milton saw his daughter had come back alone, he sent her back out to *retrieve the duke*. I overheard him say those exact words."

"Gossiping is beneath you, Maggie."

"I do not gossip. Gossiping is for people who try to make themselves look important. I report the truth."

Worried about what else might have taken place that she was unaware of, Della questioned Maggie further. "What happened after that?"

"After Miss Putnam returned, she whispered something to Lord Milton, and he turned so red I thought he might pop. When Miss Putnam looked as though she might cry, Lord Milton practically dragged her from the ballroom."

Della shook her head. "Poor girl."

"Poor girl? Poor Royce! It is obvious Lord Milton is scheming just so he can say he is the father of a duchess. And since Royce delayed his and Miss Putnam's announcement, he probably thinks that a duke is slipping through his fingers."

"Do you know why Royce delayed the announcement?" Della asked.

"I am afraid I do not, nor does anyone else."

Della let out a quiet sigh of relief to know that the Ton was still not privy to the details or that she was involved. She needed advice, and who better to receive it from than your best friend?

Besides, if Maggie found out some other way, she would never forgive Della for withholding such information from her.

"What would you say if I told you I know the reason?"

Maggie pulled Della to a stop. "Then I would say you need to tell me this instant."

"Even if it involves someone you know that is not Royce?"

"Well, now you must tell me."

"You are sworn to secrecy, Maggie...you cannot tell anyone."

"I swear on your favorite lemon tarts, I will not say a word!" Maggie held up her right hand.

"I am the reason," Della mumbled.

"What?" Maggie asked, her eyes widening in surprise.

Della took a deep breath. "I said, I am the reason Royce postponed everything, or at least I am *part* of the reason."

Maggie stood there, stunned by the news. "What do you mean, you are *part* of the reason? Royce still plans on marrying Miss Putnam, yes?"

"Shhhh, I do not want anyone to overhear." Della explained what all had transpired, not leaving out a single detail, except for the fact that she and Royce had kissed. That was something that Maggie need not know. "And yes, he is still planning on marrying Miss Putnam."

"But I do not understand what Royce could possibly help you with. He does not want to marry for love—you do."

"I do, but lately, I have wondered if I am asking for too much. Perhaps I should marry someone I...like." Della shrugged. "Maybe it would eventually grow into love."

"You *could*, I suppose, but where would the excitement be in that? Please, I beg you. Do not make me have to bear witness to my best friend agreeing to a marriage that she does not want. I must already deal with the fact that my brother will be forever connected to the blustery viscount."

They laughed, making their way toward the Duchess, where she spoke with Lady Ferndown, the Marchioness of Stilton.

"What do you suggest I do about Royce?" Della asked.

"Royce should not have agreed to begin with, but should have just stood firm and told your father no. But I also understand why he might have felt obligated to follow through. In a sense, it could have made him feel as though our father was still with us, still a part of our lives." Maggie smiled sadly. "If it were me, I would confront Royce about it and be done. It would allow both of you to be free from the agreement between our fathers. Should be easy enough. It is not as if you are in love with him."

Della laughed, as though it was an absurd notion.

"Will you be all right? Do you need me to say something to my brother for you? Maggie asked.

"No, I need to be the one to say something to him," Della said, wondering if now was a good time to admit to Maggie the feelings she had secretly harbored for Royce; that the thought of marrying him did not sound absurd to her. "It is only that I am..." Della's words were cut short when she heard someone call out their names.

"Miss Rowntree! Lady Derrington!"

"Lord Haddock." Della smiled as she looked at the gentleman approaching them.

Lord Haddock's appearance was marked by his dark, almost black eyes, his pale skin, and a mouth that was always turned up in distaste. Although he had always been polite to her, Della found herself unable to shake off the feeling of uneasiness that washed over her whenever he was near.

"I was reading my book under that tree when I spotted you and thought I would say hello." He pointed toward a large tree where a book lay open, a light breeze ruffling its pages. "Lovely weather we are having."

"Beautiful. I am envious that I did not think to bring a book as well." Della smiled thoughtfully at him. "I am sorry for not claiming our dance at the Bellamy's ball. I had to leave early because I had an unfortunate fall and sprained my ankle."

"Yes..." Lord Haddock's eyes seemed to narrow, making Della somewhat uncomfortable. "I saw His Grace carrying you to the carriage and offered my assistance, but he turned down my offer. I do hope your ankle is on the mend."

"It is, thank you." Della nodded, exchanging glances with Maggie, practically begging her to somehow bring this conversation to an end.

"Lord Haddock!" Della turned to see the Duchess approaching them. "How nice to see you."

"Your Grace." He grinned as he bowed over her hand. "You look lovely, as always."

"Ever the flatterer," the Duchess said. "I wonder, Lord Haddock, we are visiting the ruins the day after tomorrow and need another gentleman to even things out. Would you be interested in joining us? Miss Putnam and Lord Aynesworth will be coming along as well."

"I would be delighted."

"Wonderful!" the Duchess exclaimed, handing Lord Haddock her card. "Please arrive at this address at eleven o'clock."

"Thank you, Your Grace. I look forward to it. If you ladies will excuse me, I have somewhere I must be." Lord Haddock glanced at Della, and left without saying another word, leaving his book lying forgotten beneath the tree.

"You had to invite *him*?" Maggie looked at her mother incredulously.

"What is wrong with Lord Haddock? He is a perfectly fine gentleman," the Duchess said.

"There is something about that man that does not sit right quite right with me. He always lurks in the shadows or shows up at the most peculiar moments, much like he did just now."

"Oh, pshaw. There goes your overactive imagination again. I invited him because I dislike uneven numbers."

"Mother, you are not to play matchmaker for Della or me."

"I was doing nothing of the sort."

"Of course not." Maggie rolled her eyes.

Della walked over to pick up the book that Lord Haddock had left behind. She loved books and could not allow it to stay out here exposed to the finicky London weather and ruined. The book was a lovely deep red with an embossed silver print across the front.

She would return it to Lord Haddock during their trip to the ruins.

They had just arrived back at the Derrington home when the sudden feeling of being watched came over Della as she stepped down from the carriage.

She spied a large shire horse strolling by, pulling a hackney with a large yellow stripe, and attempted to look into the darkened interior as it continued down the street. But she could only make out the nondescript silhouette of a person sitting within.

Paying more attention to the carriage than where she was going, Della stepped into a small hole in the pavement, causing her ankle to bend awkwardly... "Drat!" she cried out, stumbling a bit. A firm hand grabbed her by the arm, pulling her up sharply.

"I...uh...thank you, Your Grace." Della smiled sheepishly up at Royce.

"That was fortuitous timing, my dear," the Duchess remarked.

"Indeed it was," Royce said, his brows furrowing as he looked at Della with concern.

"We were just in Hyde Park where we chanced upon Lord Haddock. Our numbers were uneven for our trip to the ruins, so I invited him to join us," the Duchess continued, as though nothing had happened.

As soon as Lord Haddock's name was mentioned, Della saw a slight tick in Royce's jaw and felt his hold on her arm grow tighter. When she tried to pull free, Royce looked at her in apology and released her, letting his hand fall to his side.

"Shall we go in?" the Duchess asked.

"I think I shall see myself home. My ankle is bothering me a little." Della grimaced as she tried to put weight on her foot.

"Oh dear, why did you not say something?" the Duchess reprimanded. "But of course Royce will see you home."

"I thank you, Your Grace, but I will be just fine on my own."

"Be that as it may, I must insist he does," the Duchess spoke assertively, making it clear that she was not willing to accept a refusal. "Royce, come find me once you see Della safely home." With that, the Duchess and Maggie went through the gate and up the stairs.

"Shall we?" Royce held his arm out and Della placed her hand in the crook of his elbow. "I would like to apologize for the other night."

Della was silent for a moment. "We are both to blame, Your Grace. Neither of us behaved as we should have."

"It is true you should not have been out in the garden alone, but I blame myself partly for your current condition, too. I also wanted you to know that I do not see you as a temporary lapse in judgement. I...well, what I am trying to say is..." Royce hesitated, as if searching for the right words, when loud shouting interrupted their conversation.

Glancing over her shoulder, Della saw people attempting to jump out of the way as a horse and hackney careened around the corner. She immediately recognized the large yellow stripe as the one belonging to the hackney that had passed by a few minutes earlier.

The horse thundered ahead as its driver cracked a whip, encouraging it to go faster. Della could not help but feel increasingly worried about the people desperately trying to flee from this madman's destructive rampage.

Royce seemed to share her concern, and without saying a word, he placed his hand at the small of her back, silently urging her to quicken her pace. But her ankle throbbed with every step she took, and she had to stop, if only for a moment.

Royce walked a little further before realizing Della had stopped and began to walk back when the angry shouting grew louder. Both of them turned their heads just in time to see the hackney narrowly avoid colliding with another cart.

The driver continued to crack his whip, urging the horse even faster as it charged forward, not caring about the destruction he left in his wake.

Struggling to make sense of the situation, Della tried to walk as quickly as she could. They needed to get somewhere safe until the danger had passed.

"Della, move!" Royce yelled.

The hackney came hurtling toward her, its wheels grinding against the uneven cobbled pavement, leaving her with no time to escape, and her heart sank. *This was it—she was done for*, Della thought as she closed her eyes, preparing to be trampled.

With a great deal of force, something hit her from the side and Della found herself sprawled on the ground, dizzy, and unable to move. The impact having knocked the air from her lungs, leaving her gasping for breath.

"Della, look at me," Royce whispered soothingly as his face came into view. "You need to breathe."

"Ouch," was all she could manage to say as her lungs recovered from the shock.

"Is this going to become a common occurrence when I am around you?" Royce softly laughed as he gently caressed her cheek and brushed a loose strand of hair behind her ear.

"The hackney?" Della asked.

"Gone, thankfully."

Della stared at those captivating eyes. She would have gladly stayed like this forever with her body firmly planted on the ground beneath him. But she also wanted to give him a piece of her mind about this being a common occurrence, and would have, had she not heard Maggie and the Duchess approaching.

"Della? Royce? Good heavens, are you two all right?" Maggie asked when she saw them lying on the ground.

"We heard all the commotion and came out right as you knocked Della out of the way, Royce! Honestly!" the Duchess exclaimed, placing her hands on her hips. "Is no one to be trusted anymore? I just sent a few of our footmen to see if they could find out who drove that hackney and bring him back for a few questions."

Royce helped Della up into a sitting position. "Can you walk?"

"I believe so, now that I can breathe again." Della saw the bystanders staring at them.

"I am sorry, but I could see no other way to get us out of the way of that lunatic, whom I would gladly kill should I ever get my hands on him," Royce snapped.

"Royce, please inform Della's father and aunt of what has occurred and see that she is taken care of. I shall wait for your return and to see if our footmen can find out who that imbecile was." With that, the Duchess turned back inside, with Maggie close behind.

"Well, this time, I might be a damsel in distress," Della joked. "Could my knight in shining armor help me up?"

With a warm smile, Royce held her hands, helped her stand, and immediately swept her off her feet. Evidently, the pained expression on her face had been noticeable.

"This knight in shining armor will carry you to the carriage and take you home."

"Put. Me. Down." Della demanded sharply.

"Must we go through this again?" Royce released an exasperated sigh as he carried Della the short distance back to his home. He located the groom and asked for the carriage to be brought back.

"I suppose this goes along with your lecture the other night about me needing someone to protect me," Della said, crossing her arms. "Well, one incident does not mean that I—"

"Two," Royce interrupted.

"Two?"

"You said one incident. The count is now two. First the garden and just now with the hackney. Two incidences in which you needed someone there to watch over you."

"Is it really two when you just admitted that the incident in the garden was *your* fault? I could walk to the carriage if you would just allow me to use you as a prop," Della said with a huff. "It would not surprise me if this incident graces the papers in the morning, labeling you as a hero. Miss Putnam will be all the happier to align herself with the tall, dark, handsome, hero duke."

"Handsome?"

"Did I say handsome?" Della laughed nervously. "I meant mediocre, somewhat decent looking…" she waved off her comment. "The point is, I have already endured this embarrassment once at the Bellamy's ball. Do not make me do it again." Della looked up at Royce pleadingly. "Please, put me down."

"Very well."

Royce held onto Della until she could balance herself and gingerly placed her weight on her ankle. It hurt, but she would not give Royce the satisfaction of asking to be carried after she demanded he put her down. So, she hobbled along at a snail's pace until they reached the carriage.

Royce's conscious had been bothering him since the moment he had made the agreement. He had told Miss Putnam that honesty was the best way forward. And even though had promised Mr. Rowntree he would say nothing to Della, it would be hypocritical of him if he were not honest with her as well.

But the time to speak with her about it had not presented itself…until now.

"Royce?" Della looked at him with concern. "Are you all right?"

He had wanted to carry Della, but she had insisted on walking on her own to avoid gossip. Royce understood, but his arms had hesitated when he set her down, seeming reluctant to let her go.

Feelings he had never thought he would have for Della had taken root, and it was getting harder to ignore them. Perhaps they had always been there, and he had just been too blind to notice. But these feelings could not go any further. He had to marry Miss Putnam. The sooner, the better, for everyone involved—especially for himself.

Royce shook his head...right, Della had asked him a question. This was his chance. He was going to tell her about the agreement with her father.

"Yes, I am fine," he replied. *Damn! I am a coward,* he thought to himself. "Just a lot on my mind, as you can imagine. I am sure we will both suffer a few bumps and bruises from today's mishap. Your ankle, notwithstanding, of course."

"I am sure we will," Della said, giving him a small smile. "Well, here we are."

"Allow me to help you." Royce let Della lean on him as she climbed down from the carriage. "Is there a problem?" he asked when she hesitated.

"Stairs." Della motioned toward steps leading to the front door.

Taking advantage of the moment, Royce scooped Della into his arms and practically ran up the steps, setting her back down once they reached the top.

"That was well done of you. I did not even have the chance to—"

"Object?"

"Yes." Della turned to knock, but the door was already open.

"Miss Rowntree, Your Grace." Croxton bowed, moving to the side to allow them entrance. "Has something happened?" he asked, closing the door.

"Oh! There you are, Della!" Tilly exclaimed. "I was wondering when you might return from your walk. We needed to discuss...Oh! Your Grace, I did not notice you standing there. How lovely to see you."

"I am afraid Miss Rowntree and I had quite the scare with a runaway horse and hackney. Unfortunately for us, we were directly in its path, and we barely managed to get out of the way before it hit us. I would recommend she rest, as she seems to have injured her ankle again."

"Oh, poor dear. First, you sprained your ankle at the ball, and now you were almost trampled to death." Tilly held a hand over her bosom. "Have pity on my heart. You must take better care of yourself. You have been extremely fortunate that His Grace has been there to keep you safe...twice."

Royce hid his laugh behind a cough as Tilly continued to talk and looked at Della. He could tell from the way she glanced at him from the corner of her eye she was not amused by his earlier statement being proven correct.

"Let us not make it thrice, hmm?" Tilly said, turning to speak with Croxton.

Della leaned toward Royce and whispered. "Does anyone say thrice anymore?"

Royce just shrugged. "Apparently."

"Do not worry about Della. I will make certain that she is well taken care of."

"I am to go to the ruins with His Grace's family the day after tomorrow," Della informed her aunt.

"Only if you get upstairs and rest," Tilly said, planting her hands on her hips. "My sincerest thanks for protecting Della, Your Grace, but you should get home and rest yourself."

"I think I am being dismissed," Royce said, a small smile playing about lips.

Tilly left to retrieve a few things as Royce bowed and walked to the door. "Della, follow your aunts' orders. Let us not make it thrice."

"Oh!"

That was all Della could say before Royce stepped out and quickly shut the door behind himself. And he could not help but laugh as a loud thump resonated from the other side.

Chapter 11

Stretching as she stood, Della greeted the morning with a smile and went to the window, throwing open the curtains. It was cloudy, but at least it was not raining; still nice enough to get out of London and away from city life.

With a purposeful stride, she walked over to her wardrobe and sifted through her dresses. Unless one was in a fussy ballgown or other finicky contraption, getting help to dress seemed rather unnecessary. She took pleasure in dressing herself whenever she could, which often annoyed her lady's maid, Abigail.

Della decided on her cream-colored walking dress with a green spencer and her most durable walking shoes. The clock on the mantel chimed the hour as she finished slipping the last button through its loop.

Checking over everything in the floor-length mirror, Della started making her way to the dining room and was halfway down the stairs when the smell of chocolate greeted her. Even if nothing else went well today, she would at least start the day off with something sweet.

The spread Mrs. Walmsley had prepared was wonderful: coddled eggs, bacon, toast with plenty of butter and jam, and a pot of chocolate. She quietly sipped her chocolate, contemplating how the day's events would go, when she heard a knock at the door.

"I am here to see Miss Rowntree, if you would be so good as to announce me?"

"Of course, my lady. If you would follow me. I believe Miss Rowntree is in the dining room." Their footsteps echoing as they made their way into the room.

"Lady Derrington to see you, Miss."

"Thank you, Croxton."

Maggie walked through the door so sedately, Della found it hard to contain her amusement and almost let out a burst of laughter as she watched Croxton's eyes widen in confusion.

"Of course, Miss." Croxton bowed and turned to leave while simultaneously shaking his head, as though he was trying to understand what had just happened.

Maggie plopped into the chair next to Della. "That..." she paused for dramatic effect, "was excruciating! But so very worth it to see the look on his face."

"I do not know which is worse. A vexed Croxton or a confused Croxton. When you finish toying with his head, Maggie, he will not know which way is up and which way is down."

They both burst into laughter at that thought as Maggie helped herself to a sip of Della's chocolate.

They pulled up to the ruins of an old forgotten church about an hour outside of London. A large oak tree provided an abundance of shade, making the area below its branches ideal for a picnic. Blankets were carefully laid out and hampers, filled with all sorts of food for the occasion, were arranged in front of them.

Then gentlemen allowed the ladies to choose their seats before seating themselves. Royce sat next to Miss Putnam, and Aden next to Maggie. Della looked up at the remaining gentleman and smiled at Lord Haddock, scooting herself closer to Maggie as he seated himself next to her.

The Duchess sat with Mrs. Cora as they watched Samuel, Victoria, and Cornelia play a game of tag. When asked where Grayson and Desmond were, the Duchess had simply scoffed and mumbled something about sons who should spend more time with their family and less time on cards and drink.

They all talked animatedly as they chose different items from the wonderful assortment Mrs. Ivers had put together for their outing. Everything looked delicious, and Della did not know which to choose first. Finally, she decided on the cold roasted beef on a slice of toast with mustard.

When the main course had been consumed, the footmen tidied up and laid out the sweets. Della could not contain her excitement when she spotted the petite duchess' amongst the selection and noticed Royce staring at her. She pointed at the pastry and smiled at him.

"Miss Rowntree," Lord Haddock said, offering Della a lemon tart. "If I recall correctly, these are your favorite." He looked at her with a dark glint in his eye.

"How kind of you to remember." Della smiled, even though she could not remember ever telling him about her fondness for lemon tarts. "Oh, before I forget, Lord Haddock. You left your book in the park the other day. It is waiting in the carriage for you."

"Very considerate of you, Miss Rowntree. I thank you," he said, staring at the lemon tart in Della's hand.

Not wanting to be rude, Della took a bite. The bright, tangy flavor of lemon burst forth, covering her tongue in a tart sweetness. A delighted moan threatened to escape, but she remained silent, looking anywhere but at Lord Haddock.

Della noticed Royce staring agitatedly at the man beside her, before her gaze shifted and she saw Miss Putnam looking directly looking at her.

"Shall we explore the ruins?" Miss Putnam asked, breaking eye contact with Della, to look at Royce.

"What a wonderful idea!" Maggie agreed, turning to the Duchess to ask if she would join them.

The Duchess declined, stating that she was close enough to keep an eye on things, but wanted to remain with the younger set.

They all stood and made their way into the ruins of what Della was sure had been a beautiful church. It backed up to a dense copse of trees with lots of overgrown thicket surrounding the outside.

Large wood beams lay on the dirt floor, the ceiling having long since fallen, but the outside walls and bell tower remained. Along the inside wall, a staircase curved upwards toward the bell tower overlooking the open fields.

"I say we split off into pairs to explore," Miss Putnam suggested. "His Grace and I will take the lower level. Lady Derrington and Lord Aynesworth can take the outside grounds, and Miss Rowntree and Lord Haddock can take the bell tower. I hear the view up there is breathtaking."

"Shall we?" Lord Haddock motioned for Della to go up the stairs ahead of him.

Agreeing to meetup shortly to switch areas, they all went their separate ways. As Della slowly climbed the stairs, she saw Royce and Miss Putnam walk by the dilapidated altar and out of sight.

Making her way to the top, Della could not help but be in awe of the circular stone room. Dust motes danced across the beams of light, shining down the ivy that grew up the walls, across the bare beams, and down over an old brass bell that still hung from the rafters.

Running her fingers over the stone's smooth surface, she looked to her right at the three lookouts that framed the land in small, picturesque scenes. Each one looking like a carefully curated piece of art hanging in a museum. And to her left, she saw the stone archway of a corridor leading to another section of the abandoned church.

"Beautiful," Della whispered.

"It is," Lord Haddock agreed, coming up behind her.

Della hurriedly walked to a lookout point and marveled at the vast expanse of rolling fields stretching as far as the eye could see. The rise and fall of hills reminded her of gentle waves on the ocean. But Lord Haddock did not seem to care about the view.

The way he nervously moved around the room, restlessly pacing back and forth, made him look like a caged animal plotting its escape. And the corridor across the room seemed to hold particular interest for him, though for no reason she could understand.

"Have you seen a ghost?" Della asked, breaking the silence.

"A ghost?" Lord Haddock repeated.

"Yes, you keep looking down the corridor, and I thought perhaps you might have seen a ghost or something."

"No, no ghosts. I am simply taking it all in," he coolly replied.

"Um, p-perhaps, we should find the others." Della turned to the stairs as Lord haddock reached out and grabbed her by the arm.

"They can wait. There is something I must ask you."

"Oh?" was all Della could say as a sense of unease slithered down her spine.

"I had hoped to have the opportunity to talk with you during our dance at the Bellamy's ball, but once I saw the duke carrying you out, I knew I had missed my chance. It was fortuitous that the Duchess invited me today." He cleared his throat as he got down on one knee and took Della's hand in his. "Miss Rowntree..."

"My Lord?" Della slipped her fingers out of his chilly hands and took a step back.

"Would you do me the honor of becoming my wife?" Lord Haddock's forced smile, which conveyed anything but eagerness to enter into an engagement, rendered Della speechless.

She had only danced with him a handful of times, and the conversations with the gentleman were just as sparse. How could he even think of asking her to marry him? They did not even know each other—nothing beyond mere acquaintances.

"Did I hear you correctly, my lord?"

"Indeed, you did, Miss Rowntree."

"But you do not even know me," Della said, taking another step back.

"I do realize this, yes, but given time, I believe we could make a go of it." He stood; his black pants now smudged with dirt.

"Make a go of it?" Della repeated. "My lord, I am flattered, but I am afraid we do not know each other well enough to *make a go of it*. Therefore, I am sorry, but I am afraid I must decline your offer."

"My dear Miss Rowntree, you would be wise to accept my offer. There may not be many proposals left for you to turn down," he said in an ominous warning. "So, I will ask you again. Will you do me the honor of becoming my wife?"

"Again, I must decline, my lord. Now, if you will excuse me..." Della turned and was about to make her way down the steps when he appeared in front of her.

"If I cannot convince you with my words, perhaps I can convince you with this."

In a surprising and forceful gesture, Lord Haddock grabbed onto Della and pulled her closer, pressing his body against hers. As he attempted to kiss her, Della desperately tried to push him away, but he was too strong

"My Lord! My lord, please stop!" Della shouted, shoving as hard as she could against his chest as he tried pressing more kisses on her. She did everything she could think of to stop the onslaught of his so-called convincing...except for one thing.

"Lord Haddock?" Della said in a softer tone as she moved her hands up to his shoulders to distract him.

"Yes?" he responded, pulling his head back to look at her.

"How is this for an answer?" Della kneed him hard between the legs, and he slumped to the floor, howling in pain as Royce came running up the stairs.

"Della!" Royce propped himself up against the stone wall, gasping for air. "I heard yelling and..." He looked down to see Lord Haddock cupping his manhood and whimpering.

"I will not ask where you learned that."

"Maggie," Della simply stated.

Royce rolled his eyes heavenward. "I probably have one of my brothers to thank for that, but the more important thing right now is that you are okay. Now you—" Royce said, pulling Lord Haddock to his feet—"need to leave. Della?"

"I will be along shortly. I just need a moment to regain my composure."

Royce nodded and headed down the stairs with the still whimpering lord.

It was a shame that such a beautiful day had to be overshadowed by the vile behavior of that beastly man. Softly, she hummed to herself while taking one last look through the lookout at the top of the stairs before going down to meet everyone when she felt a firm shove against her back.

Despite her best efforts to regain her balance, Della stumbled forward, her arms flailing as she desperately tried to grab onto something to prevent her fall, but her hands only grazed the smooth surface of the stone.

But somehow, even with her legs entangled in her dress, she managed to twist herself around so she could at least see where she was going. She spotted Royce and Lord Haddock still descending and silently prayed they would reach the bottom before she crashed into them.

Just as Royce was making his way down the stairs, a sharp gasp broke the silence, startling him. He looked up, and a surge of panic overcame him as he saw Della struggling to regain her footing. Despite her best efforts, her foot slipped, causing her to pitch forward.

Without hesitation, Royce shoved Lord Haddock down the remaining steps, confident that a fall from such a short distance would not cause too much harm. However, given the man's actions today, it was not even half of what he deserved.

As Royce raced upward, he noticed Della had managed to turn herself around on the stairs and was now facing forward.

She reached out for him, and he quickly grabbed onto her, pulling her close as they tumbled the rest of the way down. The impact of her body against his had hurt like hell, but he was determined to protect her from any more harm.

"What happened?" Royce asked after regaining some of the feeling in his backside that the fall had rendered temporarily numb.

"I am not sure," Della replied, her voice filled with uncertainty, as she pushed herself up to sit. "One minute, I was about to follow you and Lord Haddock, and the next, it felt as though someone pushed me from behind."

"Pushed?" Royce stood and bounded up the stairs two at a time, not caring how his body protested. He searched everywhere, but there were few places for someone to hide besides the corridor.

He turned in a slow circle, looking for some sign there had been another person here, when his eyes landed on a rope hanging over the edge of one lookout. His eyes scanned the fields, searching for any hint of an uninvited guest, but found only the peaceful stillness of the countryside.

Damn! Whomever it was must have headed toward the trees. Slapping his hands against the stone, he let out a frustrated growl.

Making his way back down, he saw Maggie and Aden helping Della, looking a little worse for wear, to stand up. Miss Putnam appeared indifferent to the situation, standing off to the side with her arms crossed. Lord Haddock, on the other hand, was still lying in the spot where he had landed.

"Aden, please take Lord Haddock back to the carriage and send him on his way. I will explain later."

Aden saluted, and grabbed Lord Haddock by the arm, practically dragging the disgraced lord to his carriage.

"Are you well enough to walk?" Royce asked Della.

"I am, Your Grace. No carrying required."

Royce almost laughed out loud, but decided it was not the time to do so as he held his arm out to Miss Putnam and guided her out of the ruins.

"Must you always be going to Miss Rowntree's rescue?" Miss Putnam whispered harshly to him once Maggie and Della were far enough away not to hear. "Her ankle, the hackney, and now this?"

"It is not as if she did any of those things on purpose," Royce stated.

"Hmmph. I feel like she is just doing these things to get attention."

Royce pulled Miss Putnam to a stop as they reached the carriage.

"So, you are saying she endured Lord Haddock's advances and falling down the stairs solely for attention?"

"I am saying it is a possibility. No one witnessed what happened with Lord Haddock—it is her word against his. Perhaps she gets herself into these situations, so *you* will notice her," Miss Putnam said, her agitation showing.

"Do not be ridiculous," Royce scoffed.

"Ridiculous? Do you not find it odd that these things always seem to happen when you two are near one another? I see the way she smiles at you, the way you look at her when you think no one is watching. Perhaps you might be better off asking for her hand in marriage. Though a woman of her…caliber, would never fulfill the role of your duchess as well as I could." She straightened her spine, challenging Royce to respond. "I will see myself home, Your Grace."

Royce waited for Miss Putnam to climb into her carriage, then slammed the door behind her. Although they had not been acquainted for a long time, he could not deny that he was getting to glimpse an entirely different side of Miss Putnam.

And the more familiar he became with her, the harder it was for him to ignore the fact that maybe her true colors were beginning to show. If that was the case, perhaps he should step back and rethink what a marriage to Miss Putnam would look like.

His family meant more to him than anything else in this world, and to marry a woman who seemed so inclined to tear someone else down did not seem the type of person he wanted anywhere near his family.

Royce stormed off, seething with anger at the woman in the carriage behind him, and consumed with worry for the woman in the carriage in front of him. He reached into his pocket to check if the item he had gotten from the footman before they left was still there, and he smiled.

Although the day's events had taken a sour turn, there was still a chance for something sweet to make it seem a little better.

Chapter 12

Della showed herself to the carriage while waiting for everyone to get situated. Maggie and Samuel chased the two youngest Derrington children as they ran in circles around the Duchess. Finally, Maggie grabbed hold of Victoria, placed her in a carriage, and went back for Cornelia.

She laughed at the scene before her when she heard two people arguing. Peeking her head out the window, Della saw Royce and Miss Putnam off to the side, talking angrily—again. Miss Putnam turned to climb up and Royce slammed the door shut behind her, looking enraged. Della ducked back in as he started storming in her direction.

A few moments later, Royce climbed in. "I hope you do not mind if I ride with you and Maggie. Miss Putnam is going directly back home."

"Oh, of course not." Della smiled.

Royce sprawled on the seat across from Della. Her carriage was smaller than the ducal one—now occupied by the Duchess and the children—but it still felt spacious. However, that spaciousness seemed to disappear with a man of Royce's stature.

He had now come to her aid several times, never complaining or berating her for her carelessness. But that was the kind of man he was, strong, dependable, and protective. The dukedom was safe in his hands. But a tinge of guilt gnawed at her.

These incidents, it would seem, had created some tension between Royce and Miss Putnam. His recent arguments with Miss Putnam appeared to confirm this, as she had never witnessed him so visibly agitated and flustered.

She wracked her brain about what she might say to comfort him when a small item wrapped in white cloth was laid on her lap.

"That is for you. I noticed you did not get one after accepting the lemon tart from Lord Haddock. So, I took the liberty of having the last one saved for you."

Smiling at Royce, Della picked the item up and gently unwrapped it...a petite duchesse. "Thank you."

"You are most welcome, Della." The slight darkening in Royce's voice made Della's heart race.

"Right then, off we go." Maggie flung the door open and clamored in, sitting next to Della. "Oh! Might I have a bite?" she begged. "I wanted one so badly, but mother told me I was to wait until everyone else had the chance to eat one...because someone partook before the picnic," Maggie said, eyeing her brother. "Sometimes being a lady is so difficult."

"If you can call yourself that," Royce quipped.

Maggie kicked him in the shin. "If I cannot call myself a lady, then you most assuredly cannot call yourself a gentleman, sprawled as you are. Would you please sit up so Della and I might have some space?"

Suitably chastised, Royce pushed himself into a more proper sitting position as he scowled at his sister. Della split the pastry, giving half to Maggie.

"Oh, I meant to ask you if you would like to stay with me tonight since the Ravensdale's ball is tomorrow. Please say you will! It will be like when we were little girls! We can send one of the footmen to fetch your dress." Maggie looked at Della expectantly as she took a bite of her half.

"I will get my dress myself. Besides, Father and Tilly should be made aware of what happened today. And I would like to tell them myself—"

"I will accompany you," Royce offered.

Della stared at him but continued, "...before word gets out, as it inevitably will, once your mother tells her circle of friends what a horrid man Lord Haddock is."

Glancing down at her hand, Della spotted some chocolate still on her finger and looked around for the cloth, but Maggie was already using it. Instead of doing the ladylike thing and waiting her turn, Della stuck her finger in her mouth to lick it off.

Della raised her head and felt a nervous flutter in her stomach at the intense look in Royce's eyes.

Her cheeks grew warm as she realized what she was doing, and she pulled her finger out of her mouth. He cleared his throat and shifted in his seat, his eyes darting toward the window.

"I never cared for the man," Maggie said, seeming unaware of the heated exchange between Della and Royce.

"Nor I." Della shook her head and frowned. "Even less so now, especially after today."

"He is what I consider an opportunist." Royce said. "After the rumor was spread about postponing the announcement with Miss Putnam, Lord Haddock saw his chance to offer for her. I overheard someone say that Lord Milton refused him."

"But why would he ask for my hand so quickly after asking for Miss Putnam's?"

"Your dowry," Maggie mentioned without hesitation. "It is common knowledge that your father has settled on a considerable amount for your dowry."

Della's smile faltered as she looked at Maggie and then at Royce. "Is my worth now solely measured in terms of money?"

"You are worth far more than any sum your father could offer. And those men are idiots if they cannot see that," Royce said, his gaze fixed on her as he spoke.

"Does that include yourself?" Maggie asked, drawing simultaneous looks from Della and Royce.

Royce did not respond to Maggie's goading and looked back out the window. "Stay away from Lord Haddock. He does not seem the type to give up easily. But if he knows what is good for him, he will come nowhere near me or mine."

Despite her best efforts to get comfortable, Della could not relax. The pain from her fall had set in, making her toss and turn. Luckily, she only had a couple of minor scrapes and bruises, in addition to the incident with the hackney, but her ankle appeared unharmed.

The weight of the day's events left her mind feeling heavy and drained. All she wanted to do was to forget Lord Haddock's proposal and that slobbery wetness he called a kiss. Just the mere thought of it made Della sick to her stomach.

Lord Haddock's anxious behavior had seemed odd, constantly looking down the corridor as if expecting to find something. She never would have guessed there might have been another person hiding in the shadows.

And even though Royce had found a rope hanging from a lookout, perhaps there had not been another person. Maybe her body's natural reaction to falling had made her feel as though she had been pushed.

A small laugh bubbled to the surface as she recalled the expression on Royce's face after he saw Lord Haddock curled up on the floor. She had found herself in a difficult situation when that abhorrent man had tried to kiss her, and she had defended herself the only way she knew how.

Though the actions of Lord Haddock were unforgivable, Della struggled to make sense of the other events that had occurred. But it all seemed to be just a bout of bad luck. Hopefully, she had endured enough, and her bad luck would soon be over.

Della stared at her ceiling, knowing she would not fall asleep anytime soon. Maybe a dull book would help. Pulling her dressing gown on and grabbing a candle from her bedside table, she tip-toed into the darkened hallway, down the stairs, and into the library.

Setting the candle down, Della made her way over to the shelves, reading each title as she looked over books of various sizes. Once she had made her selection, she realized it was out of her reach and looked around for something to stand on. There was no ladder, so she climbed the shelves to give herself a boost.

"That should do it," Della said out loud to an empty room and gently let herself down, being careful not to agitate her ankle.

She curled up with a blanket on the settee and had barely begun reading the third page of her book when she heard the doorknob turn.

Royce rubbed his eyes with the palms of his hands and leaned back in his chair. After helping Della retrieve her dress, he had gone straight to his study, where he busied himself with the household accounts, and asked for a meal to be brought to him—staying hidden until everyone had gone to bed.

The carriage ride back from the ruins had been torture as he sat across from Della while she had eaten the pastry he had given her. The image of her licking the chocolate off her fingers was seared into Royce's mind, making him shift uncomfortably in his chair as a certain appendage made itself known.

Della was completely unaware of how her innocent gesture had affected him, or how he had longed to bring her fingertips to his own lips and lick them...one...by...one.

Royce could not recall Miss Putnam ever evoking such a response in him, and that is the way he had wanted it, what he had desired. But his father's words kept echoing in his head: *remember, what we think we want is not always what we need.*

It had not gone unnoticed that Della had handled everything that had happened to her recently with incredible grace—and stubbornness—while Miss Putnam had shown how selfish and uncaring she could be. Though he did not want to marry for love, he did not want a cruel wife.

What if his father had been right in making that agreement with Mr. Rowntree? What if Della was the answer to what he wanted in a marriage, *and* what he needed? If so, what was he to do about Lord Milton and Miss Putnam?

With more questions than answers, he stood and stretched, his muscles protesting. A few bruises had formed from his fall, but that aside, the only reminder he had from earlier was a slight stiffness in his back. He sighed and went to the sideboard for a drink.

It had been a trying day, and sleep was calling his name. He hoped Della had found some rest as well. Blowing out the candles on his desk, Royce picked up his coat where he had discarded it, slung it over his shoulder, and walked into the foyer.

Approaching the stairs, he saw a faint light coming from under the library door. Either a person was in there, or someone would be in trouble for not ensuring all candles had been snuffed before retiring for the night. Making his way to the door, Royce raised his hand to knock, but decided to just open it up and go in.

"Your Grace!" Della exclaimed, holding the book against her chest as she scrambled up from the settee. "You frightened me!"

"My apologies. I was heading to bed and saw a light from under the door. I thought that someone might have left a candle lit in here," Royce said, using an arm to prop himself against the doorframe. "What are you doing up at this hour? And in your dressing gown, no less?"

With a gasp, Della ran behind the settee to hide herself. "I-I could not sleep, so I can down here to find a book that might bore me enough so I could."

"Ah, and what did you deem boring enough to lull you into slumber, hmm?" Royce pushed himself away from the door and walked closer, tilting his head to read the title of the book she was holding. "A Treatise on Carriages," he read aloud. "Interesting choice."

"Yes, well...I really should get to bed. Let me just put this back."

"I know on what shelf that book sits. Not to mention that my youngest siblings broke the ladder during one of their wild games of tag through the house, and we are waiting for the new one to arrive. So, now I need to know how on earth you got it," he stated, his eyes fixed on Della as she padded across the floor.

"I, uh, I climbed," Della said over her shoulder without looking at him.

"Climbed what?"

"The bookshelf," she grunted with each attempt to put the book back.

"Della..."

Della bowed her head and let out a heavy sigh. "Could you help me, Your Grace?"

A small smile tugged at the corner of Royce's mouth as he came up behind Della and placed his hand over hers, helping ease the book up to its home.

"It was quite impressive how you dealt with Lord Haddock today," Royce said, bringing his hands down on either side of Della, caging her between his arms. "Remind me never to get on your bad side."

"It would serve you well to remember that, Your Grace," Della said in mock sternness as she twisted around to face him.

"Royce..."

"Royce," Della repeated softly. "I believe I owe you an apology and a sincere thank you."

"Whatever for?"

"You took the brunt of my fall today—again—so thank you. I have also been remiss in asking how you are faring, and for that, I am sorry. It must be vexing to constantly be coming to my aid when you have more important matters to worry about."

"Della, no apologies are necessary, nor do I require thanks. The wellbeing and safety of those I care about will always be my priority." He leaned in, touching his forehead to hers. "I do not know what we would do if something happened to you."

"We?" Della whispered.

"We," he whispered back.

"Royce?"

"Hmm?" was all he could manage, his heart feeling as though it would beat right out of his chest.

"Kiss me."

Royce was not sure if that had been a question or command, but when he saw the earnest look in her eyes, he found himself unable to resist. He kept his touch gentle, letting his hand rest softly at the small of her back, while the other hand delicately cradled her cheek, allowing her a moment to decide if this was truly what she wanted.

He knew *he* wanted to kiss Della, to part her lips and delve into her depths, but that was not what she needed, not after that disaster with Lord Haddock. Taking a subtle approach, he leaned closer and tenderly brushed his lips against hers, being mindful to not overwhelm her the way her mere presence overwhelmed him.

Despite this, it seemed Della had a different opinion on what she needed at that moment as she grabbed onto his untied cravat and pulled him in closer. Their kiss grew more intense, their bodies eagerly pressing against each other as if they were determined to eliminate any space that separated them.

With a guttural growl, Royce lifted Della up, wrapped her legs around his waist, and pinned her against the bookshelf, unable to restrain himself from responding to her less-than-subtle demand.

He explored Della's mouth and slid his hands down, cupping her backside. Tightening his grip, he thrust his hips against her most sensitive spot, causing both of them to moan.

How long they had remained like this Royce did not know, but all too soon, the lustful haze that inhabited his head began to clear. With a mischievous grin, he lightly nibbled on Della's bottom lip before lowering her down to the floor.

"Goodnight, Della." Royce let her go and gripped hard on the bookshelf, his knuckles turning white in their bid to keep from pulling her back to him.

"Goodnight, Royce," Della whispered breathily, dipping out from between his arms and making her way to the door. "Sleep well."

With her white dressing gown flowing behind her, she slipped into the darkness, disappearing as though she had been nothing more than a beautiful apparition.

Sleep well. Ha! Sleep would be the last thing that would occupy his mind as he lay in bed. The only thing he would think of was the warmth of Della's body pressed against his own or the sound of frustration she had let escape when the gentleness of his kiss had not been enough.

Royce placed his hands on his hips, letting his head fall back on a sigh. What a mess...

Chapter 13

The following evening, Della and Maggie wandered around the yard, waiting for their chance to greet their hosts.

Lord and Lady Ravensdale's home had a certain air of dignity and stateliness to it. Candles glowed warmly in every window, casting dancing shadows over the lawn as servants offered refreshments to the waiting guests.

After making their way to the front of the line, they graciously thanked their hosts for the invitation and made their way inside.

Walking into the lavishly decorated ballroom, Della's eyes quickly located her father, talking to a gentleman she had never seen before.

"Good evening, Father." Della smiled, praying she and Maggie had not intruded on his conversation.

"Della! Lady Derrington!" Her father beamed. "Let me introduce you! Lord de Courtenay, this is Lady Derrington, sister to the Duke of Exeter."

"My Lord." Maggie curtsied.

"And this is my daughter, Miss Della Rowntree."

"My Lord," Della said, dipping into a curtsy as well. "It is a pleasure to meet you."

"The honor is all mine, I assure you." Lord de Courtenay smiled, bowing his head.

He was a striking gentleman, Della noticed—probably about the same age as Royce, if she had to guess. And it was obvious, by the smile on her face, that Maggie was just as aware of how attractive Lord de Courtenay was.

"Do you remember the business meeting I had to attend?" her father asked. "Well, I purchased some new ships in Topsham. Lord de Courtenay was in London and was kind enough to bring the paperwork for me to sign."

"How thoughtful." Della smiled, hooking her arm through Maggie's. "If you will excuse us, we would like to get a drink before the first dance starts."

"Of course, of course! Go have fun," her father said, turning back to the conversation at hand.

As they turned to leave, Lord de Courtenay spoke. "Lady Derrington?"

"Yes, my lord?" Maggie answered.

"Would you honor me with a dance later this evening?"

"I would consider it a great privilege, my lord."

Lord de Courtenay signed his name on Maggie's dance card and placed a kiss on the back of her hand. A tinge of pink rose into Maggie's cheeks as she smiled at him.

Excusing themselves once again, they maneuvered their way across the room to the refreshment table and selected Ratafia. Della took a sip, enjoying the berry sweetened wine.

Even though it was watered down, it was still better than the concoction Lord and Lady Bellamy had served at their ball.

"What do you think of Lord de Courtenay?" Della asked.

"He is handsome, to be sure. And, by the look of it, he has already amassed enough women searching for a husband that he could have his own harem." Maggie shook her head. "If one simply looks at his smile, they could see it does not reach his eyes. He is not interested in them," she uttered, turning back to have her drink refilled.

"No, but he certainly seems to be interested in you," Della said, seeing Lord de Courtenay staring straight at Maggie.

"What?" Maggie turned abruptly.

Della saw Maggie smile, nodding her head in acknowledgement, and Lord de Courtenay bowed his in return. The women surrounding Lord de Courtenay all looked in Maggie's direction and glared at her.

When they turned back to the handsome lord, Della could see the sudden shift in their faces. Their looks of excitement quickly changing to ones of disappointment, realizing they no longer held his attention.

"When will those women understand that chasing a man only makes him run the other way?" Maggie laughed lightly. "Oh dear, my mother is waving at me to go to her. Hopefully, it is not another introduction. I had enough of those at the last ball," she said, rolling her eyes. "I will find you later."

Della nodded and was left to wander about the grand ballroom alone.

Eventually, Mr. Green, a taciturn and unassuming gentleman, approached and asked her for a dance. She agreed, and when the dance had concluded, Mr. Green escorted her to where Tilly was sitting, engaged in a lively discussion with a group of women.

To avoid the probing questions her aunt's friends were sure to ask about her marital status, Della hastily made her excuses and left. Gradually, she made her way across the room to the open doors. She noticed an empty bench that had been beautifully carved in the balustrade and sat on it, watching the treetops sway back and forth gently in the breeze.

"Good evening."

Della started when Aden appeared before her. "Good evening, my lord."

"May I join you?"

"Certainly." Della gathered her dress and moved over to make space for him to sit. "Lovely night, is it not?"

"Indeed it is," Aden agreed as he played absentmindedly with the signet ring on his finger, a clear sign he was nervous about something.

Della cast a thoughtful look in Aden's direction. Behind his cheerful façade and mischievous personality, there always seemed to be an air of secrecy that followed him.

She was familiar with his father, fully aware of the man's despicable nature and cruelty. And despite the close friendship she and Aden had shared over the years, she understood there were aspects about his life he chose not to discuss.

She was uncertain if Aden desired a conversation or if he was content just to sit with her in the peaceful silence, so she remained quiet as the orchestra's discordant notes wafted through the air, signaling the beginning of the next set.

"Would you care to dance, Miss Rowntree?" Aden asked, standing suddenly. "I am positive that—"he glanced at her dance card—"Mr. Farley would not mind."

"He does not exist. I always put a fictitious name on my card for the waltz. But if he *was* real, I am sure he would take great offense to someone trying to steal his chance to sweep me off my feet." Della laughed. "The true reason I sit the waltz out is that I do not know how to waltz. Father once hired a tutor for me. He was horrible and told me I had the gracefulness of a chicken. Father told him where he could stuff his chicken and fired the man."

"That sounds like your father," Aden chuckled. "I seem to remember a dance with a certain young lady at her debut," he said, holding out his hand to Della.

"Yes, but you seem to have forgotten how many times I stepped on your toes."

"All you need to do is let yourself feel the music and follow my lead. I will not let you fall—I promise."

Della smiled and placed her hand in his. "I am trusting you, and that trust will be irrevocably broken should you let me embarrass myself."

"If I should allow you to stumble or fall, you have my permission to stomp on my foot as hard as you can," Aden joked, a small smile forming at the corner of his mouth as he led them out onto the dance floor. "Just follow my lead, but if you should desire to count, a waltz is in three-four time; one, two, three, one, two, three, and so on."

Della nodded and took a deep breath, letting Aden lean her into the first spin. She remembered he was a talented dancer, although he did not dance often, and this time was no exception.

"I have something I would like to speak with you about."

"Oh?" Della asked, looking up at him.

"Yes, err, will you walk with me?"

"But we just started dancing."

"I must be an excellent partner to have you protesting about stopping a waltz." He smiled, lightening the mood.

Placing her hand on Aden's arm, she let him guide her off the dance floor. Carefully weaving in and out of the crowd of dancers, they eventually arrived back at the bench on the terrace.

"I have a question to ask you," Aden said as he paced. "Well, it is a question and not a question at the same time. What I mean to say is this will sound sudden coming from me, and if you say no, I will understand."

"I am afraid you are not making any sense. What seems to have you so out of sorts?"

Aden rubbed the back of his neck and sighed. '*Out with it man*,' he whispered aloud. "Della...will you do me the great honor of becoming my wife?"

The words seemed to leave him in a rush.

"I am sorry," Della said, not sure if she heard correctly. "Did you just ask me to...marry you?"

"I did," Aden said matter-of-factly, with that sideways smirk of his.

"I am not entirely sure what I expected you to ask, but it was most assuredly not that." Della paused before speaking. "May I ask why?"

"Well..." Aden said, fiddling with the gold ring on his finger again. "You may have noticed that my father has not been seen in public for a while now. He is not well, and I fear the time for me to step up and take his place will be here sooner than I would like. I cannot say I am happy about it, but if it means I no longer must deal with his tyrannical ways, then so be it."

"I understand your fears. It cannot be easy to deal with that sort of situation, and I will be glad to help where I can. But why ask me to marry you? What does one have to do with the other?"

"I guess I want someone there beside me when the time comes. Someone to share it with. Someone I care for and whose opinion I respect."

"Why not ask Royce?"

"I already did. He said—and I quote—that he would rather be married to a horse's arse. I know he would set anything aside to help me, but I could not ask that of him. He has his own estate to run and family to take care of. Not to mention the situation with Miss Putnam."

Della looked at Aden and could see the sincerity in his eyes. Until now, she had rejected offers without a second thought, but was not sure she could reject him so easily.

"Listen," Aden said, gently taking Della's hand. "I know I am not the best man to ask for your hand in marriage. Hell, I would turn myself down flat if I were in your shoes." He laughed depreciatingly.

"You need not give me an answer now. I know my proposal probably came as quite a shock. But I cherish our friendship and I think we could make a marriage between us work. Just promise me you will think about it, hmm?"

She looked at Aden's sweet face. He was such a dear friend, and as far as basing a marriage off their friendship, well...most people did not even have that much.

"I will think about it." Della smiled. "I cannot tell you when I will give my answer. But I am flattered that, of all the women you are acquainted with, I am the one you asked first. Wait—am I the first one you asked?"

Aden threw his head back and let out a sharp laugh. "You see, Della, that is why I think we could make a marriage between us work. You can make me laugh without even trying. Which is more than I can say for most of the women who parade around these ballrooms.

"If it puts you at ease, you are the first person I have ever asked to marry me. Well," he said, "except the one time I asked Royce."

"What?"

"That is a story for another time." Aden chuckled as he held out his hand.

"I guess it is time we rejoined the swirling masses."

"If we must," Della sighed. "I see Maggie over there."

Walking over to Maggie, Della thanked Aden for the dance.

"And I thank you for the honor of your company, Miss Rowntree." Aden brushed a light kiss over her knuckles.

His kiss to the back of her hand did not kindle the same fire in her it had with Royce but filled her with the fondness of a long-standing friendship.

Della saw his walls come up as he straightened and glanced in Maggie's direction. How many people ever had the privilege of experiencing the true Aden? As far as she was aware, she and Royce's family were the only people who truly knew him, or at least the version of himself he allowed them to see.

"Della dear, how was your dance with Lord Aynesworth?" the Duchess asked. "I must admit, you made a handsome couple out there on the dance floor. Could there be an understanding between you two in the offing?"

Maggie's head whipped around to look at them.

"We are just friends, Your Grace. I do not think there will be an understanding between us." Della did not dare mention that Aden had just asked her to marry him. If the Duchess were to find out about Aden's proposal, Della knew she would be strongly urged to accept his offer.

The Duchess smiled and said, "I would not be so sure. Like I said, you two make a handsome couple. We have all known him since he was young, and I admire him. I can vouch for his character, unlike that reprobate father of his. Lord Aynesworth would treat you well, Della. It is something to think about." With a tap of her fan on Della's shoulder, the Duchess turned to speak with a group of ladies that had joined them.

Della stood there contemplatively for a while when she spotted Royce returning what looked like a very unhappy Miss Putnam to her father. As he turned and made his way over to Aden, Della could not control how her heart felt at the mere sight of him. How badly she had wanted him when he gently clasped his hand over hers, helping her guide the book back onto the shelf.

She had practically pleaded with Royce to kiss her, yearned for his touch to erase the horrible memory Lord Haddock had left behind. But his kiss had been too gentle, and she had wanted something that would steal her breath away. Something that would assure her that good men still existed.

Without thinking, she had grabbed his cravat and pulled him closer, showing him exactly what she desired. It might not have been the most sensible answer to her problems, but it had felt right in the moment.

When Royce had come to his senses and released her, she had hastily said her goodbyes and fled the library, knowing she had left her heart in the room with him.

Della knew she was in love with Royce, had been for a good while. But the weight of that knowledge did not change the inevitable outcome. Because, despite how she wished it were otherwise, Miss Putnam was the one he had decided to marry.

Della watched Aden and Royce as they spoke to one another and reflected on what the Duchess had said to her. If she married Aden, she would have a new life and family to occupy her. And perhaps, in time, the heartbreak would be more bearable when she witnessed Royce and Miss Putnam together.

Royce would still be in her life, even if it was only as a friend. And sometimes, loving someone meant having to accept they would never care for you in the way you cared for them.

Her hands trembled a little as she ran them down the front of her dress and forced herself to take a deep breath. It did not take her long to realize that the Duchess was right. Accepting Aden's proposal was the sensible choice—even if she was not in love with him.

In doing so, she was giving Royce the ability to marry Miss Putnam as he had intended. He never needed to know she knew about the agreement—which he had failed miserably at. Not to mention, her father held Aden in high regard and would be overjoyed to learn that she had accepted a proposal from him.

Della had to speak with Aden quickly, before she changed her mind. But before she could take more than a few steps, she felt a firm tug on the back of her dress.

"I take it from the look on your face that your dance with Miss Putnam did not go well," Aden said nonchalantly.

"It did not," Royce grumbled as he leaned against the wall. "I have been thinking."

"I hope you did not hurt yourself too badly."

"This is serious, my friend," Royce said sternly.

"My apologies." Aden nodded.

"I have been thinking," Royce repeated. "About my understanding with Miss Putnam. After speaking with her and the things she has said about the incident with Della and Lord Haddock at the ruins—"

"What did she say?" Aden interrupted.

"She all but blamed Della for everything that has happened, including Lord Haddock's unfortunate proposal—that it had all been an act to gain attention."

"We are speaking of Della, yes? She is the least attention seeking person I know. The absurdity of the accusation is so great it is hard not to laugh."

"My thoughts exactly. Miss Putnam has proven herself to be unkind. Almost hateful. I cannot imagine bringing such a person into my family, especially with my younger siblings. I am thankful she has shown who she truly is before we took things any further."

"Thankful indeed." Aden paused a moment before continuing.

"Does this mean you plan to recant on your agreement with her and her father?"

"I am afraid it does."

"Lord Milton will want recompense."

"I know." Royce sighed, nodding in agreement.

"And what about Della?"

"I do not know. I have done *nothing* to help her."

"Oh, I would not say that," Aden said, twisting the signet ring on his finger.

"Why not?" Royce looked pointedly at his friend.

"Because Mr. Rowntree requested your help to draw attention to her and I know one person in particular who *has* taken notice."

"Lord Haddock?" Royce guessed.

"He was not who I was thinking of."

"What other gentlemen have noticed her?"

"Do you honestly need me to answer that?" Aden looked at Royce as if he was being deliberately ignorant.

"I have seen only a few gentlemen approach her, other than you and—me." Royce took a deep breath as the realization hit him.

"I was beginning to wonder when you would finally accept that you have done what you promised. Just maybe not in the way you thought you would," Aden chuckled.

Royce pushed away from the wall without saying another word. It had taken this conversation with his best friend to make him see the truth and to acknowledge that he no longer wanted Miss Putnam by his side. He wanted Della; her smile, her caring nature, and her resilience when faced with difficult situations. Not to mention that his family adored her.

Looking around the room, he spotted Della bent over, attempting to pull her dress out from under a gentleman's foot. He laughed, recalling a similar situation in the garden. Finally, she freed her dress when Royce noticed Miss Putnam approach her.

Watching intently, he met Della's eyes as Miss Putnam spoke to her. Della's complexion grew visibly pale, her expression showing just how much Miss Putnam's words were affecting her.

After Miss Putnam had gone, Della stood there, alone, her gaze remaining fixed on him as if she was uncertain of the next steps she should take. Shaking her head, Della looked away and disappeared into the crowd.

The need to watch over her, to protect her, carried Royce across the dance floor in search of the woman he desired...but she was nowhere to be found.

Chapter 14

Della pulled at her dress, attempting to remove it from underneath the gentleman's shoe. She had tried tapping him on the shoulder to get his attention, but he was speaking to someone and ignored her. *How rude!*

Giving one last desperate tug, Della pulled herself free. Sighing, she looked down at another ripped hem when Miss Putnam appeared in front of her.

"Miss Rowntree, just the person I was hoping to talk to," she said with a sickeningly sweet smile.

"Miss Putnam."

"He is quite handsome, is he not?"

"To whom are you referring, Miss Putnam? There are many handsome men here tonight."

"Why, His Grace, of course," she said, pointing at a figure in front of them.

Della looked up to see Royce standing there, watching them.

"His Grace and I will announce our engagement soon." Miss Putnam fluttered her fan. "I had hoped we would announce it at the beginning of the season, but as we all know, these things do not always go as planned. No matter," she said, snapping her fan shut. "What I would like to know is what His Grace's fascination is with you."

"Your pardon, Miss Putnam, but I know not what you are referring to. His Grace has no interest in me, I assure you. Indeed, we have known each other since we were young, and we are friends, as I am friends with the entirety of His Grace's family. This fascination you think you see is nothing more than friendship. I am afraid you are mistaken if you think it is more than that."

"Ah, but you see," Miss Putnam said with a hint of warning in her tone. "I do not believe I am. I saw how he looked at you in the park, how he always seems to notice your every move and ignore me. And that... will simply not do."

"What do you mean?" Della asked, trying to appear indifferent.

"His Grace is mine—not yours, *mine*," Miss Putnam whispered so only Della could hear. "I want you to stay away from him."

"That would be impossible. Lady Derrington and I are best friends."

"Then it is time you found a new friend," Miss Putnam snidely remarked. "You might want to fix that." She pointed to Della's dress before she walked away, leaving Della standing there, speechless.

Della looked at Royce, emotions high as tears welled up. *Stay away from His Grace...find a new friend...*that is what Miss Putnam had said. Turning away from Royce's gaze, she went to the side of the ballroom and found an empty chaise to sit on, away from the prying eyes that might see her in distress.

She let out a quiet sob as she looked for something to wipe away the tears that fell, but there was nothing to be had. Turning to face the wall, she bent down to grab the torn hem of her dress and quickly dabbed her eyes.

"Della?" a voice called softly.

"Oh, Maggie, I was just, um," Della paused, wiping away some more tears. "I just had the strangest conversation with Miss Putnam."

"Here," Maggie said, handing her a handkerchief.

"Thank you."

"I saw Miss Putnam talking to you and thought I would make my way over to help. She looked to be speaking rather intently, but by the time I got here, she had already left. Your face went pale, and I was worried. What did she say that upset you so?" Maggie asked, laying a comforting hand on Della's shoulder.

"I need to get out of this ballroom. Is there somewhere we can talk?" Della asked, trying to hold back more tears that threatened to fall.

"The gardens, the balcony, the retiring room?" Maggie listed a few places.

"I just need somewhere quiet to hear myself think."

"I know!" Maggie exclaimed, drawing some displeased glances in their direction. "What I mean to say is," she whispered, "we can try the study. Sometimes Lord Ravensdale leaves it open for gentlemen who may want something stronger to drink. I also happen to know where the key is hidden."

Della knew better than to ask, but she did anyway. "And how would you know this?"

"I heard Royce and Aden talking about it the last time Lord Ravensdale hosted a ball. I followed them and accidentally bumped into a vase sitting on a pedestal. Fortunately, I caught it before it hit the ground. When I put it back, I saw the key sitting there. Not the most imaginative place to hide a key."

"We could be caught."

"We could," Maggie agreed. "Listen, if we get there and it is occupied, we will simply come back here."

"I was on my way to discuss something with Aden before someone stepped on my dress and Miss Putnam intervened."

"Pfft, Aden can wait." Maggie waved her hand dismissively. "Look, the orchestra is getting ready to play again, now is our chance."

Grabbing Della by the hand before she said anything else, Maggie led her toward two doors; one leading to the retiring room and the other that led into the foyer.

"Maggie! Miss Rowntree!" they heard someone call.

Both Maggie and Della turned to see Royce trying to get their attention. Della was unsure of what he was thinking after witnessing her exchange with Miss Putnam, nor was she sure she wanted to know.

"I did not have the chance earlier to ask if you would honor me with a dance, Miss Rowntree," Royce said as he approached. "I also have something I must speak with you about."

"Apparently everyone does," Della mumbled to herself. "I would be honored, Your Grace. But we were just heading to fix the rip in my dress," she said, pointing down. A plausible excuse, but she hated the deception.

"Then I shall wait until you return."

Della smiled and nodded. Once more, Maggie grabbed her hand and acted as if she was guiding her toward the retiring room. She quickly checked over her shoulder to make sure Royce was not watching them, then smoothly slipped them through the other door.

The foyer was dark, save for a few candles lighting the way for the servants that came and went from the kitchen below. Della trusted Maggie knew the way and followed her quietly, trying not to give their presence away in the part of the house where they had not been invited.

"The study is just there." Maggie pointed to the door across from them.

"The door is shut," Della whispered.

Maggie walked over to where a large blue and white vase sat on a pedestal and picked it up. There lay the key, exactly where she said it would be. "Get the key so I can set this down."

Della picked up the gold key, feeling the weight of it in her hand, and watched Maggie carefully place the vase back.

"I will knock first. If anyone answers, we will say we got lost and be on our way." Maggie raised her hand and knocked.

"Perhaps there is someone in there that would not like to be disturbed."

"Do not be silly," Maggie said, holding out her hand. "No one answered."

Quickly glancing around to make sure they were alone; Della handed the key to Maggie. And just when Maggie was about to turn the key in the lock, the door fell open slightly.

"Hello?" Maggie asked, pushing the door open further. But silence was the only thing that greeted them. She waved Della in and shut the door. "It appears as though we have the room to ourselves."

"It would seem so," Della said, staring at the curtains fluttering by the open window.

After sitting down on the settee, Della could not help but let out a long sigh. The warm light from the fire, combined with the rich mahogany of the room, gave the room a cozy and inviting feeling. Baubles and trinkets were scattered across every available surface, and must have come from Lord Ravensdale's many tours abroad.

He had told Della about his travels in his youth during an alfresco luncheon the Duchess had hosted. An elephant carved out of ivory, a wooden ship in a bottle, and a beautifully crafted chess set were but a few things she saw.

"Oh, dear. I know you want to talk, but I just realized I left my reticule on a chair in the ballroom. I must go retrieve it before someone finds it," Maggie said, rushing to the door.

"Then I should go back with you," Della said.

"No, you stay here where Miss Putnam will not bother you again. I will not be long. Here." Maggie placed the key in Della's hand. "Lock the door after I leave. When I return, I will knock four times so that you know it is me and not someone else."

"The quiet *is* nice," Della admitted. "Fine, I will stay here, but please be quick and make sure Royce does not see you. He is waiting for me to return, if you recall, and will wonder why I did not come back with you."

"I will be careful. I promise." Maggie left, closing the door behind her.

Immediately, Della locked the door and sat back down to wait for Maggie. She studied the chess set in front of her, leaning forward to get a better view in the limited light. Picking up the queen, she twisted it around, taking in the tiny details. It was ebony with gold filigree, magnificent in its simplicity, and the other pieces were just as beautiful.

She marveled at the smooth black-and-white checkered surface of the board with ornate carvings along its edges. Maggie would love a set like this. Maybe she could discreetly inquire where Lord Ravensdale had acquired such a unique piece.

"Pretty, is it not?" came a voice from behind her.

Della cried out in alarm and bumped into the table, knocking it over and causing the chess pieces to scatter as they hit the floor.

"Who is there?"

"Come now, surely you have not forgotten me so easily?"

"L-Lord Haddock, w-what are you doing in here?" Della's voice wavered as she laid eyes on the one man she fervently wished never to cross paths with again, stepping out from the shadows of the curtains.

"I have been avoiding the Duchess and His Grace all evening," he slurred. "They did a magnificent job painting me as a villain, and I tired of the contemptuous glares thrown at me in the ballroom, so I came in here to—"

"Hide?" Della attempted to finish his sentence.

"That makes me sound like a coward, Miss Rowntree." Her name escaped his lips in a hiccup.

"An apt description for someone who all but attacked me." Della attempted to use her most commanding tone to mask the fear that she felt.

"Attacked?" He tsked. "I know you felt something for me back at the ruins. Do not deny it." Lord Haddock grinned menacingly as he staggered closer to Della with an unmistakable wickedness in his eyes.

"If I remember correctly, you were the only one who felt something," Della said, bumping into things here and there as she backed away. Somehow, as drunk as Lord Haddock seemed to be, he made his way to the door with surprising quickness, successfully blocking her means of escape.

"What is the hurry?" His hands clamped down on Della's arms as he spoke. Spinning around, he pinned her against the door, running a clammy finger down her cheek. "I have been trying to figure out how to get you alone all evening. Imagine my surprise when you arrived here in the study with Lady Derrington, only to remain behind and completely alone."

"Lord Haddock, please let me leave. If someone should find us here—"

"Then you will have no choice but to marry me. Should you refuse, let us just say that things will not turn out well for you."

Della recoiled as his warm, spirit-scented breath tickled her nose, making her stomach churn. Lord Haddock attempted to kiss her, but she wiggled out of his grasp and slapped him across the face, the sound of it reverberating off the walls of the room.

"That was a mistake. Much like your refusal of my first proposal." He gripped her hard by the wrists and pinned them to her side. "You *will* be my wife, or I will ruin you so that no other man will want you."

"No!!" Della screamed and lifted her knee to strike him between the legs, but he quickly caught on to what she was trying to do and stopped her. No doubt remembering how their last encounter ended.

Bang, Bang, Bang, Bang

Lord Haddock paused at the sound of four knocks on the door. "Who is it?"

"It is the Duke of Exeter."

"Go away! This room is occupied," Lord Haddock hissed.

"Royce! Hel..." Lord Haddock cupped his hand over Della's mouth, cutting off her plea.

"Hush, you have already caused enough trouble," he sneered.

Della did not know if Royce had heard her before Lord Haddock had placed his hand over her mouth. She had to think of something; anything to allow Royce access to the room. As she glanced out of the corner of her eye, she noticed a glimmer of light reflecting off a shiny object. And there, lying on the carpet, was the key Maggie had given her. She must have dropped it in her haste to get away.

She continued to fight against Lord Haddock's punishing restraint as a distraction and stretched out her leg as far as she could to grab the key with the tip of her slipper. With a backward slide of her foot, Della shoved the key toward the door, and prayed that it reached the other side.

Chapter 15

Maggie and Della have been gone a while, Royce thought to himself, looking down at his timepiece. Tiring of standing in one place, he decided to see if perhaps he had missed their return to the ballroom and went in the direction where they had supposedly gone.

But when he asked some ladies standing outside the door if anyone had seen Maggie or Della, they all said no.

Royce felt a pang of concern surge through him as he craned his neck to search the room, hoping he could see them. Surely, they would have come back by now...but it was Maggie. And she would have thought it funny to linger just long enough to annoy her older brother.

However, Della had said she would return to dance with him, and for as long as Royce had known her, she had never been one to go back on her word.

He looked out over the room in one last attempt to locate them. Perhaps his mother might know where they had gone. He spotted her with a gathering of ladies and was about to go speak with her when he heard a door close softly behind him.

Spinning around, he glimpsed Maggie silently slipping through the door, not from the retiring room, but from a door leading to another part of the house.

"Where did you go?" Royce asked perhaps a little louder than he had intended.

"Calm down. You are drawing attention," Maggie said, smiling at some people nearby. "Your Miss Putnam evidently said something that upset Della, and she wanted to go somewhere quiet. I took her to the study since Lord Ravensdale leaves the room available for gentlemen to use."

"How do you know about that?"

"We women know more than you think. I may have also followed you and Aden at the last ball he hosted."

"Why am I not surprised?" Royce rolled his eyes. "Did you leave her there, *alone?*"

"I gave her the key and told her to lock the door behind me. I only came back because I left my reticule on a chair and needed to retrieve it. She will be fine."

"I shall go get her," Royce said, heading for the door.

"Really, there is no need. Della is perfectly safe." Maggie stepped in front of him. "No one else was in the room with us when I left. Like I said before, she is *not* your responsibility."

"Perhaps I want to change that." Royce attempted to walk around Maggie.

"What?!" Maggie looked at him as though he had sprouted two heads.

"Now, who is drawing the attention?" Royce asked her sarcastically.

"What do you mean you want to change that?"

"It does not concern you." Royce tried to pass her again, but Maggie raised her hand to stop him.

"It most certainly does," Maggie whispered harshly. "She is my best friend."

"And as her best friend, you should want what is best for her," Royce argued.

"I do! But who are we to decide what is best for her? Is that not her decision to make?"

What else could he say without giving too much away? Royce had not meant to say what he had, but Maggie had this way of finding the tiniest crack and wheedling her way in.

"You are correct," Royce agreed. "But I must speak with her and apologize for whatever Miss Putnam might have said.

"Fine. I told Della I would knock four times when I return. Wait here, let me get my reticule, and we will go together so that nothing untoward is suspected."

Royce watched Maggie disappear into the crowd. Once she was out of sight, he slipped through the door into the darkened foyer, making his way to the study.

Knock, Knock, Knock, Knock

"Who is it?" a voice from the other side of the door asked.

"It is the Duke of Exeter," Royce replied.

If what Maggie had said was true, and there was no one in the room other than Della when she left, then why was there a man replying? Maybe Della had made her way back into the ballroom and someone else was making use of the study?

But, there was something about the situation did not sit well with him.

"Go away! This room is occupied!" the man yelled.

"Royce! Hel..." another voice screamed before it was cut off.

Royce's heart thumped in his chest at the sound of Della's voice. He turned the knob, praying the door was unlocked, but no such luck. Unable to come up with another idea to get into the room, he backed up a few paces and ran full speed, ramming his shoulder into the door, but it did not budge. Royce grimaced, rubbing at the pain radiating up his arm, and let out a grunt of annoyance.

Without the key, there was no other way of getting to the room, unless... If he remembered correctly, there was a window overlooking the front lawn; perhaps he could get in that way.

"What on earth is going on?" Royce turned to see Maggie walking through the foyer. "You were supposed to wait for me."

"It is a good thing I did not wait! There is someone in there with Della!" Royce wanted to yell at Maggie, but that would not help the current situation. He began to make his way outside to check the window when the sound of metal scraping across the floor reached his ears and a key slid from beneath the door, hitting the side of his boot. "Go find Aden!" He demanded, picking up the key.

Royce unlocked the door and attempted to push it open, but it did not move. He tried again, still nothing. With all his might, he tried a third time, and the door finally gave way as two figures tumbled to the floor.

"Della!" Royce ran to her side.

"Royce, thank you. I, LOOK OUT!" Della yelled as Lord Haddock approached them with a marble statue raised above his head, preparing to strike. Della kicked her foot out, landing a solid blow to Lord Haddock's nether regions.

With a loud grunt, Lord Haddock dropped the marble statue onto his own head and fell to the floor, unconscious.

"Again?" was all Royce could say, checking to make sure the man was still breathing.

"Royce? Della?" Aden came running into the room. "Maggie came and got me, said that you needed help. Ah, but I can see I am too late. What happened?"

Della quickly filled Aden in on everything that had transpired, including how Lord Haddock had come to be lying on the floor.

"Let me just say that you may have saved us all from the stupidity that is Lord Haddock. His ability to reproduce has likely been diminished, and for that, the world owes you a great deal of gratitude."

"Now is not the time for your joking," Royce grunted, trying to lift Lord Haddock.

"Pfft. The man must have had enough drink to supply the entire British Navy," Aden said as he helped hoist Lord Haddock up.

"Let us get him out the front door and to his carriage before anyone sees us. Maggie, go inform Mother, Della's father, and

Tilly. Della shut the door and lock it. Do not open it for anyone but me."

"Should I not go back with Maggie?"

"Just do what I ask," Royce said, a bit more harshly than he intended. "Please," he added, softening his tone.

"Very well." Della said, as Maggie hurried off to do what was asked of her. "But how will I know it is you?" she asked, following them into the foyer.

"I will say 'petite duchesse,'" Royce grunted as they dragged Lord Haddock's limp form toward the door.

Della watched Lord Haddock's feet disappear around the corner and stepped back into the study, turning the key once she was safely inside. She rushed over to shut the window and checked behind the curtains where Lord Haddock must have been hiding and drew them closed. Heaven knows she did not need another repeat of tonight or of anything else that had recently happened.

She vigorously rubbed her arms, attempting to reassure herself that she was not in danger as she walked over to the toppled table. Pulling it back into its upright position, she set the chess board back on top; placing each of the scattered pieces back in their respective places as she found them. When she checked it over, she realized the queen was still missing.

"Ah, there you are," she said out loud, spotting the piece lying under a chair.

Knock, Knock, Knock, Knock

With a start, she whirled around, causing the chess set to topple over once again.

"Della...Della?"

Della walked to the door but did not respond.

"Petite duchesse." Della cracked the door open and peered out to see Royce standing on the other side.

"Where is Aden?" she asked, letting him in.

"He is keeping an eye on Lord Haddock and making sure he does not wake up and start creating more trouble before they have retrieved his carriage." Royce stalked into the room, raking his hands through his hair. "Della..."

Della held up her hand. "Please, do not lecture me. Do you think I would have remained here alone if I had known someone was hiding behind the curtains?" She plopped onto the chaise, feeling defeated.

"You lied to me about fixing your dress," Royce lightly scolded as he shut the door.

"Yes, and no. I did need to fix it, but I had already decided to come in here before you asked me to dance," Della admitted as she bent over to pick up the chess pieces again. "All I wanted was some peace, without people constantly asking me about marriage or trying to tell me how to live my life. Somewhere I could clear my head and think."

"You usually do your thinking in a garden." Royce smiled.

"I do, but I need a place where I would not accidentally stumble upon another unfortunate incident. But you see how well that turned out," Della said sarcastically, setting each piece down a little more forcefully.

"None of this is *your* fault, Della. Do not blame yourself for Lord Haddock's actions. That is his burden to bear." Picking up a chess piece, Royce placed it on the table, then kneeled in front of her, taking her hands in his. "And as easy as it would be for me to be angry and blame Maggie for bringing you here in the first place, I know she was only trying to help comfort her best friend."

"She was," Della agreed. "Please do not be mad at her. You may think her reckless, but she cares a great deal more than anyone gives her credit for."

Royce nodded. "You were attempting to free your dress when I saw Miss Putnam speaking with you, and I find myself curious to know what she said that made you so upset."

Della shot up from the chair and walked over to the desk by the window. She tried not to let the negative behavior of others affect her ability to stay calm and level-headed, even in the most difficult situations. And engaging in hysterics would not help the situation, as it often created more issues than it solved.

Her heart had leaped with joy for a fleeting moment when she thought Royce had taken notice of her the way Miss Putnam had suggested. However, that feeling was short-lived when she realized that Miss Putnam was warning her to keep her distance. She understood, but it hurt.

Della saw no reason to tell Royce the words only intended for her. Nor did she want to sound as though she were trying to undermine Miss Putnam or talk Royce out of what he believed was the right path for him. What purpose would it serve?

Prior to the agreement with her father, Royce had probably not even thought of her as a potential duchess. And no matter what she said, his decision would stay the same.

"I will not repeat what was meant for my ears alone." Della turned her back to Royce, taking a deep breath before continuing. "But you must speak with Miss Putnam. She is upset and one can hardly blame her."

"Why?" she heard Royce ask.

"Why?" Della repeated. "Why would you not? You have an understanding with her, and it is her expectation that you will announce your engagement soon."

"I understand that, but why do you care about how she feels? She has obviously shown no kindness toward you."

"No, she has not. But my only concern is that she makes *you* happy."

"And what about you?" Royce inquired.

"What about me, Your Grace? There is no point in seeking my opinion regarding matters associated with your marriage. Nor do my feelings have any bearing on the situation," Della said, attempting to swallow past the lump in her throat. "And I am sure Miss Putnam will expect to make many decisions regarding you and your household after you are married."

"And what do you expect, Della?"

Della shook her head, unwilling to look at Royce as tears streamed down her face.

"I expect to be sitting in the pew at your wedding with your family, Your Grace—if Miss Putnam will allow me to do so. Then, who knows what the future holds?" She shrugged her shoulder. "Perhaps I will find someone to marry and hope you will return the favor." Della would not mention that Aden had proposed, or that she planned to accept his offer.

"I wanted to speak with you earlier, when you promised me a dance."

"I know, and I had every intention of coming back." Della nervously bit her bottom lip, staring at the floor as she turned around. "You can speak to me now, if you would like."

"I could, but I would rather ask you a question." Royce said, coming to a stop in front of her.

"A question?" Della looked up at his handsome face.

Royce nodded. "May I kiss you again?"

Royce looked into Della's gorgeous eyes, and was filled with a quiet, yet intense anger, knowing she had dealt with the unwanted attentions of Lord Haddock more than once.

He softly held Della's face in his hands, tenderly wiping away her tears with his thumbs. His entire being was longing to have her in his arms, to experience the sensation of her lips pressed against his own once again.

"Yes," Della whispered.

He felt his heart swell in his chest with that single word, and he closed the distance between them, pressing his lips against hers. Letting the kiss be a physical expression of his concern for her safety and proof of his conviction that he wanted her as his Duchess.

Moving his hands down her back, he felt her body quiver beneath his touch. He ached to rip away the fabric between them, to feel the warmth of her skin against his.

Della wrapped her arms around his neck as he placed her on the desk behind them, and slowly slipped his hands beneath the edge of her skirts. His fingers moved sensually over curves of her legs as if engaged in a mesmerizing dance. He would be more than satisfied to touch her like this forever.

"You are not mine," she uttered, gently pushing his chest as he leaned in for another kiss.

"What?"

"You are not mine," she repeated. "We have to stop."

Royce looked at her, desire still clouding his head as he continued to hold her. Della was unaware that he had decided to no longer pursue Miss Putnam as his duchess. And he was about to tell her, could feel the words on the tip of his tongue, but the abrupt opening of the door interrupted them.

Chapter 16

R oyce quickly pulled his arms away and stood in front of Della as she scooted off the desk.

"Explain yourselves!" Lord Milton exclaimed as he stormed into the room. "I came in here to get away from all the insipid conversation and enjoy a drink, only to find the man who is supposed to marry *my* daughter carrying on with this...this strumpet!" He gesticulated wildly at Della.

"Remember whom you are addressing!" Royce boomed. "I will not have the good name of my future wife slandered in such a way."

"Wife? *Wife?* My daughter—"

"Your daughter, Lord Milton," Royce interrupted, "has shown herself to be selfish and unfeeling, much like yourself. If I had known her true character, I would have never offered for her. My family is the most important thing in my life, and I cannot imagine what havoc she would wreak upon them if I were to marry her."

"Well, I never!" The fleshy, mottled complexion of Lord Milton's face jiggled in his outrage.

"What is all of this shouting about?" the Duchess asked, appearing in the doorway

Maggie, along with Della's father and aunt, stood behind her, attempting to peer into the room.

"I found His Grace in a compromising position with this...this..."

"I would choose your next words wisely." Mr. Rowntree glared at the viscount.

Though Lord Milton outranked Mr. Rowntree, Royce had to commend the man for how he stared the viscount down, daring him to say anything against Della.

The Duchess looked at Royce and then at Della. And Della's face blushed under her scrutiny.

"I see," she said, without giving away her true thoughts on the situation. "Royce, you know what must happen now."

"I do, and I have already informed Lord Milton as much."

"We had an understanding!" Lord Milton barked. "You!" he said, shaking a finger at Della. "You have ruined everything!"

Royce guided Della further behind him, shielding her from Lord Milton's wrath.

The Duchess turned to face the angry viscount. "My Lord, I am sorry for any distress this situation may cause you and your daughter, but what is done cannot be undone." She kept her expression neutral as she straightened her spine like she was preparing to put the viscount in his place should he step out of line again.

"You will regret this, Your Grace. Mark my words!" Lord Milton roared, charging out of the study.

"Well, that was enough excitement for one night," the Duchess said after making sure Lord Milton was gone.

"Maggie told me about Lord Haddock. I will make sure that man never graces another ballroom or Ton function again." She smiled at Della. "Welcome to the family, my dear."

"So, what did I miss?" Everyone turned as Aden popped his head just inside the room.

"Della and Royce are to be married!" Maggie exclaimed.

"Ah—well, I now see my marriage proposal is a moot point." Everyone's gaze immediately fell on Della. She moaned and plopped her face into her hands. "I shall show myself out, since my presence no longer seems to be needed." Aden bowed and left.

"Royce, take Della home. The rest of us will return to the ballroom to mitigate any rumors should they arise." The Duchess sped out of the room with a determined air.

"Eeeee, now we will truly be sisters!" Maggie squealed.

"Maggie!" the Duchess's voice called from the foyer.

"We will talk later!" Maggie added before she ran out.

"Della," Mr. Rowntree said with a small smile, his arms opened wide.

Royce watched Della practically run into her father's arms. "I am sorry."

"Maggie informed us about everything. You are safe, and that is all that matters," her father said, squeezing Della a little tighter.

"We will go see if Her Grace needs our help and shall see you at home." Tilly hugged Della. "Everything will be just fine," she said, her voice filled with warmth and reassurance before she departed.

"Is there anything you need before we leave?" Royce asked.

"No, I think I would just like to go home," Della stated, making her way to the door.

Royce tried to think of something to tell Della that would ease her worry, to assure her that everything would work itself out, but he could not seem to find the right words. So, he fell into step beside her, hoping his presence alone would be enough to bring a sense of comfort.

They had said nothing to each other as the monotonous sounds of the carriage filled the silence. This evening had been a whirlwind and Della had been proposed to, encountered Lord Haddock again, and become engaged all before the night was over.

"When did Aden propose to you?" Royce asked, breaking the silence.

"Earlier this evening. You were dancing with Miss Putnam," Della said, looking out the window.

"Did you accept?"

"After giving it some thought, I had decided to accept his offer, and was on my way to tell him as much before Miss Putnam spoke to me."

"May I ask why?"

"Why did I decide to accept Aden's offer?" Della asked, still staring out the window. "Because I realized there was not another gentleman in that ballroom who wanted *me* instead of my dowry. And I trust Aden."

Slowly, she glanced in Royce's direction, her eyes glossy with unshed tears.

"Although I want to marry for love, the thought of spending the rest of my life alone gave me reason enough to consider his proposal. Even if he does not love me, at least I would know I was marrying someone who *cares* for me. It is a more desirable outcome than to remain a spinster and simply observe the world as it changed and moved on."

"You do not believe there was any other man who desired you for who you are, rather than the amount of money you would bring with you in marriage?" Royce asked as the carriage pulled to a stop.

Della shook her head before looking down at the floor of the carriage.

Royce was silent as he exited and helped Della alight. Turning, he informed his driver he would make his way home on foot, and heard the carriage pull away as he guided Della to the front door.

"Good evening, Your Grace, Miss Rowntree." Croxton bowed. By the look on his face, it was clear he had become accustomed to Della arriving without her father or Tilly. "Is there anything I can do for you, Miss Rowntree?"

"I believe that will be all for the evening, thank you. Father and Tilly will be back later," Della said, giving Croxton a small smile.

"I will see His Grace out myself," she added.

Croxton glanced at Della, seeming to understand that nothing else needed to be said on the matter. "Daisy will be up shortly to dampen the fire in the study, and I will keep an eye out for Mr. Rowntree and Mrs. Blatchford's arrival." He bowed, taking the stairs leading down to the kitchen.

Royce shifted his gaze to see Della standing there, her hands shaking as she tried to take off her gloves. He walked over and gently grasped Della's hand, pulling one finger at a time until he slipped the glove off her hand.

Tenderly, he brushed his thumb over the tops of her knuckles, marveling at how perfectly her hand fit in his.

"Come with me." Royce gently pulled Della toward her father's study and guided her to a chair before making his way to the sideboard and pouring two drinks. "Here." He held a crystal glass out to her. "It will help calm your nerves. After the night you have had, you deserve it."

Della took a large swig from the glass, and suddenly started to cough and sputter, her face turning bright red as she lowered the glass.

"Small sips, that is the key. Large gulps like the one you just took, and you will be just as soused as Lord Haddock was in no time."

Royce saw Della cringe at the mention of the man, and she quickly set her drink down on the table.

"I do not want to think of that odious man. If he ever comes near me again..."

"I will not allow it." Royce sat next to Della, taking her hand in his.

Della nodded but remained quiet for a while before speaking. "What now?"

"We do what the Ton will expect of us once word gets out."

"To hell with what is expected, Royce! How are you not tired of others dictating what you should and should not do? I know I am. Besides, we both know I am not a wife befitting a man of your station."

"Says who?"

"Everyone!" Della exclaimed. "I have no title, nor does my father. It does not matter to them that I grew up with your family, it only matters that I do not aim too high. That aside, I know you do not want to marry me."

"What I want—"

"What you want," she interrupted, "is to marry Miss Putnam. And that is what you would have done until that request from your father, and the stupid agreement you made with mine!" Della yelled as she stood abruptly and walked away.

"You know?" Royce asked, searching his memory for how she would have found out, and then it came to him. "The shattered glass."

"Yes."

"Why did you not tell me?"

"And tell you what exactly, Royce? That I had been eavesdropping? That the agreement between you and my father is laughable because you have only been helping me by somehow being near every time something happens?" Della paused for a moment. "I ruined everything for you, just like

Lord Milton said." She looked at him, hurt radiating from her eyes.

"No," Royce replied, walking over to Della, and gently grasping her by the shoulders. "The only thing you ruined was a marriage that would have made my life and my family's life miserable. I already knew my feelings about marrying Miss Putnam had changed, and I was coming to tell you."

"You were?" Della asked, tilting her head in confusion.

Royce leaned forward. "I was," he whispered over her lips.

"Is that all?"

"No, I was coming to ask you—"

Click, pop, snap

The sudden thud of a log dropping in the fireplace startled them as it sent sparks flying up the chimney. The moment gone; Royce saw Della try to stifle a yawn behind her hand.

"Let me see you to your room and then I will see myself out." Royce saw Della hesitate, but when she nodded, he followed her from the study.

He watched her hips sway from side to side, unable to look anywhere but her backside as she climbed the stairs. Once at the top, Della turned right and went to the third door on her left.

"Well...this is where I say goodnight." Royce leaned closer to Della and gently planted a small kiss on her forehead.

Della closed her eyes and smiled to herself as Royce placed another kiss on her cheek, then her lips. She felt the strength of his arms wrap around her as the smoky flavor left from his drink danced across her tongue, warming her from the inside. Oh, but his kisses were like a melody that played on her lips and spoke to her heart.

Della reached behind her, fumbling around for the doorknob. When she finally opened the door, Royce let out a deep moan, and pulled away from the kiss, propping his hand against the doorframe.

"I must stop here. If I go through that door, I cannot be responsible for my actions."

"What if I want you to come in?" she asked shyly.

"Do you know what you are asking of me?" Royce said darkly. "I am trying to be a gentleman, trying to restrain myself from taking you into that room and exploring every inch of you. To keep myself from throwing you on that bed and plunging into your depths with my tongue until you beg for release."

Royce's words resonated within her, stirring up a sensation she had never felt before, and she smiled warmly up at him, wrapping her arms around his neck. She kissed him with everything she was worth, to show how much she wanted him, how much she had always wanted him.

"Della?" a voice called out.

"Oh, no." Della's eyes went wide, knowing there was no way for Royce to leave without being seen. Luckily, his carriage had already left, so neither Tilly nor her father would know he was still here. And she trusted Croxton would not say anything.

Seeing no other option, Della pulled Royce into her room by his lapels and shut the door as quietly as she could. Pressing her ear against the door, she heard the stairs creaking, followed by the soft tread of footsteps coming down the hall.

"Is this what you looked like when you were eavesdropping on my conversation with your father?" Royce asked.

"Shhh." Della waved a hand at him.

"Della, are you awake?" Tilly asked from the other side. "Della?"

Della wanted to talk to Tilly, but since Royce was in her room, she thought it better to just wait until morning. Eventually, she heard Tilly's footsteps fade and a door close in the distance.

"That was close." Placing a hand over her heart, she backed away from the door and turned to see Royce sitting on her bed with a small smile on his face. "What are you smiling about?"

Royce shrugged. "Can a man not smile?"

"Not like that. That kind of smile promises nothing but trouble." Della motioned to Royce's face.

Royce smiled at her again.

"Stop that. Now, if you would kindly leave, it has been a long night, and I would like to rest."

Royce let out a deep chuckle as he rose from her bed. "First, you wanted me in here, and now you are kicking me out?"

"You had me out of sorts!" Della took a step back each time Royce took a step forward. "Besides, a woman may change her mind. It was a moment of weakness that will not be repeated," she said, bumping into a chair.

"As of this night, Della, you and I are engaged to be married. Do not pretend there is no attraction between us. We have found ourselves *entangled* on more than one occasion: the alleyway..." He held up his hand and started ticking off the places as he continued to walk toward her. "The garden...the library...*tonight*."

Della averted her gaze so Royce could not observe the effects of his words on her, or the blush that was creeping into her cheeks. Why did she have the desire to run away from Royce, yet also crave to be captured by him? Her legs mirrored the confusion, unwilling to take another step back as Royce drew nearer, so she pulled the chair she had bumped into between them. But he merely kicked it with his foot, shoving it to the side.

"Should I add all the dreams you have inhabited," he continued, "or the times I thought of you as I did things to myself?" Royce's hands gently cradled her face, as his thumb slid across her lower lip, leaving tiny sparks in its wake. "Tell you what I imagined when I saw you licking the chocolate from your fingers during that carriage ride from the ruins?"

He leaned in closer, placing a kiss on the sensitive place below her ear, and whispered, "Tell me to leave, Della; tell me to leave, and I will."

Della almost moaned as he continued to press kisses to the side of her neck. Her heart ached for him to remain, but her thoughts were scattered, distracted by recent events and the warmth of his arms around her. "Royce?"

"Hmm?"

"I think you should leave." Royce paused and looked at her. "A lot has happened tonight, and if my father or Tilly should catch you in here..."

He sighed, placing his forehead on her shoulder. "Goodnight, Della."

Royce kissed her cheek, and after checking the hall, he left. Della took a deep breath and sat down on the edge of her bed, wondering how this night had gotten so out of hand. Despite how much she loved Royce, she had her doubts whether marrying him was a wise decision.

Della undressed and went to her wardrobe to select a nightgown. Finding the one she was looking for, she slipped into it and looked down at the threadbare fabric dotted with the occasional hole.

Abigail, her lady's maid, had begged for the garment to be thrown out. She claimed she had patched up the holes so many times and the fabric was so worn that it refused to hold any more repairs. But Della did not care; she loved it and had never found another that had quite the same feeling.

Della lifted the blanket on the bed and climbed in, praying sleep would come quickly. But as she lay there, she could not help but think about how things were about to change. Some say, *be careful what you wish for*, that every silver lining has its dark cloud.

Her deepest wish was coming true, a wish that seemed too impossible to even dream of. Yet, the happiness she thought she would feel was tinged with sadness, knowing that Royce did not love her in return.

Chapter 17

Della felt the mattress dip as if someone or something had joined her. Her eyelids were heavy, her vision blurred and unfocused as she slowly opened them.

"Good morning!"

"Ahhh!" Della jolted awake at the sound of another voice in her room.

"Oh, do calm down. It is just me. So, how did everything go after Mother and I left last night?" Maggie inquired, bouncing excitedly on the bed.

"Must we talk about right now?" Della asked groggily, rubbing her hands over her eyes.

"If not now, when?"

"Maybe when I have had the chance to get some more sleep and eat something?" Della pulled a pillow over her head to block out the sunlight.

A knock sounded, and Maggie bounded off the bed to see who it was.

"Mistress Tilly thought Miss Rowntree might be hungry when she woke and had me bring something up for her."

Daisy, the housemaid, entered the room and set the silver tray down on the table by the fireplace.

"Thank you, I will take it from here," Maggie said.

Daisy curtsied and shut the door quietly behind her.

"Well?" Della heard Maggie's muffled voice through the pillow.

"Could I at least eat while we talk?" Della asked, throwing the pillow to the side of the bed.

"Of course!" Maggie nearly skipped to a chair by the fireplace and made herself comfortable. She poured two cups of tea, Della's with cream and sugar and hers with just sugar.

Settling back into the seat, Maggie took a sip and sighed contentedly. Della laughed as she sat next to Maggie, perusing the assortment of food brought up for her.

She spread some butter and a good amount of jam on the toast she had selected, took a bite, and looked up to see Maggie staring over the rim of her teacup.

"I am not sure what you expect me to say," Della said, taking one more bite of her toast before picking up her tea. "Royce brought me home as your mother asked."

"And…" Maggie prompted.

"And we simply…talked," Della said matter-of-factly. "I told him I knew of his agreement with my father."

"Was he angry?"

"No, actually. Perhaps surprised, but not angry. He almost seemed…relieved."

"That is good, I supposed. But how do you feel about marrying my brother?"

"Nervous? Scared? I fear what might already be circulating about last night."

"Do not let anyone make you feel you are undeserving of being Royce's wife. You deserve it more than any of the women who practically threw themselves at his feet." Maggie said without hesitation, pulling Della in for a hug. "But I cannot believe you said nothing to me about Aden proposing! You had two men vying for your hand in one night—well, three if you count Lord Haddock." Maggie grimaced. "I have had one in the past month, and my mother said no before I could."

"You act as though I have achieved something great. I assure you, I have not."

"When you mentioned needing to speak with Aden last night, is this what it was about?" Maggie asked, suddenly turning timid as she idly played with a lock of her hair.

Della regarded Maggie, remembering the dejected look on her face when the Duchess had inquired about an understanding with Aden in the future. Was it possible Maggie had some sort of affection for him?

She decided now was not the best time to discuss what was sure to be a sensitive subject, but thought it best to answer Maggie's question honestly.

"Yes, I had decided to accept his proposal."

"Why, when you have been holding out to marry someone you loved?"

"Because I thought about Royce's agreement with my father, how he had plans of his own regarding his marriage to Miss Putnam. I did not want to be in his way any longer, nor did I want to turn down so many offers that I remained unmarried forever. Aden is a good friend to all of us. If one cannot marry for love, then a marriage based on friendship would be preferable to a marriage with someone you barely know or ending up alone."

"I had not thought of marriage that way before," Maggie said, looking at Della with a sad smile.

"I never got the chance to talk to Aden again until the incident in the study. Though he gave me a reason, I am still curious why he would ask me when there are far better choices than I."

"He asked you because you are smart, beautiful, and kind."

"As are you," Della said.

Maggie smiled as though the returned sentiment made her uncomfortable and changed the subject. "The day is still young, and we have much to do. My mother and Tilly are downstairs, eager to start planning your wedding. They sent me to inform you the wedding will take place two weeks from today."

"Two weeks?!" Della choked on her tea as her cup clattered against the saucer in her hands.

"Do not worry. I will be with you every step of the way!"

"That seems an awfully short time to plan a wedding."

"Have you met my mother?" Maggie joked. "Now, let us get you dressed!"

"First and foremost, we need to see Madame Delphine for your trousseau and wedding dress. We will have to pay extra for the rush, with the wedding in two weeks, but I am sure she will accommodate us," the Duchess said as she and Tilly looked over their lists.

Della marveled at the Duchess. Even though the Derrington household would soon be plunged into chaos, she remained calm and collected. Their lists included cleaning, dusting, counting the silver, and every other detail Della would not have thought of.

"Your Grace, this is all too much." Della gestured to the lists.

"Nonsense! You are to become a duchess and should shout your new rank from the rooftops, announcing your arrival. You and Royce deserve no less," the Duchess said.

"I agree." Tilly nodded.

"B-But I..."

The Duchess held her hand up. "Della, you are my daughter now. I would not have one of the most important events in your life, or my son's, be anything less than spectacular. I know this would have been an exciting day for your mother. Please, let me and Tilly do this for you...for her." The Duchess discreetly wiped away a stray tear. "My husband would have said the same, were he here."

Della smiled and simply nodded in silent acquiescence.

"Wonderful!" the Duchess exclaimed, clapping her hands together. "Royce told me he would take a separate carriage and meet us outside Madame Delphine's after he talks to your father about some last-minute arrangements and speaks with his solicitor.

"Ow!"

"Well, if you will stand still, 'zen I will not stab you with 'ze pin, mademoiselle."

Della did her best not to fidget, but she had been a living pincushion for the past several hours and was growing restless. She could tell madame Delphine was growing weary of her constant movements.

"Et Voilà!" Madame Delphine smiled. "Pièce de résistance, oui?"

"Oui, Madame." The Duchess looked at Della from head to toe. "Oh, Della, you look magnificent! Madame Delphine, you have outdone yourself! This will truly be a dress to remember. I cannot wait to see the finished piece!"

"Merci, Your Grace. I shall have my masterpiece finished by next week and her trousseau, of course." A light tinkling of a bell rang in the distance, and Madame Delphine ran to the front to greet her customers.

The Duchess, Tilly, and Maggie excused themselves to look at some more fabric in another part of the store, leaving Della standing there alone in her wedding dress.

She always liked less ostentatious designs when choosing a dress, and this dress was the exact opposite. But she felt beautiful in it, the way the faint pink fabric shimmered and sparkled as the light bounced off the glass beading, the way it swayed elegantly as she walked.

"Please head to 'ze back. I have your dress waiting for you." Della heard Madame Delphine say.

As the curtain swayed open, Della felt a tightness in her throat as she beheld Miss Putnam's eyes narrowing in anger, her face contorting with disgust at the sight of Della standing there in her wedding gown.

"I thought I was coming to the best modiste, but if she has you as a customer, then perhaps I was wrong." Miss Putnam clucked her tongue. "Not the most flattering color on you, Miss Rowntree. Madame Delphine must have lowered her standards considerably to create this...well, I guess you could call it a dress," she sneered, walking around Della.

"If this is what future duchesses are wearing, I had better thank my lucky stars I am not becoming a duchess after all. For I would not be caught wearing something such as that!"

"That is quite enough!" the Duchess's voice said authoritatively from where she stood with Madame Delphine, Tilly, and Maggie. Miss Putnam paled. It was apparent she had not meant what she said to be heard by anyone other than Della.

"Madame D-Delphine, Y-Your Grace...My apologies. I did not see you standing there."

"Well, 'zat is quite clear." Madame Delphine snorted indignantly. "Since my creations are so disgusting, 'zen you will not be wanting 'ze one you ordered."

"Oh, but I-I..."

Miss Putnam was at a loss for words, and Della could see that she was on the verge of tears. She might have tried to present a hard exterior, but Della could sense the hurt that lay beneath. It must have been a heartbreaking experience to have your father inform you that you no longer had an understanding. To know the person who you were supposed to be engaged to was now engaged to someone else.

"Madame Delphine?" Della called out.

"Oui, mademoiselle?" Madame Delphine paused to look at Della.

"You would not want a gorgeous dress such as that—" Della pointed at the lovely periwinkle dress trimmed with white lace flowers. "—to go to waste. Despite her words, she would not have come to you were you not the best modiste this side of France. Please, allow her to purchase her dress. The words she spoke were meant for me, and rightfully so." Della turned to face Miss Putnam. "I am sorry that I made your father angry and for any pain I may have caused you. I hope that with time, you may forgive me for my mistakes. However, if you cannot do so, I will understand and accept it gracefully."

Della excused herself and went behind the curtain to change. Gathering all her items, she passed by Miss Putnam without another word, and made her way out to the carriage.

"Oh, Royce! There you are," the Duchess said as they exited the modistes behind Della.

"I hope your outing was successful." Royce smiled.

"It was! Della is going to make a lovely bride!" Tilly replied.

"Of that, I have no doubts." Della blushed under Royce's praise.

"Royce dear, Tilly and I must run next door to the milliner to pick up our hats. Would you mind waiting for us?" the Duchess asked.

"Of course. I have a shop I must go to as well," Royce said.

"Perfect. Della and Maggie, you can take our carriage back. We will not be long."

Maggie climbed into the carriage and Della was about to do the same when she felt a gentle hand placed on her shoulder.

"Della, before you go…"

"Yes, Your Grace?"

The Duchess leaned in close and whispered so that Royce could not hear her. "I just wanted to say how proud I am of you for how well you handled the situation with Miss Putnam."

As if on cue, Miss Putnam exited the shop and, without saying a word, dipped into a quick curtsy and left.

The Duchess continued speaking as if nothing had happened. "Your response showed compassion for someone you believe you have wronged, which is the making of a true duchess. Well done, my dear."

Della merely smiled and nodded before climbing into the carriage and sitting next to Maggie.

"We will not be far behind. See you at home," the Duchess said before waving them off.

"I would not have been so gracious," Maggie mumbled as she searched through the items she had purchased from town.

"But I have wronged her, Maggie. Surely you must have some sympathy for the position she is in."

"Be that as it may, there is no reason one must be as horrible as she has been this season."

"Has she been horrible to you?" Della asked.

"She has been horrible to everyone! Except my brother Grayson, apparently, though I cannot fathom why. He is always so serious," she said, still searching through her purchases.

They sat silently for a while when they heard rain hitting the top of the carriage.

"Just when you think you get a break in the weather." Maggie tsked. "When I marry, I will ask my husband to take me somewhere that always has sunshine. London's weather is always so dreary. I—"

"Whoa, Whoa there!" they heard the driver yell.

The whinnying of the horses gave Della pause as the carriage lurched forward and they both grabbed onto the leather handles above them. Maggie pressed her face against the window, attempting to see what was going on, but tumbled into Della as the carriage careened around a sharp turn, barely balancing on two wheels before slamming back down to the ground.

"Hold on!" Maggie reached for the handle again, her voice lost in the clatter of the carriage doors flying open as it turned another corner.

With a loud snap, they saw a wheel fly off into the distance, and felt the carriage collapse to its side. The trees went by in a blur of green and Della tightened her grip on the leather handle, the rushing sound of wind filling her ears as the doors continued to swing open and closed. But when they hit a large hole in the road, her hands slipped, and Della felt her heart sink deep into her chest as she fell from the carriage.

Over and over, Della's body rolled down the unforgiving road, causing waves of pain to shoot through her, until she eventually found herself lying in a large puddle of water. Her head ached, and her senses dulled as the rain continued its staccato rhythm upon her body, causing her dress to cling as though it were a second skin.

"Della!" The voices were faint, as though they came from a long distance. "Della!" she heard again.

"Send for help!" a deep voice commanded.

"Maggie?" Della mumbled as the sharp metallic taste of blood formed in her mouth.

"Shhh. Do not speak. Maggie will be okay, as will you. Please, stay awake," the deep voice begged, and Della felt herself being lifted from the ground. "Stay with me!"

"Hurt too much," Della murmured, attempting to do what the voice demanded. But the pain was more than she could bear, and she let herself slip into a dreamless sleep.

Chapter 18

Royce drummed his fingers on his desk; he could not focus. Every time he heard a knock at the door, his heart raced in anticipation, hoping it was news about the state of Della's health.

He, his mother, and Tilly had caught up to the carriage Maggie and Della were in and could only watch in sheer terror as the driver did everything within his abilities to get the frightened horses under control. Fortunately, the driver's skillful maneuvering had prevented Maggie from sustaining any serious injury, but Della had not been so lucky.

Royce forcefully slammed the ledger in front of him shut as he ran his hands down his face and leaned back. According to the doctor, Della had suffered a blow to her head hard enough to render even a large man unconscious. But his prognosis was cautious, yet hopeful, given her young age and overall health.

He had wanted to visit Della every day, but the thought of standing at the foot of another bed, silently begging for her to wake up and assure him she would be okay, was too much for him to handle.

So, his mother had kept him informed, and while the swelling had gone down as of last night, her fever persisted, and she had yet to wake.

A loud knock on the door startled Royce, nearly causing him to fall from his chair.

"Enter!" Royce said, regaining his composure.

"Y-Your G-Grace?" Mr. Milby timidly entered the room. "I have looked over the damage and what it would cost for repairs and think it would be best to have a new carriage built instead of fixing this one."

"I expected that would be the case," Royce said.

A look of relief washed over Mr. Milby's face. Royce had the carriage brought back, knowing it had been badly damaged. Despite its condition, he held onto the hope of salvaging it, knowing his father had commissioned it.

"I-I thought you might also like to know that upon further inspection, I believe someone may have tampered with your carriage."

Royce's head jerked up. "What do you mean, tampered with?" he asked darkly.

"I-I can show you," Mr. Milby stuttered, his hands trembling as he motioned for Royce to follow.

Royce did not hesitate. With determined steps, he followed Mr. Milby to the side of the stable where the carriage had been stored.

"If you look at it from here, one would t-think that the carriage simply threw a wheel, possibly from hitting a nasty bump in the road." Mr. Milby circled around to the side and got closer. "But. if you look here, you will s-see a small cut in the axle. I am not exactly sure how an individual could do this unnoticed, but..." he paused for dramatic effect. "I believe t-that someone sawed through the axle just enough t-that the weight of the occupants would cause it to s-snap, allowing the wheel to separate from the carriage. The top of the cut here is smooth, not jagged, as one would expect with a sudden break."

Royce stared dumbfounded at the carriage and took a deep breath before speaking. "Why did it break with only two people in the carriage when four of them rode earlier?"

"T-That I am afraid I-I do not know, Your Grace," Mr. Milby said. "Perhaps with four of them, it weakened the cut enough so that less weight was required later for it to snap."

"Thank you for going over everything so thoroughly. I shall inquire with my men if they saw anything out of the ordinary. Please let me know when you have the figures on a new carriage."

"Glad to be of service, Your Grace." Mr. Milby left as the head groom came barreling out of the stable, saddle in hand, nearly knocking Royce over.

"Oy, Yer' Grace, I did not see ya standin' there." The man set the saddle down and stood next to Royce. "Righ' nice carriage this was." The man clucked his tongue. "Guess the only thing it be good fer now is firewood, ay'?"

"Mr. Birks, have you or any of the stable lads seen a person lurking around here that did not belong?"

"Nah, cannot say I 'ave." Mr. Birks paused a moment, then snapped his fingers. "Hold a moment...now ye mention it, there was a fella 'ere a few days ago. Said he were lookin' fer work. But somefin' about him did not seem quite righ'."

"How so?" Royce asked.

"He looked like a worker but spoke like a toff." Mr. Birks shrugged. "I told 'em if he wanted a job, he needed to inquire at the 'ouse. I lef' after that and when I came back, he were gone. I figured he decided that workin' here was maybe no' what he were lookin' fer."

"Thank you, Mr. Birks. Please have this broken down and burned."

"Of course, Yer' Grace. But before ya go, may I inquire as to the healf' of Miss Rowntree? I 'eard she were in a bad way from the accident."

"The Duchess has been keeping me informed. Until then, I am afraid all we can do is wait and hope she wakes up soon."

"S'naught right," Mr. Birks said, rubbing his scruffy beard. "Things like tha' should no' happen to people as kind as 'er. If there is anythin' I can do fer ya..."

"I appreciate the offer, Mr. Birks."

Royce bent to look at the sawed-through axle as Mr. Birks left. When would someone have done this without being noticed?

He could not help but wonder if all the unfortunate incidents—apart from that evening in the garden—that Della had gone through were somehow related. Though the only common thread he could think of was Della herself.

There *was* Lord Haddock, but he had not been driving the hackney that had nearly run them over, nor had he been with

Della when she fell down the stairs. Still, some things were not adding up.

"Royce!" He heard his mother call out. "A letter just arrived from Tilly, and I figured you would want to know right away. Della's fever has broken, and she is awake!"

As Royce read the letter, all his thoughts regarding the incidents were forgotten. Wasting no time, he dashed into the house and asked for Titan to be prepared at once.

"How long has it been since the accident?" Della asked Tilly.

"Nearly a week," Tilly said. "I was so worried about you! Your father has been a mess, and His Grace demanded that we keep him informed about how you are faring. I already sent him a letter this morning, stating you had finally woken up."

"Has he responded?"

Daisy appeared in the doorway. "His Grace has arrived, along with the Duchess and Lady Derrington as well."

"Thank you. Please show His Grace upstairs."

"Yes, ma'am." Daisy curtsied slightly and left.

"Well, I guess you have your answer." Tilly rushed around the room, grabbing this and that, attempting to make the room presentable.

"Would it be okay if I just moved to sit in front of the fireplace? My body can tell it has been idle for far too long, and I need to move." Della looked at Tilly imploringly.

"The doctor said you should stay abed for a few more days, at least."

"But the doctor does not always know what is best," Della said grumpily.

"I do not disagree with you, dear," Tilly said, patting Della's leg. "But I believe the doctor's orders should be followed."

"If I must."

"Do not worry, dear. You will be up and about in no time." Tilly said, fluffing a pillow behind Della. "The only reason I am allowing this visit to your bedroom is because you are engaged to be married. Otherwise, he would have to wait just like everyone else.

A short while later Royce appeared in the doorway, and Della smiled, her heart skipping wildly at the sight of him.

"Good afternoon, Your Grace," Tilly said, propping one more pillow behind Della's back. "Is your mother here?"

"She is." Royce smiled at Tilly.

"Then I shall go downstairs and speak with her to see what wedding details still need to be taken care of."

Tilly exited the room, putting on a grand display of closing the door, but a moment later, they heard the door pop back open.

Della noticed Royce trying to conceal his smile at Tilly's poor attempt at being subtle, all in the name of maintaining propriety and creating the illusion of privacy. But when Tilly's footsteps faded away, Royce pushed the door closed.

"You are going to get us into trouble."

"Well, then I guess you will have to marry me." Royce chuckled, sitting in the chair next to the bed.

"You are awake!!" Maggie exclaimed, her voice filling the room as she burst in with her usual dramatic flair.

"Do you ever knock?" Royce asked his sister.

"Of course, I do! At least when it is warranted."

"And your best friend talking to her future husband is not one of those times?" Royce looked at Maggie questioningly.

"No, it is you we are speaking of, after all," Maggie replied sarcastically.

"Could you let us speak for a little while in private?" They both stopped bickering and turned to look at Della.

"You heard her! Out you go!" Maggie tried to shoo Royce out of his seat.

"Actually, Maggie, I was talking to you."

"Me? B-But I..." Maggie huffed.

"I know. But I need to speak with your brother first."

"Fine, but do not take too long. I will go downstairs with Tilly and my mother and wait for you to finish your conversation with my *dear* brother." Maggie glared at Royce as she left the room.

"One day, she will choose not to knock on the wrong door," Royce laughed.

"I can only hope it will not involve us." Realizing what she implied, she quickly changed the subject. "The doctor told me I need to remain in bed for a few more days, and Tilly agrees with him, but I simply cannot. Could you find it in your heart to turn a blind eye if I were to get out and sit by the fire?"

"If you wish." Royce smiled, offering his arm to her.

Della swung her legs over the side of the bed and gently walked to the chaise, using Royce for support.

"Comfortable?" Royce looked worriedly at her as he sat on the chaise next to her.

"Yes. I am a bit sore, but it feels good to finally move. Thank you."

They sat in companionable silence for a while, watching the flames flicker in the fireplace.

"Royce..." "Della..." they said simultaneously and laughed.

"Please, you go first." Della smiled at Royce.

"Right." Royce cleared his throat. "I do not feel like it would be a good beginning for our marriage if we continue to withhold information from each other as we did before."

"I agree," Della said.

They talked for a while before Royce mentioned some things that did not quite make sense. First, he talked to her about the rope at the lookout. How it had seemed to be placed there so someone could escape without being seen. Second, the out-of-control hackney that had nearly run them over.

"Thrice." Royce laughed, and Della smacked him playfully on the arm. "The carriage ride that nearly cost you and Maggie your lives." His expression quickly grew serious as he told her about the cut Mr. Milby had found on the axle.

"Della...my mother, Tilly, and I witnessed the entire thing. We could only watch in horror as you two were tossed about. But when I saw you fall out of that carriage..." Royce gently took Della's hands and turned them over, placing a kiss on each wrist.

"Everything will be fine. I am a little worse for wear, but I am on the mend," Della assured him.

Royce kept Della's hands in his as he continued. "There were still many things we had yet to discuss prior to the accident. I was unsure..."

"Royce?" Della asked softly, encouraging him to continue.

"I was going out of my mind with worry and tried to keep myself busy while waiting for news that you had finally woken up. The biggest thing we had yet to discuss was where we would live once we wed. I looked at several properties, but none seemed quite right, until I came across a house with a stunning garden that made me think of you. I spoke with my solicitor and purchased it, hoping to surprise you by having it fixed up."

"Oh, Royce!"

"I have had it fully furnished—which you are welcome to change if you wish. I have hired new staff, whom you will meet when we arrive on our wedding day. Some of my current staff will be there as well until things have settled. I hope you do not think it presumptuous of me for making such an important decision without you." Royce looked at Della with uncertainty in his eyes.

"Of course not. Everything was in such disarray before the accident, and I had not thought of where we might live."

"If you do not care for the house, we can look somewhere else—"

"Shhh, Royce." Della smiled and kissed him on the cheek. "I am sure it will be wonderful."

Chapter 19

"Here you go, Miss Rowntree," Abigail said, handing Della a cup of tea. "Sugar and a splash of cream—just how you like it."

"Thank you, Abigail."

"My pleasure, Miss Rowntree. Oh! But I should start calling you, Your Grace."

Della plopped down in the chair closest to her, causing tea to splash over the rim and drip down the side of her hand. Abigail kindly took the cup, handed Della a handkerchief to wipe her hands, and handed the cup back.

"Abigail, could you help me put the finishing touches on her hair?" Maggie asked. "We cannot have Della being late for her own wedding."

Della sat there patiently and drank her tea, while Maggie and Abigail dashed back and forth across her room, trying to add details she was sure no one would notice.

Amid the hustle, Della realized this would be the last time she would be in her home as an unmarried woman. Soon, she would become the Duchess of Exeter.

Tilly had come to talk to her earlier in the morning before everyone started arriving. Della had expected the discussion would be about what would happen on her wedding night, and her assumption had been correct.

"*I will tell you the basics,*" Tilly had said.

A few years ago, Della had been searching the shelves at a bookstore and stumbled upon a plainly bound, unassuming book. Curious, she opened it, and was completely unprepared for what it contained.

It was a picture book with descriptions, and not a picture book for children learning how to read, or how to do needlepoint; it was a book detailing many *things* couples could engage in.

She probably should have put the book back as soon as she had seen what was inside, but she wanted to know. Some pictures had made her heart race, others had made her blush, and some, well...some she would rather have not known about.

"*He will want to...*"

Della pretended to listen intently to Tilly's '*explanations*' when all she wanted to do was laugh. She knew Tilly had meant well, but after seeing that book, her explanation seemed very chaste and innocent, when the act itself was anything *but*.

"*Beyond that...best let your husband guide you.*" Tilly had said.

Della's stomach was in knots. She had barely eaten anything that had been brought up to her earlier, and it now growled in protest. But she was afraid if she ate something, it might not stay put.

"Finished! Come see for yourself!" Maggie exclaimed.

Della handed her cup back to Abigail as she stood and went to the floor-length mirror. The sight of the woman standing before her left her completely stunned.

"You are a vision!" the Duchess said, sweeping into the room.

"Maggie, Abigail, please make sure the carriages are ready. I would like a quick word with Della." Once they had left, the Duchess motioned for Della to sit down.

"After Royce told me he was searching for a wife, I tried to introduce him to women I thought might step up to become the duchess he needed. I must admit I was worried when he decided on Miss Putnam so quickly. She was one I was hoping he would not choose, but she was eligible, and the daughter of a viscount, so I could not exclude her."

Della was unsure why the Duchess felt it was necessary to inform her about the choices she had made for Royce.

From the moment Della had accepted that she was marrying Royce, she had felt like an imposter living in a dream world; a placeholder until the women who was supposed to become Royce's wife showed up.

But it had not escaped her notice that she had not been one of the women the Duchess had presented to Royce as a suitable choice.

"I am sure you are wondering why I did not suggest you as a choice to Royce," the Duchess said.

"N-No," Della stuttered, wondering how the Duchess always seemed to be one step ahead.

"Do not lie to me, Della Rowntree. I can see that very question written in your eyes. The truth of the matter is that I *very* much wanted to suggest Royce ask you. You know this family inside and out, the family adores you, and I have always thought of you as the best match for him. Even when you both were younger, I could tell you two would be perfect for each other.

"But I know my children—better than they know themselves sometimes, I think. If I had told Royce about my true thoughts on the matter, he would have laughed in my face because he was blind to what had been right in front of him...and that was you. I do not know the details leading up to the night at the Ravensdale ball, nor do I need to. I just wanted to tell you I cannot express the happiness I feel knowing you will continue to be part of this family in a more permanent role. You will rise to the challenge, my dear, of that I am certain."

"Thank you, Your Grace," Della said, as a tear streamed down her face.

"We will have none of that on your wedding day," the Duchess said, wiping the tear away. "I believe your father is waiting to speak with you." She bussed Della on the cheek. "This is your time to shine. When you are ready, we will be waiting downstairs."

Della smiled at the Duchess as she left the room, and her father entered.

"You look beautiful," her father said warmly.

"Thank you. You are quite handsome yourself."

"I would have to agree with you." Mr. Rowntree showed off as he slowly spun around and laughed. "Are you ready?"

"As ready as I will ever be, I guess." Della held her hand to her fluttering stomach. "I love you."

"I love you too, my darling girl, which is why I feel I must apologize."

"Apologize?"

"Yes," he said, pacing across the room to look out the window. "I wanted to apologize for my agreement with His Grace and his father. It is unlike me to keep things from you, and I am sorry. He informed me you knew and suggested I speak with you about it, and I agreed. Though today was probably not the best day, I thought it best to clear the air so you could start this new stage of your life without secrets."

"I understand you were only trying to help, and I appreciate everything you have done for me," Della said as tears welled up again. "Though I wish mama could be here."

"So do I." Mr. Rowntree smiled sadly. "She would be so proud of you."

"Proud of the way this all came about?"

"I think she would be proud of the lady you are, of the Duchess you will become, regardless of how it came to be. His Grace is a fortunate man, and I hope he knows that," he said, giving Della a hug.

Della smiled, trying to hold back the tears threatening to undo all of Abigail and Maggie's hard work.

Her father produced a handkerchief and held out his arm. "Your carriage awaits, *Your Grace*."

"I now pronounce you man and wife."

Royce was her husband now...

Uttering those words felt strange to her, and Della knew it would take some time for her to fully grasp their significance.

The Duchess had intended to invite several members of the Ton, but after the carriage accident, she and Tilly had decided that perhaps a smaller wedding might be best and invited only family and close friends.

Della had not looked over the guest list but was confident that neither Lord Milton nor Miss Putnam had been invited. So, it came as a surprise when she spotted Miss Putnam standing alone, about four rows back from the front of the church. Della could not imagine what it would have been like to witness a wedding that should have been your own.

She should have paid more attention to Royce waiting for her at the altar, but Miss Putnam's saddened, far-off look pulled at her heartstrings. It did not go unnoticed that she wore the lovely dress Madame Delphine had made for her.

"Is everything okay?" Royce whispered in her ear as they stood on the steps of the Derrington home.

"Yes, of course. I was just thinking about Miss Putnam. I did not realize your mother had invited her," Della said quietly to him as she greeted a few more guests.

"Nor did I."

"Well, my dears, here we are!" The Duchess said happily, clapping her hands together after they had greeted their last guest. "When you are ready, come eat, celebrate, and enjoy yourselves. This day is about you two, after all." She swept through the doors that led to the terrace, leaving Royce and Della alone together for the first time since they had exchanged their vows.

"Good afternoon, wife," Royce said playfully, pulling Della's hand up to his mouth to kiss it. "I have not had the chance to tell you how utterly breathtaking you look."

She shivered with anticipation as he gently skimmed his lips and tongue over her knuckles. Closing her eyes, Della took a deep breath, and let Royce's gentle touch calm her nerves.

"Della?"

"Hmm?"

"There is a slight problem I must rectify before we do anything else."

"A problem?" Della's eyes quickly opened, her heart racing as the intimate moment was quickly replaced by a feeling of panic.

"Yes, you see, I did not give you the type of proposal you deserve." Royce got down on one knee and held up a little box. "Your Grace, will you do me the honor of becoming my wife?"

"But we are already married," Della said, laughing lightly as the panic subsided.

"Yes, but I wanted to propose properly." Royce carefully opened the ornate box, and laying on a velvety cushion was a delicately braided gold ring encrusted with diamonds, and a large teardrop emerald gracing its center. "I am sorry I did not give it to you sooner, but its design proved to be a little difficult."

"It is gorgeous and more than I ever expected, but you need not have gone through so much trouble. The gold band I received during the ceremony was more than enough."

"So, will you marry me?"

"Yes! Of course I will!" Della laughed.

Royce stood and started to remove the gold band from her finger, but she stopped him.

"Can I keep this one as well? It may seem silly, but this is the one we said our vows with, so it should stay closest to my heart. Just place the other one above it on the same finger. That way, I can admire them both at the same time." Della held up her hand to get a better view after Royce slipped the ring on her finger. The precious stones glittered as the light bounced off their many facets. "It is perfect. Thank you."

"Shall we?" Royce held out his arm as he smiled.

"You go ahead. I need to visit the retiring room. When I am finished, I shall meet you on the terrace."

"You are not sending me out there alone, so I shall just wait for you here."

"Are you saying you need...*protection*?"

"Possibly..." Royce mumbled, not looking directly at her.

"I will return this time." Della placed her hands on either side of Royce's face and guided it back to look at her. "I promise," she whispered before she kissed him and left.

Della rounded the corner as two people emerged from a room, talking in hushed tones. Not wanting to interrupt, she ducked behind a large potted palm. *What was it with her and hiding behind plants?* she thought to herself, peering through the fronds. *Maggie? Aden?*

"Your brother would *kill* me if he knew!" Aden said through clinched teeth.

"Then do not let him find out! I will not tell him, so that would mean he would only know if *you*," Maggie poked her finger into Aden's chest for emphasis, "told him."

Maggie stomped off down the hall and out of sight. Aden waited a few moments before doing the same.

Della was unsure of what she had just witnessed, but she did not want to risk being caught accidentally eavesdropping...again. Dipping around the palm, she ran down the hall, opened the door, and quickly shut it behind her. When she headed toward another door leading to a more private room, she heard a quiet sob coming from behind the folding screen in the corner.

"Hello?" Della said, walking over to see if the person might need some help. "Is there anything I can...Miss Putnam?"

"What do you want?" Miss Putnam sniffed, dabbing at her eyes with a handkerchief.

"Are you all right?"

"I will be fine. Please, just leave me alone...wait!" she said and turned to look at Della. "I-I would like to apologize to you, Miss Rowntree. I mean, Your Grace. I have behaved abominably, and I want you to know that is not who I am."

Della walked slowly over to the cushioned bench and sat down next to Miss Putnam. "What do you mean?"

"I mean, the person I *truly* am and the person you have known since our debut are not the same," Miss Putnam said, twisting the fabric of the handkerchief in her hands. "According to my father, kindness is a weakness, so I pretended to become the person he wanted me to be. I am not the cold and unapproachable person I portray. And despite what everyone believes, titles and money mean little to me, it only matters to my father."

"So, your understanding with Royce—"

"Was what my father wanted." Miss Putnam dabbed at her eyes. "After my first engagement ended so horribly, my father was determined to see me wed as soon as possible. Once he learned of Her Grace's intention to hold a ball in honor of His Grace's return to London, he immediately set his sights on me becoming the next duchess."

Della remained silent, offering Miss Putnam the chance to speak without interruption.

"When His Grace approached my father, requesting to postpone everything, I panicked and started the rumors to force his hand. But as time passed, I noticed how much His Grace was falling for you. His eyes always searched for you, even when he danced with me. And though I am ashamed to admit it, you presented the perfect opportunity to thwart my father's wishes. I acted as horrible as I could so His Grace would no longer want to marry me. It was difficult to behave in such a way, knowing I did not mean a word of what I said."

"Why not just tell His Grace you no longer wish to marry him?" Della asked.

"I had fallen in love with someone else," Miss Putnam admitted hesitantly. "And I figured that if His Grace was the one to break our understanding, he would have the power to stand up to my father's anger."

"Did it work?" Della asked, concerned.

"Not really. My misjudgment was that I did not fully understand how much my father wanted to use me for his own gain or how much he wanted to be absolved of all responsibility for me." Miss Putnam laughed depreciatingly. "I know I was not invited today, nor does my father know I am here. But I spoke with your aunt before the wedding because I wanted you to know the truth and that I harbor no ill will against you or His Grace."

"Thank you for telling me this, and I am glad you came. But I hate to think about how angry your father will be if he finds you gone."

"What else can he do? He has become blinded by his anger, and according to him, I am a failure and of no further use. I am to go live with some relatives in Scotland until he sorts things out—though I do not know what he means by that." Miss Putnam smiled sadly. "In case I do not get another chance to speak to you, I would like to say how sorry I am for everything that has happened."

"Do not give it another thought. All is forgiven, Miss Putnam." Della patted her hand.

"Please, call me Emma. I know it will take some time, but I hope we can put the past behind us and become friends."

"I would like that, and you must call me Della. Madame Delphine creates the most beautiful dresses. It looks lovely on you. Will you join us for luncheon?"

"Thank you, but I must be going." Emma grabbed her reticule as she turned to leave. "Please, do not let me keep you. His Grace must be wondering where you are," she said, walking to the door. "I hope our paths may cross again someday."

Della sat in the quiet, feeling lighter after their unexpected conversation and hoped that one day Emma would find happiness of her own.

Chapter 20

"And that is why you simply must introduce my Beatrice to your other sons. I am sure she would make a fine wife for any of them."

"Andromeda," the Duchess kindly chastised. "I just married His Grace off. Please give me time to let things calm down before the matchmaking begins again."

"My apologies! Please, do let me know if you find any of your other sons are starting their search!" Andromeda politely excused herself and walked toward the refreshment table, striking up a conversation with Lady Ferndown, the Marchioness of Stilton, and her *very eligible* son.

"Bravo," Royce whispered to his mother.

"My dear boy, once you have been around these people as long as I have, you learn a thing or two," she said in a playfully condescending way.

"I will—for the sake of knowing what is best for my health—bow down to one more knowledgeable than I."

The Duchess smacked Royce on the shoulder with her fan. "Do not mock me. You may be a duke, but I am a duchess and *your mother*. I was here long before you, and I can ensure I am here long after you as well." She walked down the steps to chat with some of the wedding guests.

"My mother terrifies me," Royce said, making Della laugh. "You think that is funny, do you?"

"Not in the slightest. Your mother is something to be feared."

"Should we try to sneak out of here? I doubt anyone would notice our absence, at least not for a while," Royce asked, leaning toward her.

"Please?" Della whispered.

"Follow me." Royce took Della's hand and guided her to the side of the house. "This door leads to the kitchens directly."

"I have never noticed this door before."

"Really? Even in your late-night raids with Maggie to the kitchen when you were younger?"

"How do you know about that?"

Royce laughed. "Because late one night, Aden, Desmond, Grayson, and I decided we were hungry, and apparently you two were as well. We thought about scaring you, but decided it would make too much noise, so we hid until you left."

Making their way down the stairs, Royce had a flashback of himself with Desmond, Grayson, and Aden hiding around a corner after finding Maggie and Della in the kitchen. He remembered all of them laughing when they discovered girls were not immune to the call of their stomachs, either.

Once the girls had left, the four of them snuck into the kitchen when they heard someone clear their throat. His father stood there, unkempt from a late-night working in the study.

Royce had expected to be reprimanded for being out of bed and tried to devise an excuse to lessen their punishment. But his father did not say a word before he started going around the kitchen to get plates and forks from the cupboard, then into the pantry, where he found leftover strawberry tarts and gingerbread.

Within minutes, the five of them were sitting around the table in the servant's hall, eating, joking, and laughing. It was probably one of the fondest memories Royce had of his father.

Royce and Della came to the bottom of the stairs, only to be greeted by the kitchen servants and Mrs. Ivers. Everyone froze, not knowing how to respond to the newly married duke and duchess showing up unexpectedly.

"Your Graces." Mrs. Ivers curtsied, and the rest of the staff follow suit. "We did not expect you down here. I hope you found everything acceptable for your big day." She looked at them with hopeful eyes.

"Everything was absolutely divine," Della assured her. "I cannot express enough gratitude to you for all your hard work." Mrs. Ivers' smile stretched from one ear to the other at Della's praise.

"I must agree with my *wife*. Everything was excellent." Mrs. Ivers' face turned several shades of red from Royce's compliment. "We came this way to avoid being seen by any guests."

"I saw nothing, Your Grace. But perhaps you would like to take some cake with you?" Mrs. Ivers asked. "It will not take but a moment." And she hurried around the kitchen, grabbing some cloth, string, and a knife. She spread the cloth out on the table and turned to cut two large pieces of cake. Placing the cut pieces down, she wrapped them up and secured a sting around each one. "Now off you go." She giggled, handing the cakes to Della.

"What?!" Royce heard Mrs. Ivers exclaim as they left. "There is nothing to see! Get back to work, the lot of you. We still have guests out there that need to be fed."

Royce laughed as they raced up to the other side. "Stay here," he told Della, and peeked out to see if the foyer was empty. He turned back and pulled Della out the front door, and they ran to the carriage that was waiting for them. Following her in, Royce sat on the plush, well-cushioned seat next to her.

"Your mother will wonder where we have gone."

"Whose idea do you think it was to use the servant's entrance to make our getaway?" Royce asked.

Della's face revealed her shock, and Royce chuckled.

"I had wondered why our escape seemed so easy, but I cannot complain, for we now have two pieces of cake!" Holding up the neatly wrapped parcels, Della smiled brightly.

The giddy excitement Della had felt as they made their pretend covert escape was wearing off. It had been all talking and laughter, but her nerves had started to make themselves known as she thought about what lay ahead. And suddenly, she did not know where to look or how to act.

"Abigail packed your belongings and brought them to our new home. She has assured me everything will be in place when we arrive," Royce said, breaking Della away from her thoughts. "I hope you will be as pleased as I am with how everything turned out."

"I am sure everything will be wonderful." Della smiled at Royce and quickly changed the subject. "Is this the carriage you had built to replace the other one? It is lovely."

"It is yours to take wherever you wish to go."

"What?" Her shock was almost enough to make her forget how nervous she was. "This is mine?"

"Yes, a wedding gift from me to you."

"But you already gave me this ring," she said, holding up her hand and sighed. "I did not get you anything."

"Della." Royce turned in his seat to face her more fully. "You deserve everything and more. Besides, it will be nice to know when Maggie needs a carriage, she will not steal mine...she will steal yours," he chuckled.

Della smacked Royce playfully on the arm as she laughed, too. "I knew there must have been a reason for such a grand gesture."

"If Maggie should commandeer your carriage, you are more than welcome to use our other one."

"Our other one? You mean yours?"

Royce shook his head. "No, I mean ours. Mine implies I will be riding alone; ours implies I shall be in the carriage with you."

His playful demeanor vanished, replaced by a heated intensity in his eyes.

"Will you be in *my* carriage with me for occasions other than today?" Della leaned in closer.

"I am sure something could be arranged."

Royce claimed Della's lips as his own as he smoothly pulled her onto his lap. But soon, their kiss turned into a passionate collision that ignited a whirlwind of desire and excitement within her. Della grazed her fingers along the edge of his collar, relishing the velvety texture of his skin and the silkiness of his hair as she tangled her hands into the darkened strands.

But the moment Royce dipped his finger into her bodice, the world beyond their carriage ceased to exist. He continued to brush kisses along her neck as he teased her nipple to a peak; allowing every lingering pass to be a whispered promise of better things to come.

Overwhelmed by the sensation, Della nearly let out a loud moan when the carriage came to an abrupt halt, causing her to jump from Royce's lap and look in the mirror mounted on the carriage's wall.

Her lips were red and swollen, her color high, as she tucked a tendril of hair behind her ear. She hoped the staff would assume her flushed cheeks were from the excitement of her wedding day and not from the heated moment they had just shared.

"Royce, it is magnificent," Della said as the door was whisked open. Her eyes widened in awe at the sight of the place she would now call home.

The combination of brick and stone walls with white-washed windows gave it a dignified presence. Staff had arranged themselves along the wide, sweeping stairs that ascended to a white door with two tall columns on either side.

"May I present to you, your new duchess? A few know Her Grace, but many of you do not, and I will introduce you in due course. All I ask is that you make her feel welcome and do your best to be helpful while we are all adjusting." Royce's voice was authoritative but kind.

The staff dispersed as Royce led Della up the stairs. *I can do this*, she thought to herself. But before she could step inside, Royce scooped her up and carried her over the threshold, through the opulent foyer, and into what she assumed was now his study. Once inside, he put her down, turned the key in the lock, and leaned his head against the door.

"Is something wrong?" Della asked.

"What do you think?" Royce asked, turning to face Della.

Everything about him seemed normal as Della looked over his form, her gaze traveling down his body until it settled on the telltale sign of his desire. "Oh," she said nervously, biting her bottom lip.

"This is what has been wrong every time I dream about you, every time I see you...every time I *think* about you." Royce looked down at himself. "There has been no relief for me. All I need to do is picture your eyes, your lips, and I am undone. Unable to slake the lust you incite within me with anything other than my own hand."

Moving with deliberate slowness, Della closed the distance between herself and Royce. "Well," she said, feeling her entire being on the verge of melting from the sheer intensity of his gaze. "Here I am."

Royce wasted no time. The moment the words escaped Della's mouth, he swiftly twirled her around and pressed her firmly against the door. Fear had consumed her when she last found herself in this position, as Lord Haddock made yet another attempt to force her into marriage. But here, in this moment, with the only man she ever wanted, she felt safe and protected.

Royce lightly pulled at the front of Della's dress and trailed his tongue across the tops of her breasts, where they strained beneath her stays, begging to be released.

"Della." Royce's breath was hot against her skin. "We cannot do this here." He whispered as his tongue continued its exploration. "I want to take you on every surface in this room. The desk." He trailed his lips up, meeting hers in a fiery kiss. "The chair." His hand skimmed upward, cupping her breast. "Against the wall." He kissed her again. "I do not know how many more times I can start and stop and not explode from sheer want of you. But, for our first time, I think it best to do this somewhere a bit more comfortable."

The multitude of new sensations that Royce was eliciting from her was enough to make her feel dizzy. And his deep, resonating voice sent shivers down her spine, awakening a longing she never knew existed. Royce pressed one more scorching kiss upon her already swollen lips before reaching around her and pulling the bell, its sharp chime cutting through the air.

"Giles will see you to your room. I borrowed him until our new steward—a Mr. Jeffries—arrives next week." Hearing a knock, Royce opened the door.

"You rang, Your Grace?"

"Giles, please show Her Grace to her new room," Royce said, turning to Della. "I shall be up shortly."

Della smiled at Royce before allowing Giles to show her the way.

"Giles?"

"Yes, Your Grace?"

"Would you be so kind as to give me a tour of the house and grounds soon?"

"I believe His Grace said he would like to assume that duty," Giles said as they arrived at her room.

"But should you have questions, I shall be happy to answer them."

"Thank you."

"My pleasure, Your Grace." Giles bowed his head as he opened the door for her.

Taking in the surroundings of the room, Della noticed the ivory-colored décor, with hints of blue and green. But when she saw her bed, she excitedly darted across the room and flung herself onto its plush surface. This bed was massive compared to the one she had back at home.

Della paused—that was no longer her home. This one was. Several thoughts raced through her head, but the one that occupied the most space was that she was now Royce's wife, the Duchess of Exeter, and mistress of this house.

"I hope you find the bed to your liking."

Della bolted upright, and looked toward the door where Royce stood, silhouetted by the candlelight emanating from the hallway. His jacket was nowhere to be seen, his shirt was untucked with the top buttons undone, exposing a glimpse of what lay beneath. Her eyes swept down to his bare feet, causing her face to flush at the sight of his naked toes.

"May I come in?" Royce asked,

Della's mouth was dry, so she simply nodded.

Royce took a few steps into the room, locked the door, and froze; almost as if he was unsure of what to do next.

"I will give you a tour of the house and grounds tomorrow if you would like. This, of course," he said, motioning around him, "is your room. If there is anything you would like to change, you need only say something. Through that door," he pointed to the ivory-colored door on his left, "is your dressing room. And on the other side is a door that leads to my bedroom." He raked his hand through his dark brown locks and cleared his throat. "Would you care for a drink?"

He left without waiting for an answer and quickly returned with two glasses and a crystal decanter. "Scotch?" he asked, holding up the bottle.

"Please." Della rose from the bed and walked toward the table positioned in front of the fireplace, where Royce poured them both generous servings.

"Grayson brought this back for me when he visited an old school friend of ours whose family owns one of the oldest distilleries in Scotland. Only scotch worth having, in my opinion."

Della took a small sip, not wanting a repeat of the last time, and watched Royce swirl the amber liquid in his glass. The liquid burned all the way down, but soon, a soft ambient warmth flowed through her veins. Royce's heated gaze met hers over the rim of her glass.

Taking one more sip, she swished it around her mouth, swallowed, and handed her partially full glass back to Royce. Never breaking eye contact, Royce threw back the remaining contents of her drink as well.

"Oh, what the hell..." Della threw her arms around Royce's neck and pulled him in for a kiss. Royce let the empty glass in his hand fall onto the carpeted floor with a thud as he wrapped his arms around her waist.

"We can take this slow, Della," Royce spoke out of the side of his mouth as they continued to kiss.

Della simply shook her head, pulling him closer.

Royce placed his hands on her shoulders and pushed her back far enough so their lips did not touch.

"We *will* take this slow..." The statement sounded more like an order as Royce began backing her up toward the bed. "I will take my time with you," he growled low in her ear. "I want to make you discover things you do not even know about yourself." He placed his hand beneath her jawline.

"Things that will have you screaming out my name before the night is over."

"You seem rather sure of yourself," Della said, cocking an eyebrow.

"Oh, I am," he chuckled darkly. "But know this…should you need to stop, just say so. I want to make this enjoyable for both of us. Understood?"

"Understood," Della whispered.

"Good. Now—turn around." Royce spun his finger in a circular motion. "Please." He added when Della hesitated.

Slowly, Della did as she was asked, turning her backside to face his front. Royce gently ran his fingers across the delicate fabric of her wedding dress, carefully unfastening each button until the dress slipped off, revealing her undergarments.

"Women wear too many things under their dresses," he grumbled, undoing the laces on Della's stays. When Royce finally pulled the last length of ribbon through, he let go, allowing her stays to follow the dress to the floor.

Chapter 21

Della stood before Royce in nearly see through chemise, and he could not help but question how he would have felt if it had been Miss Putnam before him, standing there in such an intimate manner. Would he have had the same urge to claim her as his own, like he did with Della? In his gut, he knew the answer was no.

"You are absolutely breathtaking." Royce's hands moved slowly over Della's body until they came to rest just below her breasts. "These are heaven," he said, lifting them up for a closer look. Bending over, he took the tip of her chemise-covered breast into his mouth, using the fabric to his advantage.

With a soft moan, Della weaved her fingers through his hair, holding him firmly in place. With a dark chuckle, Royce moved to the other side and repeated the same ministrations, thoroughly enjoying her reaction. He was beyond hard, and as much as he wanted to sink into her core and pound away until they both found bliss, he knew he could not.

He wanted to make this night something Della would always remember. Something that, when they were old and gray, would reignite the embers and keep them burning at the mere thought of it.

Still latched onto her breast, Royce walked Della backward until the backs of her knees hit the bed, forcing her to sit down. "This needs to go," he said as pulled at her chemise. But Della stopped him before he could remove it.

"I think this is terribly one-sided, Your Grace." Della smiled. "Why am I sitting here clad only in a chemise while you remain fully clothed?"

"That can be easily rectified." Royce shoved away from the bed, grabbed the bottom of his shirt, and pulled it over his head. Keeping his eyes on her, Royce undid the buttons on his breeches. "Should I stop?" Royce quirked an eyebrow at Della.

"No..." she said in a breathy whisper.

Tucking his thumbs below the waist of his breeches, Royce slowly guided them down his legs. When he stood, Della's eyes went wide. His cock jutted forth, standing like a soldier at attention under her curious stare, and she bit at her bottom lip, tilting her head to the side as if she was contemplating something important.

With deliberate steps, he moved toward her, allowing her enough time to observe him, and eventually settled on the bed. He placed his hands behind his head, causing his muscles to flex and bend.

"Do you wish to explore?"

"Is that not uncomfortable?" Della asked, staring at his manhood where it curved upward along his stomach as she scooted over and settled down beside him.

"It can be, but in this case...no, it is not."

"I am sure there are many words that this goes by," she said, reaching down and gliding a single finger along the sensitive underside. Della jerked her hand back as Royce drew in a ragged breath through his nose. "Did I hurt you?"

"Della, it would take much more than a feather-like touch to hurt me. There are many words people use, but I will not elucidate on them tonight. And the main word used to describe that—" he looked down— "is cock."

"Cock," Della repeated, gently stoking her finger up and down over his length, his cock growing harder with every pass.

With a teasing touch, her finger traveled from his manhood, circled his naval, before finally reaching his chest, where she gently caressed each of his pale pink nipples.

Royce watched as Della leaned forward and copied what he had done to her. She ran her tongue over one, and he hissed at the contact. Inspired by his reaction, she sensually traced her tongue along his chest, gradually moving to the other side, and delicately sucked it into her mouth. The intense sensation made his hips instinctively lift off the bed.

"Good God! Warn a man before you do that!" Royce laughed at his own response.

"You did not warn me!" Della chastised, placing her hand on her hips.

"Touché. I think that is enough exploring for today."

"Oh, but..." Della protested.

"You can explore whenever you like, Della. We are married now, remember? Just say the word, and I am yours." Royce sat up and kissed her firmly. "Now...my turn." With a wicked grin, he flipped their positions and straddled her hips. "Now, who is wearing too much?"

Royce lifted Della's chemise over her head, letting it flutter to the floor as he bent to take her still erect nipple into his mouth. A soft scream escaped her lips as she lay utterly naked beneath him like an offering; much like she had done in his dreams.

"Open for me."

"What?" Della propped herself on her elbows and stared at Royce as he got up and kneeled in front of her.

"Please." He grinned, stroking his hand up and down her thigh. "Trust me."

Della laid back and hesitantly let her legs fall open; her face growing red with embarrassment, knowing Royce was staring at the most intimate part of her.

His arms wrapped around her thighs and pulled her closer before he drew his tongue up and over where she ached with desire. A whimper escaped from her as Royce hummed his satisfaction and used his arms to pin Della's hips down to the bed as she squirmed under his tongue's perusal.

"Relax Della. Just let yourself focus on how I caress you." She heard Royce say before she felt his fingers replace his tongue. "How it feels when my fingers move in and out of you."

Della concentrated on the unfamiliar sensations, taking deep breaths as Royce's fingers steadily moved in and out. And soon a slight pressure began to build, ebbing and flowing with each stroke, drawing a moan from her lips.

Seeming to understand what she needed, Royce sped up, each movement sending her higher and higher until she burst forth, her body trembling as wave after wave of pleasure washed over her.

"Perfect," Royce said, his fingers glistening with the evidence of her arousal. Lowering his hand, he took hold of his cock and placed it at her entrance. "Della..."

Wrapping her arms around Royce, Della pulled him in for a kiss. "I trust you."

With those words, a quiet tension seemed to leave him as he pushed forward ever so slightly and withdrew, driving deeper with each slow roll of his hips.

Della wanted to tell Royce she loved him but did not think now was the right time to tell him how she felt or what he meant to her. Nor did she know how he would respond to sentiments he had not wanted in his marriage.

With one more roll of his hips, Royce fully seated himself within her and stopped, his nostrils flaring slightly with each breath he took.

"Royce?"

"I am fine," he said with a slight tremor in his voice as he bent down to take Della's lips in a searing kiss. "More than fine. Are you?"

"Yes." Della nodded as Royce readjusted his stance.

His movements became increasingly more forceful, creating a sense of fullness that made her body quiver with excitement.

Soon the room felt like it was spinning; so strong were the sensations rioting around in her.

As Royce thrust over and over, the pressure built and built until it felt like water battering itself against a dam, demanding it give way lest it overflow, but give way, it would not. Della cried out, knowing what she wanted but unable to put it into words.

Without a word being spoken, Royce placed his thumb on the bundle of nerves above her entrance, using a gentle circular motion as his hips drove forward. Della's body tensed as pleasure coiled deep within her.

"Let go, Della. Let go!" Royce demanded.

Della screamed her pleasure, her body obeying Royce's words as if it were his to command. She felt Royce's grip tighten on her hips as he thrust a few more times before finding his own release, letting out a trembling breath before collapsing heavily onto her.

Della smiled as she traced her fingers along his back as they lay there, the sweat from their exertions coating their skin. Still breathing heavily, Royce pulled her closer and rolled them to their side.

"That was...that was..."

"Indeed," Royce laughed, reaching his hand up to push a damp lock of hair from her face.

A few minutes passed and neither of them wanted to move, their bodies too sated from their efforts. Royce eventually untangled himself and walked to the washstand. He cleaned himself quickly and grabbed a fresh cloth.

"Open your legs for me," he said as he dipped the cloth in the water and wrung it out.

"Already?" Della quirked an eyebrow at him.

"Many more times if I have anything to say about it, however, this is for you," he said, holding up the cloth.

Della did as Royce asked and let him lay the wet cloth on her. The cold made her gasp slightly, but it was soothing to the slight soreness she was feeling. Once finished, he threw the damp cloth onto the floor, climbed up, and slid beneath the blankets.

She could not help but find amusement in how Royce's long, muscular frame dominated the bed. Holding his arm up in invitation, Della crawled toward him and snuggled into his warmth.

"Next time, we will do this in my room. My bed is bigger," Royce said. "Better for me to have my way with you."

With each lazy stroke of her arm, Royce's lips lightly grazed Della's forehead, causing her smile to grow wider and her heart to flutter. She nestled her head on his chest, finding solace in the steady rhythm of his heartbeat, and let it lull her into a peaceful sleep.

Beams of light poured through every window as the sun peeked over the horizon. Della yawned and stretched, only to be startled by a sudden pressure around her waist, which made her momentarily panic. But memories from the previous night slowly made their way into her consciousness as the morning fog cleared.

Della turned to her side, wedging one hand between her face and the pillow, and smiled at Royce's still-sleeping form. She was sure he cared for her; he had all but said as much that night in the library after they visited the ruins. But uncertainty lingered as to whether he would ever be willing to hear the words she longed to say to him.

"Why are you staring at me?" Royce asked with his eyes still shut.

"How did you know I was looking at you? You have not even opened your eyes."

"I can just sense it," he said groggily.

"I am staring at you because I am trying to make sure this is all real, that I am not dreaming."

Without warning, Royce sprang up and rolled on top of her.

"Does this feel like a dream to you?" he taunted, grinding his hips into her. "Does this?" He leaned down and sucked one of her nipples into his mouth.

Della could only squeak in reply as she rotated more fully onto her back and let her legs fall open, inviting him into her warmth.

"Your offer is wonderful, and trust me, I am more than tempted. But for your sake, I must decline. Besides, if we do not get dressed, how are you supposed to see your surprise?"

"Royce," Della admonished.

"This really is not a surprise from me as much as it was one from Maggie. I just paid for it." He laughed, exposing a small dimple on his right cheek.

"What else could you possibly surprise me with?"

"Oh, I can think of many, many...*many* things." Royce's voice lowered suggestively as he placed a heated kiss on her lips before tumbling off the bed and headed for the dressing room.

Della watched Royce's perfectly sculpted backside disappear into the other room as she lay there in bed, smiling. She could not remember when she had last felt this happy.

With Maggie, her happiness came from knowing they would be there for each other no matter what; of time spent together and the laughs shared. But the type of happiness she felt with Royce? That was entirely different. She had never cared about being a duchess; she only ever wanted the man behind the title.

Royce came back out, almost fully dressed, attempting to button his cuff. "Could you help me? I can use my right hand with no issue, but I seem to lack the coordination with my left."

"Where is your valet, Tinsley?" Della inquired.

"I gave him a few days off to visit his mother. I did not think he would appreciate having to help me dress multiple times throughout the day."

Della rose onto her knees and let the sheet slide down her front, putting every part of herself on display.

"Give me your hand, please," Della said, reaching out for him.

She found herself captivated by Royce's penetrating stare, and in an instant, he discarded his jacket, untied his cravat, and pulled his shirt over his head.

"I thought you said no."

"I changed my mind," Royce growled.

Della shrieked as Royce charged for her, tackling her back onto the bed. They both laughed as they fell, their lips and bodies meeting in a fiery passion that went well into the afternoon.

Chapter 22

After their stomachs were full, Royce gave Della a very thorough tour of their new home, making sure to point out little hiding areas where they might partake in certain amorous activities.

"Thank you for today." Della smiled at Royce as she followed him into the study. "I can imagine you have important business to see to. So, I think I shall just go explore the garden since I have yet to see it except from the window of our room."

"Della, have you forgotten about your surprise?" Royce asked.

"No, I just thought it could wait if you needed to work."

"*Work* can wait." Royce walked behind his desk, taking a small key out of his breast pocket, and unlocked a drawer that contained a fat stack of documents. Sitting atop of those documents was another key with a bow tied around it. He tossed the key up and caught it as he slid the door closed.

"Just so you know, should Mr. Milby stop by needing information and I am not here, that is where all the documents regarding this house are located. This, however—"he said holding up the key with the bow—"is yours."

"What does this go to? You have shown me every room in this house."

"Every room...except one." Royce's eyes flicked to his left.

Following his gaze, Della's eyes landed on a set of bookshelves, which looked like many others she had seen. Their shelves held beautiful leather-bound books of all shapes, sizes, and colors, but nothing about them stood out.

"Is this a puzzle I am to solve?" Della asked, wondering what he could be smiling about.

Royce merely shrugged his shoulder in amusement. Della inspected each shelf, picking up books and baubles in search of whatever she was supposed to find.

She systematically worked her way down from the top—using the ladder provided, of course—and was just about to replace two books at the end of the middle row when she spotted a brass plaque against the back, hidden in the shadows.

Setting the books in her hands down on the table next to her, she leaned in closer to examine the plaque. Not seeing a handle, Della reached out, and noticed that with a swipe of her finger the plaque easily swung side to side like a pendulum.

Moving the plaque to the left, Della held it in place as she looked even closer and noticed a hole that was the perfect size and shape for the key Royce had given her. Grabbing the key from where it lay on the shelf, she placed it in the lock and twisted it to the right.

Nothing happened, so she turned it to the left and heard something akin to the sound of a clock being wound up.

The bookshelves popped open just enough to allow a sliver of light to pour through a tiny gap that had appeared between them. Royce swung the bookshelves open like doors and stepped to the side, allowing Della to peer into the room that lay beyond.

Hues of green, blue, purple, and gold greeted her, a colorful contrast from where they stood in the study. Across the room, Della could see windows reaching from floor to ceiling, letting the sunlight filter in as they looked out over the gardens she had yet to explore.

The curtains were pulled back, exposing a set of doors leading out onto a terrace with a marble balustrade wreathed in a riot of roses. And a chair covered in the same fabric as the drapes sat facing a blue settee, with a gold-footed table between them.

"What is this?" Della asked in absolute awe.

"That is a good question. When I bought this house, I went over everything in excruciating detail with my solicitor—every room, every closet, every creak in the floor, but one mystery remained." Royce reached around the bookshelf and pulled out the key. "We did not know what this key went to. We searched and searched and asked the seller of the home if he knew, but he said the old man would only speak in riddles and never gave an actual answer."

Royce motioned for Della to walk ahead as he continued talking.

"Naturally, it bothered me, so I searched for anything that it might go to. Then one day, I was going through the old books on these shelves. I brought several of these books with me, but the gentleman who owned the house insisted his books stayed with the house. Simply told the seller it added character.

"A few books fell over as I attempted to put them back on the shelves when I heard metal scraping. That is when I found the plaque and discovered that the key led to this long-forgotten room. I had not noticed it in my search outside the house because the windows and door had been so overgrown with vines and ivy, I thought it was just a wall."

"What was in here?" Della asked as she continued to look around.

"There was nothing, really. Just some old brig-à-brac, family portraits, and documents. I showed Maggie, and she is the one who suggested I turn this into a room specifically for you."

"Oh!" Della squeaked as Royce snaked his arms around her.

"Do you like it?" he whispered in her ear.

"I love it!" She laughed, tilting her head back to look up at the ceiling; even that was elegantly decorated. Della's eyes traced over the walls and furnishings, honored that Royce and Maggie had done this for her.

Royce's hands moved up her body, traveling from her stomach, up between her breasts and finally to the side of her face as he leaned in for a kiss.

"Ahem."

Della jumped at the sound of someone clearing their throat and looked over to see Giles averting his eyes as he placed a tray laden with tea and cakes on the table.

"Is there anything else I can get you, Your Graces?"

Royce did not say a word as he dismissed Giles with a nonchalant wave, causing Della to laugh into their kiss as he guided his hands down to grab her backside.

"I truly love it, Royce, thank you. I will have to thank Maggie as well."

"Yes, in a day or two."

"A day or two? Do we have plans?" Della asked, curious.

"As a matter of fact, we do." Royce sat on the settee, pulling her down to straddle his legs.

Della leaned in and kissed Royce with everything she was worth. The happiness she felt inside, knowing he was hers, gave her hope that one day, he would come to love her as much as she loved him.

But even if that love never came, she could share moments like this with him, and maybe that would be enough.

Over the next several days, neither Della nor Royce ventured much beyond the confines of their bedroom, choosing to have food brought up to them. The few times they had left, they had taken walks in the garden.

One walk had turned into a spontaneous game of tag, and she had lost horribly, which resulted in her owing Royce a boon at a time of his choosing.

They played cards by the fire and chatted about nothing and everything while consuming a shameful amount of desserts.

But inevitably, they would end up wrapped in each other's arms as they fell into bed.

Della was sure she could go on like this forever, but life and responsibilities had a way of sneaking up on one when all one wanted was for them to disappear.

Della swung her knees over the side of the bed and reached for her robe, but her fingers were only greeted with the wooden hook where it usually hung. Glancing around the room, she spotted it discarded in a heap with various other garments by the fireplace. She got up to retrieve it, but her attempt to get out of bed did not go unnoticed. A large hand slid up her side, cupped her breast, and pulled her back into bed.

"Royce, we have to get out of bed eventually," Della laughed.

"Must we?" he asked, kissing her on the shoulder.

"I am afraid we must. We received a letter from your mother yesterday as a reminder that we are to attend the Marquess and Marchioness of Stilton's ball tonight."

Royce sighed as he rolled onto his back. "Are we to be thrown to the vultures so soon?"

Della smacked his chest playfully. "And they say women are dramatic." She paused and took a deep breath before continuing. "I will admit I am terrified that people will say I should not be the one walking into the ballroom on your arm, but rather Emma. They will say I tricked you into marrying me and not her."

"Della, we know what truly happened, and that is all that matters; and when did you start calling Miss Putnam, Emma?"

"When she and I talked after our wedding ceremony."

"Is that why it took you so long to return to me?"

"Yes," Della said guiltily. "We have become friends...I think."

"And you did not think to mention this to me?"

"I am sorry. I meant to tell, but it was our wedding day, and I was preoccupied with other things."

Royce smirked. "What did she say?"

"She said she harbored no ill will against us and that she had been intentionally horrible to persuade you to call of your impending engagement."

"Why would she do that?" Royce asked, looking confused.

"Because she had fallen in love with someone else." Della looked straight at Royce as she said those words; when he said nothing, she continued. "But I am afraid she will end up heartbroken, as her father is sending her to Scotland to live with some distant relatives. I feel terrible knowing that we are partly to blame."

"As do I, but as my mother said, what was done cannot be undone. I hope that Miss Putnam can find happiness away from her horrible father," Royce said, sitting up. "Tonight, will be our first ball as the Duke and Duchess of Exeter, and our families will be there to show they support our marriage. If it gets to be too much, tell me, and I will bring you home." He kissed her enticingly. "I will bring you up here and make you scream my name over and over until you remember it is only you and me in this marriage and no one else."

Royce laid back down and pulled Della on top of him, her breasts plumping as she lay against his chest. Della smiled wickedly as she bent down and lightly bit his nipple. As Royce flailed and fought with the covers, Della quickly spun over the side of the bed and dashed across the room, her bare feet slapping against the cold floor.

Royce freed himself and swiftly lunged toward her, attempting to swat her bottom. "Next time...I will not miss," he jokingly declared.

"Who said there will be a next time?" Della teased and laughed as she ran to the safety of their dressing room.

Royce stood in the corner; his glare focused on the Marquess of Stilton swirling Della around the ballroom floor. She smiled at him as they chatted through their twists and turns, causing Royce to wonder what the man had said to make Della blush.

"Brooding, are we?" Aden tsked as he appeared, holding a glass of champagne.

"I am not one to brood. I am merely standing in a corner watching my wife," Royce scowled.

"I stand corrected," Aden said sarcastically, taking a sip of his champagne. "It serves no purpose staring like you want to place a dagger into the man's back. Especially not when he is hosting this ball. The Marquess of Stilton is a good man—a married man—who is infatuated with his wife and our friend. He is doing you a favor by dancing with Della, what with it being your first ball as a married couple. And you know he is an excellent ally to have in your corner."

"That does not mean I have to like it," Royce grumbled under his breath.

"No, but it proves that you have greater feelings for your wife than you care to admit."

"What?"

"You, my friend, are in love with your wife," Aden said, taking another sip. "Otherwise, you would not be over here acting as you are."

Royce sighed. "It is true I care for Della a great deal more than I ever expected to care for the woman I married," he admitted. "But I do not love her...I cannot."

"Do not and cannot, are not the same. You *do* love her, but you will not allow yourself to admit it,"Aden stated, handing his empty glass to a passing servant. "I do not pretend to know why you are so opposed to saying you love Della when it is so blatantly obvious."

"If I told her and something happened, what then?" Royce asked.

"Then something happens, but at least she would know." Aden shrugged his shoulder. "Do not let the fear of something happening make you regret the words you did not say. If I were you, I would swallow my pride and tell her before I lost her."

Royce leaned against the wall, his mood darkening as he watched the Marquess escort Della off the dance floor.

"Thank you for the dance, Your Grace." The Marquess said, bowing over Della's hand.

"The pleasure was all mine, I assure you," Della replied.

"Your Grace, my lord." The Marquess bowed to Royce and then to Aden before excusing himself.

"Royce?" Della looked at him questioningly.

"Ignore your husband. He has been over here brooding the entire time you have been dancing."

"Truly? Royce, it was just a dance. The Marquess is very kind," Della said, fanning herself as she looked out over the dance floor.

"So, what is the verdict on the newlywed couple?" Maggie asked, sauntering over to their little group.

"People will gossip, of course. They have nothing better to do with their miserable lives, but overall, it is good. Especially since we all entered together, and our sweet Della has danced with practically every lord here, including our host." Aden glanced at Royce.

"Not brooding," Royce said, moving closer to Della and placing a hand on the small of her back.

"Of course not." Della patted Royce's arm as though he were a child in the middle of a tantrum. "Maggie, I have not thanked you for my surprise! I absolutely love it, and I wanted to go into town to buy a few decorative things. Would you care to go with me?"

"Margaret did something nice for someone?" Aden asked sarcastically. "My, my, this night keeps surprising me. Even with mister broody breeches over here."

If looks could kill, Maggie would have cut Aden down where he stood, and Royce was about to do the same.

"For your information, *Lord Aynesworth*, I am far kinder than you give me credit for. The only person who seems to have issues with me is you. Why do I bother you so?" Maggie asked, tilting her head to the side. "What egregious act have I committed to offend our very own Adonis?"

Royce noticed Aden tense at being referred to by the moniker the Ton had given him. He hated the name, and Maggie knew it.

"Think about what I said," Aden whispered to Royce. "Some of us will never be so fortunate," he grumbled bitterly, his eyes narrowing at Maggie before he stormed off.

Royce looked at Maggie. "Will you be—"

"I will be fine," Maggie stated, cutting Royce's question short. "I just do not understand why Aden is always in such a foul mood when I am around." She quickly swiped away angry tears and took a deep breath. "I am so glad you like the room. I will see you tomorrow."

"Maggie..." Della reached out a hand as Maggie left.

"Let her be. I do not know what is going on between them, but it is probably best to let them figure it out on their own," Royce said, watching his sister leave. "This ball is growing tedious. Are you ready to go home?"

"Please." Della nodded.

They walked over to bid the Duchess goodnight and went outside to wait for their carriage. Royce looked at Della as they stood there, thinking about what Aden had said.

He was not sure if he could ever summon the courage to speak those three words out loud...because he was afraid.

Afraid that if he did, it would mean acknowledging his life would not be complete without her, that he would always *need* her.

And the thought of needing someone that desperately was enough to bring him to his knees.

Chapter 23

A light gust of wind blew through the open windows of the carriage as they rolled along at a leisurely pace. Royce had remained silent, staring at the houses as they passed, leaving Della wondering if she should speak first or if the silence was keeping his surly temper in check.

"I am sorry," Royce mumbled, turning to look at her.

"Whatever for?" Della asked, feigning ignorance.

"I am sorry for how I behaved tonight. It is just..." He sighed, dragging his hands down his face. "I was not prepared for how I would feel seeing you dance with other men."

"It never seemed to bother you before."

"You were not my *wife* before," he replied. "I am not proud of how I acted."

"You mean like a fool? Perhaps even a bit jealous?"

Della could have continued, but there was no need. Royce was probably berating himself just fine without any help from her.

He said nothing but gently placed a hand on her knee, drawing idle circles with his thumb in silent acknowledgement. Even through the layers of her dress, his touch sent shivers racing to all parts of her body.

"Follow me," Della whispered, her voice filled with excitement as they arrived home. She grabbed Royce's hand and guided him upstairs to their room.

At some point during their short marriage, they had silently decided that Royce's room would be where they spent most of their nights. Though occasionally they used her room for a change of scenery or because it just happened to be the closest bed.

"Wait here," Della instructed Royce. "I want to make sure everything is in place for your surprise."

"*My* surprise?" he asked.

"Yes. It is my turn to finally do something for you."

"I know something else I would like to do," Royce said with a sly smile, as he grabbed the front of Della's dress and pulled her toward him.

"None of that." Della playfully swatted his hands away. "Now, wait here, and do not come in until I tell you to."

"But—"

Della did not give Royce a chance to finish what he was saying before she shut the door in his face to keep him from following. Quickly running to the dressing room, Della spotted the translucent nightgown and robe she had requested Abigail to set out for her and undressed. She had chosen her outfit for the ball with tonight in mind so she could do everything herself.

Finally divesting herself of her clothing, Della slipped on the nightgown and robe and made her way back into their bedroom, where champagne and strawberries were waiting.

The warmth from the fireplace did little to ease Della's nerves as she sat on the settee. She truly hoped Royce would enjoy what she had planned.

"You can come in now," Della called out.

The door opened, and there stood Royce, handsome as always and looking far more comfortable than he had at the ball. He had removed his coat and undone his cravat, which hung loosely around his neck, his sleeves rolled up, exposing his forearms.

"Come sit by me." Della patted the spot next to her, and as Royce closed the door with a sharp kick, she could feel the excitement building in her chest. His eyes seemed to brighten at the sight of the champagne she offered to him…or maybe the nightgown she was wearing. She was not sure which. "To our marriage and our life together," Della said, smiling at Royce as he sat next to her.

Royce clinked his glass against hers and continued to stare at her, making Della feel like thousands of tiny butterflies were flitting about in her stomach.

"Would you care for a strawberry?" Della set her drink down and reached for a small bowl of sugar that had been crushed into a fine, almost powdery texture. "My mother used to eat strawberries this way. You simply hold the strawberry by the stem and roll it around in the sugar, like so," she said, holding it up in front of Royce.

Royce remained silent as he firmly gripped her wrist and led her hand, with the strawberry, toward his mouth. Della's throat went dry, and her pulse quickened as she watched his lips lock around the sugar-coated fruit. She was trying her hardest to seduce *him*, but it seemed like he was the one doing the seducing, as flames from the fire danced in his eyes.

Unable to resist, she set the bowl of sugar down, tossed the strawberry stem on the table, and leaned forward to lick the sugar crystals from his lips. With a low growl, Royce leaned Della back and braced himself over her. Their lips met, and her body grew excited as his hand moved toward where she craved him the most.

"No," Della said with a gasp as Royce nipped at her neck. "Tonight is for you." Della's lips met Royce's for a final kiss before she pushed him away, running her hands over his body as she sank to her knees before him.

"Della," Royce whispered hoarsely.

Della's fingers brushed against the fall of his breeches, and she looked up to see the hazy look of desire in Royce's eyes. With each button she unfastened, Della could feel her own desire building, and wondered if he would be receptive to some of the same things he had done to her. With a flick of her fingers, she undid the last button, and his cock sprang free, seeming eager for attention.

Tentatively wrapping her hand around the base of his cock, Della lightly skimmed the tip of her tongue along the sensitive underside, watching Royce's face contort in pleasure. He reached down and placed his hand over hers, demonstrating with his own movements how he wanted to be touched.

Following his lead, Della searched for a pace he enjoyed. When she found it, he released his grip, and she continued alone, determined to give him as much pleasure as she could. Her hand continued to move up and down as she slipped her lips over the tip and took him into her mouth.

Della knew tonight would not make up even a fraction of what Royce had given her, but...it was a start. She closed her eyes, letting the taste of him fill her senses as her mouth moved in tandem with her hand. Then, with unexpected swiftness, Royce took hold of her arms and lifted her up to sit beside him.

"Did I do something wrong?" Della asked, unsure if she should be upset that Royce stopped her so abruptly.

"Wrong?" Royce laughed. "By gods, Della, if you had done anything more right, it would have been over before we even got started. I need you,"—he said darkly, pulling her over to straddle him—"now."

Royce stood up, and Della felt a rush of excitement as she wrapped her legs around him, enjoying the sensation of being held so close. His powerful arms circled around her body as he placed a searing kiss on her lips and walked them over to the bed.

"This has to go," Royce said, tossing Della onto the bed.

Instead of gently pulling the nightgown off over her head, he grabbed at the neckline and ripped the gown down the middle, splitting the front in two.

"I will have you know I liked that gown," Della said, looking down at the now destroyed garment.

"I will buy you a hundred more if it means we will have more nights like this." Royce stepped back and divested himself of his clothing. "Are you willing to try something new?"

Della nodded, her skin tingling with the thrill of anticipation. Royce motioned for her to flip onto her stomach, then pulled her up on all fours so that her backside was even with his hips. Looking over her shoulder, she saw Royce place himself at her entrance before slowly pushing forward.

She felt herself sinking deeper into ecstasy with every push and pull of Royce's hips. Each movement he made feeling like a revelation as he stretched her, filled her; solidifying the love she had already had for him.

Royce's hand skimmed up her back before he gently pushed her front down to the bed, causing her hips to raise, and the sensitive tips of her breasts to drag across the fabric, creating a sensation that only sped up the climb.

Della gripped the sheets tightly as Royce picked up speed, causing her to climb higher and higher until she felt as though she were standing on the brink of something truly extraordinary. With one last thrust, she shattered, and yelled three words that brought everything to an abrupt halt.

"What?" Royce asked, not moving a muscle.

"I said, I love you," Della repeated.

"No." Royce shook his head. "You cannot, you do not."

His words had a sharpness and precision that only a skilled archer could match, piercing her heart and splintering it into a million tiny pieces. The silence in the room thick with tension as Royce withdrew from her and reached for his breeches on the floor. Della scrambled for a sheet to cover herself and stared at Royce in utter disbelief.

"But I can, and I do. I have been in love with you for many years. And even if you do not feel the same, I know you care for me, or at least I thought you did."

Royce stood in the center of the room with his breeches hanging loosely on his hips, not saying a word as he looked at anything but her. "Falling in love with me was a stupid thing to do."

Della scoffed, "Yes, stupid me. Stupid, silly girl who always hoped that a certain man might notice her as more than just a friend. Now that man is standing here, married to that stupid, silly girl as she hands him her heart." Tears welled up in her eyes as she took a deep breath and swiped them away.

"What else do you want me to say?"

"You do not need to say anything, *Your Grace*," Della said with a calmness she did not feel as she rose from the bed, keeping the sheet wrapped around her. "You have already said enough."

Padding across the floor, Della placed her hand on the doorknob and let a quiet sob escape as she looked over her shoulder.

"We do not choose who we love—love chooses us. And whether or not you want my love, you have it just the same."

She had shut the door softly, but the sound seemed to ricochet around the room like a gunshot as he absentmindedly rubbed at the dull pain in his chest. Royce had convinced himself in that moment that Della needed time to let her anger subside. But in truth, he had needed that time to gain the courage to apologize.

Eventually, he went to her room, only to find the sheet that had been wrapped around her naked body lying across the bed. He searched their home and garden, then finally went to the stables to see if Demeter was still there, but the stall was empty.

Quickly placing a saddle on Titan, Royce raced toward one of the two places Della might have gone.

He only hoped he had chosen the right one.

A short while later, Royce charged up to the Rowntree residence, practically throwing himself from the saddle as he brought Titan to a stop.

Stalking down the path leading to the garden, he found himself barred by a gate with a large lock. He knew it was of no use, but he grabbed the iron bars and shook them vigorously, anyway.

"Della!" Royce yelled, hoping she might hear him. But even if she could, he would not blame her for ignoring him. The wounded look in her eyes when he had rejected her words had made him want to carve out his heart and give it to her, but he had been a coward. He had let her leave, thinking he did not want her.

The household was probably awake by now, but he did not care as he stalked to the front door.

Bang, Bang, Bang

"Della!" Royce yelled again, beating on the front door.

Still, no answer came.

Under the mistaken belief that she had to repay him for everything he had done for her, Della had gone to great lengths to arrange a surprise for him. And though she never needed to repay any kindness he showed her, to know she cared enough to return the favor meant the world to him.

But he had ruined it. Had carelessly dismissed her words and tossed them aside as if they had meant nothing, possibly destroying the love she said she had for him forever.

Leaning against the door, Royce slid to the ground, and let his head fall back with a dull thud, wondering how long he was going to be made to sit out here looking like the fool he was. Suddenly, the door was pulled open, and Royce found himself unceremoniously sprawled on his back across the threshold.

Mr. Rowntree's kind countenance stared down at him. "Mucked it up, did you?"

Royce simply nodded.

"I was thinking you some sort of god among men that you had not messed it all up sooner than this."

"We have been married less than a fortnight," Royce said, still lying on the ground.

"That is true, but *I* only made it three days." Mr. Rowntree laughed, holding out his hand to help Royce to his feet. "Let us go to the study and talk, shall we?"

"Brandy?" Mr. Rowntree asked, pouring two glasses.

Royce shook his head.

"No? Well, more for me then." Mr. Rowntree poured Royce's portion into his own. He took a sip and wandered over to a chair, motioning for Royce to sit down.

"I must apologize for the lateness of the hour. Della—"

"Della has informed me of what happened."

"I see," Royce said, hoping Della had not told her father *everything*. "Did she tell you what an arse I was?"

"She did, among a few other things, but that about sums it up." Mr. Rowntree smiled, taking another sip.

"Della told me she loves me—has loved for many years. But how could she possibly know something like that?"

"You are not the first man to ask such a question, nor will you be the last. Love is something man has struggled with since time began. Women, on the other hand—"he shrugged his shoulder—"never seem to question it. Though exceptions exist, loving unconditionally seems to come more naturally to them."

"I care for her more than I can say. But I let her—"Royce shook his head—"I let her leave, thinking she meant nothing to me."

"What you fail to realize, Your Grace, is that we do not choose who we love—love chooses us." Mr. Rowntree stood and went to the sideboard.

Royce let out an exasperated laugh. "Della said those exact words to me before she left."

"Della is a smart woman...takes after her father." Mr. Rowntree winked. "I loved my wife very much, and still do. She always lit up a room with her presence. But when she passed, I became so consumed by my grief, I ignored everything else. Then, late one night, when I was about to go to bed, I saw Della sneak into the study. I watched her through the open door as she sat next to her mother's chair and cried. In that moment, I realized how selfish I had been. I was not the only one who had lost someone."

"Your mother may have lost her husband, but she still had you and your brothers and sisters. You are *all* a part of her most cherished memories with your father. And I know without doubt it was their love of each other and their children that made, and continues to make, her life worth living." He swirled his glass around. "My suggestion to you: do not fight it. Instead, fight for it."

Royce did not know if he could ever say those three words to Della. But as he looked at her father, he saw a man not made weaker by love, but stronger because of it.

"Well, it is time for this old man to get some sleep," Mr. Rowntree said, tossing back the rest of his drink. "Just so you know...she may be your wife, but she will always be my daughter. No matter the circumstance, my door will always remain open to her."

Royce nodded his understanding and read the meaning in words left unsaid, *'whenever you muck something up.'*

"She really does love you; you know. Do not do anything to lose it, hmm?"

With that, Mr. Rowntree left the study, leaving Royce to think over his parting words.

Royce walked over to the fireplace as the clock on the mantle chimed the hour; it was late. He was uncertain how this night would end, but standing here was not getting him any closer to obtaining Della's forgiveness.

Chapter 24

The night was still, except for a soft breeze that floated through the branches as Della sat beneath her mother's tree. Royce's reaction to her admission of love had been far worse than she expected.

His words had been harsh, dismissive, and the thought of returning home, with the knowledge of how he felt, left her feeling unsure of their future.

Letting out a deep sigh, she shivered in the chilly night air and fumbled for her wrap, but all she found was hard marble beneath her fingers.

"Della," a voice said as her wrap was gently placed over her shoulders.

"Royce!" Della put a hand over her pounding heart. "You frightened me."

"Add that to the long list of things I must apologize for," he said, sitting on the bench next to her. "I arrived a while ago."

"I heard," Della said, watching the trickling water in the fountain. "Though I am surprised you came here at all."

"Why would I not?"

"Do I really need to answer that, Royce?" Della rose to her feet and walked to the fountain, placing her hands on the coarse stone.

"No," Royce said, coming to stand beside her. "But I cannot stress how very sorry I am. I should have never let you leave thinking I do not care for you; when I do—more than you know."

"Then why push me away?" Della slowly turned her head to look at the man she loved, her heart aching to understand.

Royce tenderly clasped her hand and placed it over his heart, letting out a heavy sigh.

"My mother and father had an unbreakable bond. They were inseparable, and I witnessed their love for each other every day of my life. And I longed for the same in my future marriage. But when my father passed away, the grief nearly destroyed my mother. For a while after that, it felt as though we had not lost just one parent, but both."

"Maggie never told me." Della looked at Royce tenderly.

"No." Royce shook his head. "She would not have wanted you to worry. Della—"

"Shh, Royce. You do not need to explain—"

"But I do. I need you to understand why I reacted the way I did."

Della fixed her gaze on the spot where Royce held her hand over his heart, feeling the warmth of his touch radiating through her skin. She could tell he was struggling to express whatever he felt he had to say, so she stayed quiet, allowing him to take as much time as he required.

"I am afraid that if I allowed myself to love someone and something were to happen—especially to you—I would shatter like a mirror, unable to put the pieces back together. Left to face this life with only the shattered pieces of my former self without you by my side. Though that is no excuse for what I said or how I acted. I am truly sorry, and I will make every effort to earn your forgiveness."

Della kept her hand over his heart at Royce's admission and lovingly reached up with the other to brush away his tears. He leaned into the gentle caress of her hand and placed a kiss on her palm.

"Take me home," Della whispered, looking up at Royce.

Royce nodded. And with her hand in his, they made their way to the front of the house, only to be surprised by the sight of Titan affectionately nuzzling Demeter as they stood tethered behind her father's carriage.

"Seems to be the night for the Derrington men to make apologies," Royce joked as he handed Della up.

As they made their way back home, Della felt Royce put his arm around her, drawing her close to him, saying nothing but everything at the same time.

As the weeks went by, Della slowly adjusted to her new home, endeavoring to make the servants comfortable with her presence, and attempting to not be too demanding.

Their new butler, Jeffries, and their cook, Mrs. Barlow, had been worth their weight in gold, helping her decide on how the house and kitchens would run most efficiently.

In the evenings, after dinner, Royce would retire to his study to respond to correspondence or check over the numbers for various holdings he had invested in. And Della invited Mrs. Barlow for late-night tea in her room beyond the study.

Mrs. Barlow had disliked the idea of meeting upstairs initially, but Della had insisted they should at least be comfortable if they were to pour over recipes and menus.

"Royce! We just finished." Della smiled at him one evening as he entered the room. She bent down to place papers full of recipes and lists in a stack and handed them to Mrs. Barlow.

"Good night, Mrs. Barlow. Sleep well and thank you for your help."

Mrs. Barlow grinned and headed for the door when an errant piece of parchment sailed from the stack of papers in her hands. Royce snatched it out of the air and handed it back to her.

"Thank you, Your Grace. Goodnight." Mrs. Barlow curtsied and left.

"You two were in here quite a while," Royce said quietly as he ambled toward Della with his hands clasped behind his back.

"Yes. We will host our first dinner at the end of the week. To prevent any potential mishaps, I wanted to make sure everything was in order." Della bent down to pick up the guest list from the table to read over once more.

"May I ask who was worthy enough to make your list?" Royce asked, placing his chin on Della's shoulder.

"You and I, of course…"

"Not those two again," Royce groaned. "People have said they cannot keep their hands off each other. Quite scandalous, or so I am told," he whispered in Della's ear.

Della ignored him and continued. "Your mother, Maggie, Grayson, Desmond, Samuel." Royce's wandering hands made it hard for her to concentrate, but she kept reading the list of names as though nothing was happening. "My father, Tilly, and I invited your Aunt Imogen, uncle, and cousins."

"Sounds like a houseful."

"Oh! And Aden." Della reached down to grab the quill and quickly added his name to this list.

"You must not forget him—he would be terribly put out." Royce attempted to look serious.

"Everyone gets along. The only two I worry about are Aden and Maggie. You saw them at the last ball. Those two barely tolerate being in the same room, and I am afraid if they sit near each other, we could end up with an argument or food fight on our hands."

"That would be rather amusing, I would think."

"Oh, hush." Della lightly smacked Royce on the arm. "This is my first-time hosting and planning a menu for this many people since I became a duchess. I need it to go well. Even if it is only family. By the way, I wanted to talk to you about giving Jeffries and Mrs. Barlow an increase in their pay. I know they have not been working for us long, but they have done so much for me. I would like to do something for them in return."

"Consider it done."

Della felt Royce's hands stop their roaming as he went to open the doors leading out to the garden. A strong gust of wind blew through the room, causing the candles on the mantle to gutter, leaving the room lit by the light of the spectacularly large moon.

"Beautiful," Della said, awe coloring her voice.

"Yes, it is," Royce said, as he came up behind her, gently pressing his lips against the exposed skin of her neck.

With her head tilted to the side, Della tried to turn to face him, but he held her in place. "Stay as you are."

Slowly, Royce pulled at the hem of Della's dress, exposing her legs a little at a time. Once he had gathered the material, he tucked it against her back and pinned it between their bodies, freeing both of his hands.

"May I?" Royce asked softly, reverently.

"Mmmmm," was all Della could manage. Royce's touch made her tremble as his hand moved along the curve of her breast, while the other found the place where she wanted him most.

"You are already wet for me." He let out a low growl as he traced her opening with his fingers before sinking them into her.

Della let out a soft scream as Royce's pulled her more firmly against him, his erection pressing insistently against her backside.

She spread her legs wider, her breath quickening as Royce's fingers continued to do wicked things, then finally settling on that bundle of nerves that never failed to send her beyond. He flicked, stroked, and lightly plucked, each movement causing her to be wound tighter and tighter.

"Not just yet," Royce said, kissing her shoulder before guiding her to a chair and bending her over so she was forced to place her hands on the cushion to keep from falling over. Tossing the already bunched fabric of her dress over her waist, he smacked her behind.

"Royce!"

"I told you next time I would not miss," he growled as he undid the fall of his breeches. "Shall we continue?" Royce asked, stroking his cock along her seam. "Or shall we just go to bed?"

"Please..." Della whimpered, feeling as though every nerve was on fire.

Royce slid himself in, little by little, pulled out slightly, and plunged back in, causing Della's breath to catch. She wanted him, and he seemed to reciprocate the sentiment. Della moved her hands up to grasp the back of the chair, pushing herself into each thrust, driving him deeper and deeper.

"Royce!" "Della!" they yelled simultaneously as Royce tightened his grip on her hips.

"Now, Della!"

Della screamed at her release, her knees feeling like they would give out as Royce leaned over her and placed his hands on the arms of the chair, his heavy breathing matching her own.

"Well..." Della panted. "That was fun."

Della heard Royce chuckle as he withdrew from her and tucked himself back into his breeches. Lightly shaking out her dress, Della turned to press a gentle kiss to his lips and allowed Royce to guide her over to the settee, pulling her on top of him as he lay down.

"I love you," Della whispered into Royce's chest.

He wrapped his arms around her, neither saying another word as they listened to the sound of the night that drifted through the doors.

The sound of birds chirping outside was the first thing Della heard as she opened her eyes to the morning light. It was only when Royce attempted to turn over and unceremoniously dumped her onto the floor that she remembered they had never made it to their bedroom.

"Royce." Della patted him gently on the chest. "Royce..." Just a snore was all she received in response. "Royce!!" she yelled, smacking him in the chest with the flat of her palm.

"W-w-what?!" Royce jolted to a sitting position, then laid back down, holding his hand to his head. He opened one eye and looked around, spotting Della on the floor. "What are you doing down there?"

"You tossed me off."

"My apologies," Royce said, holding out his hand.

Della took his hand and stood, but soon found herself straddling Royce's lap.

"Good morning." Della smiled down at Royce.

"Good morning to you too," he said, pulling her in for a kiss.

"I cannot believe we slept on this tiny thing all night."

"Oh, I can believe it," Royce said, straightening his back.

"What time is it?" Della asked, looking at the clock on the mantel. "Oh, heavens! It is nearly a quarter to ten. I promised your mother and Maggie I would have tea with them at eleven." Della made to get up so she could get ready, but not before Royce pulled her back in for another long searing kiss.

"Enough," Della laughed, attempting to pull away from Royce. "If you keep that up, I shall be late for sure."

"Care to test that theory?" Royce smiled wickedly.

He tried to hold her to him, but Della squirmed out of his grasp. She grabbed a pillow from the adjacent chair, threw it at Royce, and made her escape, his laughter following her as she ran toward their room to change.

Once she was ready—in record time, according to Abigail—Della rushed down the stairs, ran into the study to give Royce a glancing kiss on the cheek, and left before he had a chance to react.

"How are the preparations for your dinner coming along?" the Duchess asked, pouring herself a cup of tea.

"Mrs. Barlow and I discussed the final details last night." Della took a sip of her tea, trying to hide the blush that threatened to show itself regarding what had happened *after* that conversation. "Imogen finally confirmed, so all will be in attendance."

"Will Aden be there?" Maggie inquired; her tone tinted with annoyance.

"Of course he will! Lord Aynesworth is practically family!" The Duchess looked at Maggie incredulously. "I believe he would be terribly offended if he were excluded."

"How horrible," Maggie grumbled as she took an unladylike bite of scone and dropped it on her plate.

The Duchess slid a glance at Della, eyebrow raised in question. Della merely shook her head and took another sip of her tea.

"Della, would you like to join me for a horseback ride in the park?" Maggie asked as she abruptly slammed her plate down on the table, causing everything to rattle.

Without waiting for a response, Maggie stood and headed to the door.

"That sounds lovely, but I came in the carriage."

"We just happened to have a horse arrive last night from Derrington Chase. The twins needed riding lessons, but our horses here are bit finicky, so I thought a more tolerant horse would be best for them. Her name is Biscuit."

"Biscuit?" Della laughed.

"Yes. I would tell you how she received her moniker, but I believe the story would be better told by the one who named

her. Do be sure to ask Desmond about it at our family dinner."
The Duchess smiled.

"Shall we be off, then?" Maggie asked impatiently.

"Only if you take two footmen with you," the Duchess said casually, brushing some crumbs off her lap.

"Must we?" Maggie sighed.

"Della may serve as your chaperone for outings, as she is now a married woman. But *you* remain unmarried. And while I trust Della implicitly, I would feel better knowing that the two of you have protection with you. No offense, Della dear." The Duchess lightly patted Della's knee.

Della smiled to show no offense was taken. She noticed Maggie seemed troubled, and from her objections to Aden joining them for the family dinner, she suspected it had to do with him.

But Della had been trying her hardest these last few weeks to take Royce's advice and let it sort itself out. It would be up to Maggie when or if she wanted to talk about it.

"Very well," Maggie said harshly before leaving.

Della smiled slightly at the Duchess and stood to follow.

"Good luck, dear," the Duchess said, taking a sip of tea as she looked out the window. "You are going to need it."

Chapter 25

Della rode on Biscuit, a very plump, tawny colored horse, and reveled in the perfect weather as they made their way through the park.

Families spread out their blankets, enjoying picnics while children laughed and played with hoops, racing each other to the finish line. People casually walked along the intersecting paths in the park, engaging in conversations with acquaintances they bumped into.

She looked over at Maggie. It was unlike one of them to not know what was going on with the other, but since Della had married Royce, things seemed...different. Maggie had become less talkative, only speaking when spoken to, and their ride through the park had not seemed to improve her mood.

The presence of the two footmen the Duchess had requested to accompany them seemed to make Maggie even more hesitant to discuss what was bothering her; even though they remained a respectful distance behind them.

The footman sauntered along on their horses, their expression betraying a hint of boredom, yet a sense of happiness at being relieved from whatever mundane duties they had left behind.

"Your Grace." Della heard the clopping of hooves as one footman approached. "I have been asked to inform you that His Grace will join you as soon as he speaks with his mother."

"Thank you."

The footman bowed his head and fell back with the other and they resumed their conversation.

"Maggie?" Della asked a few minutes later.

"Yes?"

"Royce will join us shortly."

Maggie just nodded.

"Is everything all right? You have seemed out of sorts lately. Is there anything I could help you with?" Della asked, unable to take Maggie's silence any longer.

"I am fine..." Maggie appeared to be holding back something as her voice trailed off, as if there was more she wanted to say. "Actually...no, I am not." She looked as though she was about to break down in tears, with her head hanging low.

"Would you like to talk about it?" Della asked, trying to offer comfort to her best friend.

"Perhaps another time, when we have a bit more privacy."

Della nodded her understanding before she heard the clopping of hooves once again. Squinting her eyes against the sun, Della looked at the man on the horse coming toward them as they both turned around, expecting to see Royce.

"Do you know who that is?" Della asked Maggie right before the man reached inside his coat, pulled out a pistol, and aimed directly at them.

"Della, GO!" Maggie yelled, slapping the reins, urging her horse forward as the man continued to charge at them.

Della did not hesitate another second as she nudged Biscuit in the flank, willing her to pick up the pace, and they both took off, neither daring to glance back. Della looked to her left, then to her right, trying to decide which direction they should go.

"We need to split up!" Maggie yelled even louder over the thundering of the horses' hooves as they came upon where the paths split. "He will only follow one of us. The other needs to circle back and get help."

Della nodded her agreement when a shot rang out, striking a tree as they passed. She hunkered as low as possible, grabbing the reins tighter, and prayed she did not lose her seat.

"On the count of three. One, two—"another shot rang out—"three!"

Maggie drifted right as Della went left. Biscuit slightly protested at the command but obeyed, sensing the danger. They jumped over a small stream and began weaving their way around the trees, hearing hoofbeats behind her. The unknown man had followed her, which meant Maggie should be able to go back and get help.

Della desperately wanted to turn around to see how close the man was, but she did not dare as they came to a broader portion of a stream surrounded by a hedge. Knowing the best way forward was to jump over it, Della pressed Biscuit forward, hoping the horse would understand the command.

With one last slap of the reins, she held on with all her might as they soared through the air and over the hedge.

Biscuit stumbled, her leg buckling as they landed on the other side, causing Della to scream as she was thrown into the water with a splash. She lay there, momentarily stunned, but quickly gathered herself and ran for cover.

Della did not know how long she hid behind the group of bushes as she stood there cold and shivering from her sodden dress. She looked around for Biscuit, hoping she was okay, but the horse was nowhere to be seen.

"Della...Della, where are you? Please answer me!"

Della heard a familiar voice and peeked out from behind the bushes.

"Royce? Royce!" Della picked up her skirt and ran toward Royce's outstretched arms. "Who was that man?"

"That is something we both want to know. I decided shortly after you left, I would join you all for tea, only to be told by Mother that you and Maggie had gone for a ride. I arrived to find Maggie racing toward me, yelling and pointing which way you went.

"One of footmen mother sent with you, told me what happened as we gave chase. From there, it was an all-out sprint to catch up, but we caught the bastard." Royce took a deep breath. "His horse hesitated to jump the hedge and tossed him from the saddle."

"He pulled out a pistol, and we made a run for it. Maggie said we should split up so he would choose only one of us to follow while the other got help," Della said, as she buried her face in Royce's chest, shaking at the thought of how scared she had been.

"That was the right decision." Royce cupped the sides of Della's face and tilted it up to look at him. "Are you hurt?"

"I am wet from landing in the water, but other than that, I am unharmed."

Royce bent down and kissed her soundly.

"I will question him, then hand him over to the constable—if I do not kill him first." Royce's nostrils flared in anger as he rubbed his hands up and down Della's arms. "Let us get you home and into some dry clothes." Royce lifted Della up onto Titan, then pulled himself up behind her.

"I can still ride, you know."

"I know, but Biscuit threw a shoe and has a slight limp. The footmen are letting her walk back at her own pace. Besides, I enjoy riding like this." He gently kissed her forehead and turned Titan toward their home. His lips brushed her ear as he spoke in a hushed, dark tone. "It will let everyone know if they want you, they will have to go through me first."

Royce tightened his grip around her and pulled her in until his chest was firmly pressed against her back. Sinking into his warmth, Della felt her anxieties melt away and a sense of calm take over.

When they had made it through the front door, Della was immediately ushered upstairs by Abigail, who fussed over her ruined dress and a few scratches that had started to bleed. Jeffries informed Royce that the man they had apprehended had been tied to a chair in the study, with footmen standing guard.

Royce thanked him and asked that messengers be sent out with notes to his family, Aden and Della's father and aunt, requesting they adjourn to his home with all due haste. He stalked toward the man now strapped to a chair and asked the two footmen who had witnessed everything to stay and relay what had happened to the constable.

He clenched his fists so tightly his knuckles turned white as he entered the room, fighting the urge to pummel the man within an inch of his life. As Royce circled like a hawk, he could feel his frustration growing with each passing moment the vial man remained silent, refusing to answer any of his questions.

"I ain't tellin' you nuffin'" the man sneered.

Royce's temper got the best of him, and he backhanded the man across the face, then leaned in to stare him down. "That was for my wife," Royce snarled between clinched teeth. "What will happen to you in gaol is far worse. If you tell me what you know, I may ask them to grant some leniency."

A crooked smile played across the man's face, blood dripping from his busted lip as he spit at Royce.

"Piss off."

Royce's vision blurred with rage as he kicked the chair backward and lunged at the man who dared to harm Della. He felt a surge of satisfaction with each punch and could see the footmen growing increasingly uneasy, wondering if they should intervene or not.

"Royce, that is enough!" Grayson yelled as he barreled into the room, quickly grabbing his arms and pulling him away.

"Let the constable handle it," Desmond said, helping Grayson.

Royce shook himself free from their grip but stood there, his chest heaving as he tried to calm down.

"How did you get here so fast?" Royce asked.

"We were already on our way to see you and had just arrived when one of your men came rushing out and informed us of what was going on," Grayson said.

"Imagine our surprise of finding our eldest and most loving brother pummeling a man to within an inch of his life." Desmond's eyes shifted to the man strapped to the chair on the floor.

"He had it coming," Royce growled, whipping a handkerchief from his pocket to press against his bloodied knuckles.

Soon, several police and the constable were ushered into the room, only to find the assailant already roughed up. Royce relayed the entire story, accompanied by the footmen, and said the man had suffered his cuts and bruises when he was thrown from his horse.

Royce stared the constable down, daring him to question the authenticity of his words as the rest of the police hauled the man away.

When Royce answered in the affirmative to the constable's question about pressing charges, the constable told him they would notify him of the trial date.

Royce paced in front of the fireplace, now surrounded by his mother, Maggie, Grayson, Desmond, Aden, Mr. Rowntree, and Tilly. Della had yet to come down; no doubt Abigail was still fussing over her. He had been relieved to find that Della had been mostly unharmed by her hellbent ride through the park.

It was fortunate that she was an excellent rider, or the outcome could have been much worse.

"I thought everything leading up to our marriage had been just a set of unfortunate coincidences, especially since nothing has happened since we have been married, but after today—"Royce raked his hand through his hair—"I fear that someone may be after Della."

"But who, Royce?" the Duchess looked at him with motherly concern. "Who could possibly want to harm Della?"

"Miss Putnam?" Desmond asked.

The Duchess gasped. "She may be upset, but I cannot fathom she would go to such extremes as this!"

"Have you seen the vultures who circle the ballroom, Mother?" Desmond replied, casually draping his arm across the back of his chair. "Most members of the Ton would probably commit murder if they thought they could get away with it to claim a title."

"No, I will not tolerate Miss Putnam's name being bandied about as if she were some common criminal," the Duchess huffed.

"I agree with Mother," Grayson said.

"You do not need to worry about Miss Putnam," Royce added. "She and Della made amends on our wedding day and are now on friendly terms."

"She could have lied..." Desmond retorted.

"Desmond!" Grayson snapped.

"Lord Haddock, then?" Aden interjected.

"I find it hard to believe he would have enough brains to be the mastermind behind all of this." Royce tapped his finger against his cheek. "He accosted Della twice, it is true, and attempted to force her hand in marriage to him, but to what end? Besides, he has not been heard from since the Ravensdale ball."

"I know his family has cut him off until he marries," Grayson said to no one in particular, as he looked out the window. "He carries enormous gambling debts, most of which I own. His father refuses to pay them for him. It is possible he would have resorted to something he would not have normally done, desperate as he is for funds."

"That would explain why he was so insistent on me accepting his proposal," Della said calmly as she entered the room. "But do you honestly think he would stoop to something worse than proposing? And what about the man that chased Maggie and I earlier in the park?"

"He would revel nothing." Royce said angrily as he ushered Della to a vacant chair by the fire.

"Then I can safely assume your attempt to persuade him to give you answers was in vain," Aden said nonchalantly.

"Royce, your hand!" Della grasped his hand in hers, gently brushing her thumb over his bruised knuckles.

"I will be fine," Royce assured her.

"I cannot believe I forgot..." Della said, still holding onto Royce's hand.

"Forgot what, dear?" the Duchess asked.

"Our wedding day..."

"You forgot your wedding day?" Desmond asked.

"Desmond," Royce grumbled.

"Sorry..." Desmond said, holding his hands up. "Please, continue."

"I went to the retiring room before Royce, and I came out to join everyone..."

Royce noticed Aden glance at Maggie as he fidgeted with his signet ring at Della's words; Maggie, too, had gone still. He tucked that observation away to be examined later as he listened to Della.

"Do you remember me mentioning that Emma and I spoke, Royce?"

"I have already told them you two were now on friendly terms," he acknowledged.

"Do you remember me telling you that her father has plans to send her away to Scotland to live with relatives?"

"He what?!" Grayson exclaimed.

Della nodded at Grayson's outburst. "Emma sent me a letter informing me she is to depart the day after tomorrow. But when we spoke at the wedding, she said her father was blinded by his anger for her failure to marry you, Royce. Lord Milton also said he would send for her once he sorted things out, but Emma did not understand what he meant by that."

"You do not think Lord Milton's need to 'sort things out' involves the two of you, do you?" Mr. Rowntree asked.

"I know he is not happy with me, and we all know he is quick to anger when he feels like he has been wronged, but I cannot speak as to what he might do in certain situations."

"Where does that leave us?" Maggie asked.

"I do not know." Royce raked his hand through his hair, trying to remain calm. "I can only suggest that we remove ourselves from the equation until we can figure some things out. Grayson and Desmond, cancel whatever plans you have. Mother, please send your regrets for any events you might attend and inform Imogen of the change of plans. We leave for Derrington Chase tomorrow."

"But surely whoever they are will know where we have gone," Della said.

"Then we prepare the best we can and stay vigilant," Royce said, smiling down at Della, hoping to allay some of her worries.

"That means your family dinner will be changing location, dear," the Duchess said, looking at Della. "I will talk to Imogen and let her know the details. Della, will you send notice to Scrivens to let him know the entire family is about to descend upon him? You are now the mistress of Derrington Chase, after all. Jeffries and Mrs. Barlow should be able to watch over everything here. Maggie, come along. There is much to do." The Duchess swept from the room without another word.

Royce saw Maggie stop to glance at Aden before she, too, left.

"Aden, I know it is asking a lot on such short notice, but will you join us?" Royce asked.

"If it means I can avoid my father and help you sort this out, I will happily oblige," Aden said. "I will see you tomorrow." He saluted and left the room.

"Royce, is this truly necessary?"

"Until this family is safe...until *you* are safe—"he looked at Della sincerely—"everything is necessary."

"I love you," Della said as she gently pulled him in for a kiss.

Royce growled as Della snaked her hands up the back of his neck, weaving her fingers into his hair. Savoring the moment, he held onto her tightly, grateful for her safety and the comfort of her embrace. He reluctantly stepped back from their kiss and, holding tightly to Della's hand, they headed off to make the necessary preparations before leaving for Derrington Chase.

Chapter 26

Their travel had been a very long four days, and everyone rejoiced when they pulled up to the final inn of their journey. They had arrived in five carriages, nearly bursting at the seams, inquiring if rooms were available.

The kind owners, Mr. and Mrs. Tewksbury, apologized after informing Royce that only four rooms were vacant.

Royce assured them it was not an issue and they would be more than happy to share. After receiving their keys, the Duchess took it upon herself to sort everyone between the four rooms.

The younger children slept on makeshift beds in a room with their governess', with Imogen and Archibald in their own room just down the hall. Samuel squished himself into the larger of the rooms with Royce, Desmond, Grayson, and their two older cousins, Ace and Theodore.

Maggie, Della, and the Duchess shared a room containing a large bed and a small cot. Della had insisted the Duchess and Maggie take the bed, choosing the cot for herself. This would be the first time since they married that she and Royce had not slept next to each other.

It had been a little lonely, but the three of them had fun staying up till the wee hours talking.

It was a blessing Della's father was required to remain for a few extra days because of some unavoidable meetings, which eased the need for more rooms. And Tilly stayed behind to act as a travel companion.

Aden had sent a message before they left to inform Royce he would be delayed but would arrive as soon as he was able.

The following day, the entire brood descended upon the owners once again as they made their way into a private dining room for breakfast. As soon as they had reduced the food to mere crumbs, they all filed back into their awaiting carriages.

Royce settled the bill with Mr. and Mrs. Tewksbury for their lodging, meals, and even gave them a little extra. Despite their attempts to decline the amount, Royce insisted and refused to budge. Stating that anyone who had the courage to deal with his family deserved a token of his thanks.

A few hours later, everyone piled back out of the carriages—some looking tired and some looking like they wanted to punch something. Della just laughed as she looked up at the regal façade of Derrington Chase; she had forgotten what a magnificent structure it was.

She remembered thinking the same thing when she attended a two-week retreat the Duke and Duchess had hosted. There had been excursions to the ruins of a castle, outings to town, archery, games, and all manner of food.

On the final evening, they had organized a masquerade ball, inviting people of all ranks and stations. Sadly, all the children were too young to attend, even Royce and Aden.

Della's fondest memory of that time had been when she and Maggie had snuck out of their beds while the ball was in full swing, staring down at the masks and costumes the women wore and the handsomely dressed men.

The Duke had caught them poking their heads through the railing of the stairs, looking into the ballroom and escorted them back to their room. He had not been mad; in fact, he had promised when they were older, he would throw another ball, just like this one, so they could attend.

"Every princess should be able to go to a masquerade ball," he said, tucking them into bed.

When all this mess was behind them, Della made a note to herself to plan a masquerade ball. It would be the first large formal event she would host here, and an homage to the late Duke.

And it would fulfill the dreams of two little girls who once got caught out of bed so they could witness something magical.

Over the next few days, Della became accustomed to the inner workings of Derrington Chase, and quickly realized what worked for her home in London did not always work for an estate nearly three times the size. She tried to defer to the

Duchess on several occasions, but she refused, saying it was now Della's job to change things as she saw fit.

Most women who held such a position of power would probably have balked at having their groundwork changed, but not the Duchess. She had been more than happy to relinquish all the responsibilities to Della, stating she had sacrificed enough.

"Keep the tradition, but put your own special touch on it," the Duchess had said. "That way you can leave your mark and show respect to the woman who have come before you."

Once her father, Tilly, and Aden arrived, Della had done her best to keep things in order—including her first family dinner. Back in London, their cook, Mrs. Barlow, had kindly sent all the food and supplies that had been purchased when they had completed the menu.

But when it came time for Mrs. Campbell to prepare the dinner, she had informed Della that several things had gone missing.

Evidently, the Derrington men's childhood penchant for sneaking into the kitchens and pilfering anything they could find had not changed in the slightest.

Della had laughed at the look on their faces when they realized what they had done and they immediately apologized, offering to go into town to replace everything.

Della sent Grayson, Desmond, Ace, and Theodore into town to find what they could or something that could be used as a replacement.

On the evening that followed, the dinner had been meticulously prepared according to her exact specifications. The table, under the careful guidance of Scrivens, was arranged with meticulous attention to detail. And the food was exquisite, each dish bursting with delectable flavors.

The addition of the younger set at the dinner table had been Royce's idea. Because it had been a while since all the Derringtons had gathered in one place, he requested the whole family have a meal together. It was a wonderful dinner, and everything had gone smoothly—at first.

Della had asked Desmond why he had named the horse Biscuit, and he revealed one summer while they were here at the estate, he had taken to a horse named Petunia. He visited her every day, sneaking her biscuits when the caretaker was not looking.

He noticed the horse had become plump, and one day, he found her lying on her side in the stable. Thinking he had made her ill from the biscuits he had been feeding her, he had run to get his father. But when they returned, they saw the foal she had just given birth to.

Their father had chuckled at the irony of the foal's color, which resembled that of a freshly baked biscuit, and thus the name stuck.

They all laughed at Desmond's retelling and were about to start their next course when a potato was catapulted down the table, landing with a plop in a wine glass.

One thing led to another, which resulted in wine being spilled on Desmond's lap, Maggie's toes being stepped upon by Desmond in his bid to stand up, and several guilty-looking children who were reprimanded and sent to their room for the rest of the evening.

Della had not known what to do, but the Duchess had quickly—and impressively—managed the situation with no further casualty. Once the children had left and everyone had returned, they continued their meal, sharing funny family stories about growing up at the estate.

After dinner was finished, they all chose to retire for the night.

The sky was a brilliant blue as tiny wisps of white clouds passed gently by, making everyone eager to get out and enjoy the day. After partaking in breakfast, they all elected to part ways; some went into town, some got a book from the library and sat in the garden, while others chose various things of interest.

Della, Royce, and Aden decided to walk down to the river that ran behind the estate.

They headed toward a path that had been cut down the middle of a field full of wildflowers and wisteria trees. Della stopped here and there, adding a wide variety of flowers to her basket to be used as an arrangement at the dining room table later that evening.

Della held her hand to her stomach. Breakfast had not been sitting well with her since they left London. Around dinner time, everything always seemed to subside, but the next day, it would start all over again.

"Della?" Royce looked at her, concerned.

"I will be fine," Della assured him as they continued along the path.

They had almost made it down to the river when they heard someone coming up behind them. Maggie had caught up and stopped when she saw Aden.

"Oh great, you are here," Maggie said sarcastically.

"We were just discussing the letter Royce received from the constable about how the investigation is going," Della interjected, before a fight could break out between Maggie and Aden.

"And?" Maggie asked.

"The only thing he will say is that someone had paid him for his services," Royce grumpily replied, looking out over the lake.

Royce discussed the letter and what else the constable had figured out, which turned out to be bloody nothing. The man, who still refused to talk or give his name, would not give them any other information than what they already knew.

"The have set a tentative date for his trial, but it looks like they will deport him." Royce said.

"Could you not just bribe him?" Maggie asked.

"Oh yes, try to out-bribe the person who not only paid the man to harm Della, but also ensured his silence. Short of giving him his freedom, what would make him want to talk?" Aden asked sarcastically.

"Well, if you are so smart, then what do you suggest?" Maggie crossed her arms as she glared daggers at Aden. Walking past him toward the lake, Maggie stepped into a hole, causing her slipper to fall off.

"Lose something?" Aden teased as he bent over and came up holding the slipper.

"Give me my slipper back," Maggie demanded, holding out her hand.

"You did not say the magic word...Margaret."

"I hate being called Margaret, you self-important buffoon." She stomped her foot for emphasis. "I said give me my slipper back...please," she ground out through clinched teeth.

"No, I do not think I will." The corner of Aden's mouth kicked up in a devilish smile as he tossed it back and forth between his hands.

"No? No?!" Maggie yelled. "Why you...you..."

"Cat got your tongue?" Aden asked mockingly.

Maggie took a deep breath, her eyes glistening with unshed tears. With a huff, she turned back toward the house and stumbled. Hopping on one foot, she tore the remaining offending slipper off and flung it at Aden, hitting him squarely on the side of his head.

"There!" Maggie yelled. "Now you have a matching pair!" She picked up her skirts and sprinted back through the wildflowers and into the house.

"That was poorly done, Aden," Royce reprimanded his best friend. "Whatever you two are fighting about—"Royce held up his hand before Aden had the chance to reply—"and do not say slippers. You need to fix it or call a truce. For as of right now, there are other issues we need to deal with."

"Nothing is going on between us. She is a thorn in my side," Aden said irritably, kicking at some flowers. He picked up the other slipper and put the set into his pocket.

"You are like a brother to me, Aden, but that is my sister. If I am forced to choose a side, it will always be hers."

Aden nodded, looking like a chastised child. "For what it is worth, I am sorry, and I will try to make amends. If she will let me." Aden said nothing further and fell into step with Royce and Della toward the river.

Chapter 27

They sat down to dinner, as had been their custom since arriving at Derrington Chase. Following the flying pea incident, the children were made to eat with their governesses.

However, after a week of good behavior, Royce allowed them to return to the dining room with the promise that no food of any kind was to be launched down the table.

Everyone sat idly chatting over their food when Della heard a plop and looked over to see her drink garnished with floating green peas. As she glanced up, she caught Grayson and Desmond trying to suppress their laughter while Ace and Theodore feigned innocence.

Apparently, the children had promised to behave, but the men had not.

Shaking her head at their child-like antics, Della turned to rejoin the conversation when her stomach started to rebel. Excusing herself, she shoved back from the table and walked to the foyer.

As soon as she was out of sight, she broke into a run, barely making it to the chamber pot in her dressing room before she tossed up her accounts.

Della slumped to the floor with a slight moan as she continued to hold her hand over her stomach, willing whatever was wrong with her to go away. The door quietly opened, and the Duchess let herself into the room, followed by Tilly.

"How are you feeling, my dear?" Tilly walked over to the table, poured a glass of water, and handed it to Della.

"I do not know what is wrong with me. One minute I will be fine, and the next minute I am trying to find somewhere to discreetly get sick."

"Have you said anything to Royce?" the Duchess asked.

Della shook her head. "Other than inquiring about my well-being, he has said nothing."

"May I ask a personal question?" The Duchess looked at her, waiting for a response.

Della nodded, taking another sip of water.

"When did you last have your courses?"

Della paused at the Duchess's question and tried to come up with an answer. "I-I do not remember, come to think of it."

The Duchess looked at Tilly before she smiled at Della. "I believe you might be with child, my dear. I have noticed a glow about you. You are getting ill at various points throughout the day and taking long naps in the afternoon."

"I have to tell Royce," Della said as she rose to her feet.

"You will tell Royce when you know for certain. It is late, but I will have a message delivered to our doctor tonight and have him come tomorrow morning. I will send Maggie to fetch a few things in town, and the others can distract Royce by taking him out riding. Do not worry," the Duchess said, leaning over to kiss Della on the cheek.

"You have nothing to fear. We are here for you, and Royce will be thrilled."

Della had found it extremely difficult to keep such exciting news from Royce, but realized the Duchess's suggestion to wait was probably wise. She encouraged Royce to join the others downstairs after claiming a terrible headache.

Which was true, after she tossed and turned all night, thinking about how their lives were about to change. Royce had wanted to stay with her, but Della had insisted she would be fine after a little more sleep.

A knock on the door about an hour later produced the doctor, the Duchess, and Tilly. The Duchess informed her that Royce had practically been shoved out of the house, leaving only after she promised to check on Della. She had also sent Maggie into town—with Aden, of all people—to grab a few important things.

Della had asked Tilly to stay with her to help calm her nerves, feeling like a child again when she had begged her not to leave. Doctor Thorton was quick and efficient in his evaluation and confirmed what the Duchess had suspected.

She was with child, though how far along was a little hard to determine, but he would check back in a couple of weeks. Until then, Della was to relax, go on regular walks for fresh air, and eat smaller, more frequent portions, just in case her stomach continued its current course.

"Well, my dear," the Duchess said with a smile as she closed the door behind the doctor. "I believe congratulations are in order. We will, of course, remain ignorant of the matter until you decide when it is best to tell everyone. Try to lie down and get some rest. Royce will make his way up here when they get back, I am sure."

After they left, Della sat by the window to read a book, hoping the words on the page might calm her, but her excitement soon turned to restlessness, and she decided to take a walk in the garden.

Royce had yet to return from whatever the Duchess had concocted to get him out of the house, which was fine since she had not yet decided how she was going to tell him the news.

Grabbing her wrap, Della headed downstairs, reaching the bottom step as the front door opened and Maggie came in, mumbling something, while she stared at a piece of parchment.

"Maggie?"

"Do you know why my mother sent me off for some items she deemed so *important* this morning?" Maggie asked, planting her hands on her hips as she looked up at Della.

"I have not the faintest idea." Della winced slightly at her lie. "I have been fighting a headache all morning." She desperately wanted to tell Maggie the news, but Royce needed to know first.

"I mean, how important could some of these items be?" Maggie asked, slapping the list in her hand. "Thread, various herbs for tea, and a...a...I do not even know what this is. Worse, she sent me with Samuel and Aden!"

Della had to laugh at Maggie's outrage.

"I am sure there was a need for the items she sent you for. I am about to go for a walk. Would you care to join me?"

"Of course. Let me make sure these *important* items have been delivered, and I will meet you in the garden."

Maggie hustled off downstairs toward the kitchen, still grumbling about her mother, pointless trips into town, and something about Aden, which Della did not hear as Maggie's voice faded away.

Della ambled along the pathway parallel to a row of trees, watching squirrels chase each other as birds frolicked in the fountain. The garden was perfumed with the scent of flowers, herbs, and the divine smell of bread baking in the kitchen, creating a sense of calm within her as she placed her hand over where a new life was forming.

Carefully, she stepped over the puddles that had formed from the rain that had fallen overnight, when a rustling in the trees drew her attention, causing foot to stick in a patch of thick mud.

The sound of twigs snapping instantly made her heart race when a rabbit sprang out of the trees, startling her. Her foot broke free from the mud with a squelching sound as she landed on the ground.

Laughing at her own silliness as she stood, Della attempted to wipe the mud that now caked her slipper, when a pair of powerful arms grabbed her around the waist and hauled her toward the tree line.

"Let go of me!" Della tried to scream, but a large hand clamped over her mouth, muffling her attempt.

"Della?" she heard Maggie call out.

Anger flooded through Della, and she bit down on the man's hand, causing him to curse. He tightened his grip, but her arms were still free, so she drove the point of her elbow into his ribs.

The man grunted, loosening his hold, and Della tried to scramble away, but she was not fast enough before he grabbed her again.

"Try that again and I will kill you where you stand," the man snarled as he flung her over his shoulder. He ran through a thorny overgrowth that let out onto the main road where a carriage was waiting for them.

Della landed with a hard thud on the floor, her arms wrapping around her belly on instinct as the man stepped up into the carriage and closed the door.

"GO!" he yelled at the driver. The horses whinnied at the snapping of a whip, jerking the carriage forward.

Della tried to untangle her feet from her skirt as the man held out his hand to assist her up into a seat, but she slapped the hand away and sat down, her jaw dropping in surprise as she looked up. "L-Lord Haddock?"

"The one and only." He gestured to himself. "Did you miss me?"

"Hardly," Della scoffed. "I have not given you a second thought."

"Oh, you thought about me. Otherwise, why would you and the entire Derrington family, and that pompous arse, Lord Aynesworth, have come all the way to Exeter in the middle of the season?"

"I cannot believe you have the gall to show your face after everything you have done."

"And what have I done exactly, Miss Rowntree?"

"I am the Duchess of Exeter. You will address me as *Your Grace*, and nothing else," Della said in her most commanding tone.

"Tsk, tsk. Such high-handedness." A wicked smile crawled across his face. "We are going to take care of this nasty business and fix this mess you have gotten us into."

"What business do you speak of?"

"Why the business of you becoming my wife, of course."

"In case you were unaware, I am already married," Della said, looking out the window.

"That can be easily remedied once we arrive at our final destination."

"And where exactly is that?" Della asked, trying to find out any information that might help her.

"Oh, not far at all—just a quick trip across the ocean. There is a ship in Topsham that will sail in a few hours, and there is also someone who would like to speak to you," Lord Haddock said. "I am sure His Grace will find us in short order...once he receives the note I left behind."

Della was unsure what direction they were heading, but something her father had said kept repeating in her head; something about purchasing ships in Topsham from Lord de Courtenay.

Perhaps her father could tell Royce how to find her, depending upon the information Lord Haddock had provided in his note.

A wave of nausea crept over Della, and she laid her hand on her stomach, willing it to settle. Casting up her accounts on Lord Haddock would not go over well, especially since provoking his anger any further might jeopardize the safety of her future child.

So, she did her best to stay composed and held onto the hope that Royce would find them soon.

Chapter 28

They had just arrived back when Maggie frantically ran toward them. Panicked, Royce slid from the saddle before the horse had even stopped.

"What do you mean she disappeared?!" Royce roared.

"I do not know. I spoke to Della after I arrived back from an errand mother sent Aden and me on. She wanted to go for a walk, and I told her I would meet her in the gardens once I saw the items delivered to the kitchen. When I came out to find her...she was gone. Her wrap was lying on the ground by the trees over there."

Royce looked up to see Aden dashing across the garden.

"Here..." Aden said, breathing heavily as he held out a letter to Royce. "This was delivered just before you arrived."

Royce ripped opened the seal and read the note scrawled across the parchment. "It says to meet at the docks in Topsham at a ship named—"he squinted, attempting to read the poor handwriting—"the Primrose."

Desmond snatched the letter from Royce's hands and read it himself.

"I know that ship!" Mr. Rowntree said as he, the Duchess, and Tilly joined the group.

"How?" Royce asked pointedly.

"Because I just purchased that ship from Lord de Courtenay. She is to set sail in—"Mr. Rowntree looked at his pocket watch—"six hours. I was about to leave to meet with the captain before they weigh anchor. But why do you need to meet at the Primrose? Has something happened?"

"Someone has taken Della," Maggie replied.

"Oh, my heavens." Tilly fluttered her hand. "How far is it from here?"

"Not far," Grayson said, dismounting from his horse. "About an hour by carriage; faster if you ride on horseback. If we leave now, we should be able to catch up with them."

"It says here," Desmond read out loud. "If you do not wish to become a widower this day, I would suggest coming alone."

"Like hell you will!" the Duchess blurted out, causing everyone to turn and look at her. "Bring Della back. Do you hear me?" She looked sternly at Royce.

Royce nodded. "Right. Mother, please inform Scrivens, Imogen and the rest of the family about what has happened. Desmond, Grayson, and Aden, you all will come with me. I have two sets of dueling pistols in the study, and each of us will take one. We will have to use them wisely, as it is all I have."

"I am coming too!" Maggie announced.

"No, you will stay here with Mother. I cannot have another person to worry about," Royce said, shaking his head.

"She can ride with me in a carriage, Your Grace. I know what the ship looks like, and I will not stand by and wait for answers about my daughter when I might be of help," Mr. Rowntree said sternly.

"Nor will I!" Maggie agreed.

"Very well." The urgency to reach Della weighed heavily on Royce, so he agreed to avoid wasting any more time.

His body was practically vibrating from his anger as he ran into the study to grab the pistols. With a careful eye, he inspected the pistols, ensuring they were loaded correctly before hurrying back outside. Handing one to Grayson, Desmond, and Aden, they pulled themselves into their saddles as Mr. Rowntree and Maggie clamored into the carriage and raced to the designated meeting point.

The pounding of his horse's hooves mirrored the thudding of his heart, burdened by his unspoken love for Della. With a glance at the sky, Royce whispered a prayer, begging for Della to remain unharmed until they could reach her.

He leaned forward, pressing his horse faster. He could not live without her, count not live without Della knowing how much he loved her. And the thought of losing her—Royce shook his head—he was going to get her back or die trying.

For him, a life without Della was not a life worth living.

"Let go of me!" Della shouted.

"This would go much more smoothly if you would stop fighting the inevitable!" Lord Haddock barked as he hauled Della from the carriage and pushed her down the dock.

Della could hear nothing but the distant shouts of sailors and the creaking and moaning of the ropes anchoring the ships as they bobbed in the water.

The mist that fell from the dark clouds gathering overhead dampened her dress, making it cling to her skin.

"Sit…" Lord Haddock commanded, pointing to a bench.

Della plopped down with a huff, not daring to provoke Lord Haddock any further until she could come up with a plan.

"Della?"

"Emma?" Della's eyes widened. "What are you doing here? I thought you were leaving for Scotland."

"Did he harm you?" Emma asked, running over to sit next to her. "I begged him not to do this—told him he just needed to move on. "

"Told who? Lord Haddock?" Della looked at Emma worriedly.

"Me…" an ominous voice said, as a silhouette emerged from the shadows.

"Lord Milton?"

"Yes, very astute, *Miss Rowntree,* and…where is His Grace? I am surprised he has not yet arrived."

"Yes, I have!"

A sense of relief filled Della as her eyes fell upon Royce standing next to her father at the end of the dock. Their attention was not on her, but rather on Lord Milton and Lord Haddock, who were standing behind her.

But as she looked on, she could not help but worry the day might not end as happily as it had begun.

Thank heavens Mr. Rowntree had come with them, for they had nearly gone the wrong way when the road had split about a mile outside of Topsham.

When they arrived, Royce told everyone to stay hidden. Maggie had tried to argue, but Royce had put his foot down.

Mr. Rowntree, on the other hand, had charged past him, heedless of his own safety. Royce let out an exasperated sigh and rolled his eyes. Like father, like daughter.

"I believe my letter said for you to come alone, but when can one ever expect a duke to do what he is told?" Lord Haddock inquired with a sarcastic tone.

"Let her go!" Royce boomed, taking a step forward.

Lord Milton brandished a pistol from his coat pocket. "Halt, Your Grace, or I shall shoot her right here, right now, and you will have no one to blame for her death except yourself."

Royce stood there, attempting to figure out what he was going to do next as his eyes traced down the pistol in the viscount's hand and over to Della. She smiled at him, not hinting at how frightened she must be, unlike Miss Putnam, who stared at her father, obviously terrified of what he might do if she dared move.

Not knowing what was to come, Royce let his eyes express every emotion he felt as he looked at Della.

"I love you."

"And I love you," Della said, smiling at him.

"*Touching*," Lord Milton sneered with contempt. "We are running out of time. So, here is what we are going to do, Your Grace. We—and by we, I mean *you*—are going to fake the Duchess' death. You are going to put her on the next ship bound for America under a new name. Lord Haddock's name."

He gestured to the lord, who had propped himself against a lamppost as if everything was going as it should.

"He will leave with her, as was our original plan—now that I have gotten it back on track." The Viscount said the last part as he looked at Royce's rage filled stare. "I promise to continue to let her live, so long as *she* promises never to return."

"And what about *me*?" Royce did his best to keep calm and his voice steady, though his anger was boiling just beneath the surface.

"You, Your Grace, will make up a very sad tale about how Her Grace perished by drowning or some such rot. Of course, her body will never be found, so there will be nothing to bury. You will wait a few weeks of the requisite mourning period before announcing you have decided to marry again. People will forgive your hastiness since your wife never produced a male heir before her tragic and untimely demise."

"But what if I am with child?" Della asked.

"Then you can both die here or sail across the ocean and start a new life. Whichever you choose is of no matter to me," Lord Milton spat.

"Do not worry, Miss Rowntree. We can have plenty of children once we arrive at our new home," Lord Haddock crudely remarked, winking at Della.

Royce started for Lord Haddock, but Mr. Rowntree held him back.

"How did you even know about any of this to begin with?" Royce asked the detestable man standing before him.

"It was simple, really." Lord haddock looked at Royce with an undeserved sense of pride. "When I heard the rumor of your engagement being postponed, I saw my chance and approached Lord Milton about offering for Miss Putnam. The viscount turned me down, but he offered me a sizeable amount if I could figure out why you had wavered on making an announcement. Later that evening, at the Bellamy's ball, I noticed you and Miss Putnam heading to the garden and followed you. I heard everything. Including that part where she spread the rumor to force your hand."

Royce looked at Miss Putnam, who had the wherewithal to look remorseful when she realized that her rumor had created this mess.

"Imagine my shock when I see none other than Miss Rowntree appear from behind the trees once Miss Putnam left," Lord Haddock said with a mock look of shock on his face. "Seeing you with *her*, I could not help but become suspicious."

"Suspicious of what?" Royce's tone turned to ice as he looked at the man who was like a nightmare that never fully went away.

"Your duplicity, Your Grace. I saw you kissing Miss Rowntree. I am only sorry that my sneeze interrupted the moment. It was a rather enjoyable thing to watch."

Royce shuddered in revulsion when Lord Haddock revealed he had been observing them in the garden. He obviously found pleasure in his depravity.

"The noise in the garden. That was you I heard?" Della asked, looking like she might be sick.

"Guilty." Lord Haddock grinned. "I did not know if my suspicions of there being something between you two would prove correct, so I followed Miss Rowntree as well. It was not until I heard Miss Rowntree and your sister conversing in the park that I was certain of what was going on."

"That is how you knew about the lemon tarts!" Della interrupted.

"Yes." Lord Haddock nodded his head at Della. "The Duchess invited me to join you on the outing to the ruins, and I used that to my advantage to do what was asked of me."

"And what was that?" Mr. Rowntree asked.

In his anger, Royce had forgotten Mr. Rowntree was standing next to him. It must have been difficult to stand there and listen to this man speaking of Della in such a disrespectful way, with no regard for her dignity.

"Why, to get rid of her," Lord Haddock calmly replied in an unsettling tone.

"Shut up! Say no more!" Filled with rage, Lord Milton's face contorted into a fiery shade of red. "You have done enough damage already."

"I did as you asked, and when she did not agree to marry me, I tried to remove her from the picture—" Lord Haddock pointed at the viscount— "so that your daughter could marry your *precious duke*! The man I hired did what he could, but unfortunately for us, the Duchess here is rather resistant to being killed!" He gestured wildly.

"Are you saying the man who pushed Della down the stairs at the ruins is the same man that drove the hackney, cut the axle on the carriage, and chased her down in the park?" Royce's voice grew louder as he clinched his fists at his sides.

"Yes, except the axel on the carriage." Lord Haddock scowled. "That was me," he grumbled, obviously displeased it had not had the outcome he had hoped for.

"Father!" Emma begged. "Please! Do not do this."

"Shut up, girl. You could have saved us all the trouble if you had just managed to hold on to the duke. I knew your grip was tenuous at best, and so I did what needed to be done to ensure your marriage to him," Lord Milton shouted at Emma.

"Lord Haddock found out why Her Grace was getting in the way. I told him to either secure her hand in marriage so that he might use her dowry to pay off his debts or remove her from the picture, regardless of the outcome." Spittle flew from his mouth as his words seethed out with his rage. "But time and time again, he failed."

"That comes as no surprise," Royce said matter-of-factly.

Lord Haddock had obviously taken offense at the comment and stalked toward Royce, but Mr. Rowntree stepped forward and punched the man square in the jaw, knocking him unconscious.

"That is becoming a good look for him," Royce said to no one in particular as he stood over Lord Haddock's prone form.

"I DO NOT CARE!" The pistol in Lord Milton's hand shook with his fury. "It was to be our family's blood that ran through the veins of the next duke, not *hers*..." He gestured at Della. "MINE!"

"If you think I will ever give Della up, think again. I will bring the full force of my family's name down upon your head and see they put you away for the rest of your miserable life."

"Very well, Your Grace, if that is how you want this to end."

Royce's heart raced as he heard the distinct sound of the hammer being cocked. Without hesitation, he sprinted towards Della, feeling a surge of adrenaline pumping through his veins.

Out of nowhere, a figure materialized, swiftly placing itself between Della and the pistol, as the deafening sound of a gunshot pierced the air.

The sound warbled around the ships, and Royce watched on as the figure crumpled to the ground.

Chapter 29

The faint creaking of a spring being stretched caused Della to turn away from Royce and look directly down the barrel of a pistol.

She closed her eyes and shied away as a loud scream quickly masked the sound of the gunshot. But who had screamed Della did not know.

With the silence settling around them, she turned her attention to Royce, and their shocked gazes locked in a moment of disbelief, realizing that neither of them had been harmed.

"No!" Della cried out when she glanced down to see Emma lying motionless at her feet.

All at once, several people appeared on the dock. Desmond and Mr. Rowntree surrounded Lord Milton as Maggie rushed to help Della. They ripped strips of fabric from their chemises and held them to Emma's shoulder, attempting to stop the blood flowing from the wound as much as possible.

Lord Milton looked down at Emma, who had bravely taken the bullet for Della, with disgust. There was no hint of worry or sign of remorse showing in his face for having shot his own daughter. And his attitude suggested that he held no regard for her well-being, as if whether she lived or died did not matter to him.

Della's heart ached for Emma, after seeing a glimpse of what she must have had to endure with this man as her father.

As she tended to Emma's wound, Della saw her own father press a pistol he got from Grayson against the viscount's back and guide the man away from his daughter.

And with the help of Desmond, Aden tossed Lord Haddock over his shoulder, and dumped him into the carriage at Lord Milton's feet. Mr. Rowntree offered to ride back to Derrington Chase with them to ensure they did not escape or cause any more trouble.

Accepting another loaded pistol from Desmond, Mr. Rowntree climbed up to sit in the seat next to the driver, because he was afraid of what he might do to the men who tried to have his daughter shipped to America if he sat inside with them. On a ship he owned, no less.

Della did not know what would happen to either of the men being carted away, but she did not care so long as they never graced her presence again. Grayson's hands moved with great care as he picked Emma up, making sure not to disturb the bandage that had just been placed on her wound.

"I will take her to the estate and have the doctor called immediately," Grayson said, cradling Emma's body against his. "I will see if Mother can watch over her until someone in her family can be contacted."

"The extra carriage I asked Mother to send just arrived. You can use that to take Miss Putnam back," Maggie said.

"Ever the planner, dear sister." Grayson walked down the dock and placed Miss Putnam gently on the floor between the seats, using the coat off his back as a pillow for her head, and climbed in with her.

Strong arms wrapped around Della's waist as she watched them leave and prayed Emma would be all right. "We owe Emma everything, Royce."

"I know, and I promise to do everything in our power to see she is taken care of. But right now, she is in the best of hands. Grayson will let nothing happen to her and see that she gets the care she needs." Royce walked in front of Della and turned to face her. "What I am currently worried about is the fact that I never told you that...I mean, are you...Della..." Royce could not seem to form a full sentence.

"I will be fine," Della said as she gently cupped his cheek. "As Lord Haddock said, I am rather resistant to being killed. I must be, otherwise—"she took Royce's hands and guided them to her stomach—"how are we to meet our son or daughter?"

"So, when you asked Lord Milton about being with child, you were not lying?"

The look of shock on Royce's face nearly made Della laugh.

"Oh, how wonderful!" Maggie exclaimed, clapping her hands together.

"Y-You mean, w-we are going to be...I-I am going to be—" Royce stuttered.

Della smiled and nodded. "Yes. The doctor came to the estate while you all were out, er, riding."

"Is that why mother sent me to town with Aden on that pointless shopping trip?!" Maggie asked.

Royce sank to his knees before Della until his eyes were level with her stomach and gently wrapped his arms around her. "To think I could have lost you both."

"Shh, Royce, we are alive and safe, thanks to Emma."

Royce kissed her stomach and stood, cupping her face in his hands.

"I love you, Della," Royce said, placing a kiss on her lips. "I have been such a fool." He gently used his thumb to wipe away a tear as it streamed down her cheek. "Please, do not cry. I am only sorry it took me so long to say those three words. Now that I have, I feel as though I cannot say them enough."

"I am not crying because you said you loved me, though I am overcome with sheer happiness at the thought. I am crying because you finally admitted you are a fool," Della said jokingly.

"The biggest." Royce chuckled as he smiled warmly at her.

"So, if he is a fool, what does that make you?" Maggie looked at Aden. "An idiot?"

"Better an idiot than a fool in love with you," Aden remarked dryly as he clasped his hands behind his back. The lightness of the moment dissipated with Aden's unkind words.

Maggie took a deep breath, and with fire in her eyes, she marched straight up to Aden. The sound of his face being slapped echoed around the shipyard.

"Go to Hell." Maggie met Aden's eyes in silent challenge.

"Only if you promise me you will not be there."

"Oh, I can assure you I will not be." Maggie looked at Desmond. "Will you take me home? We can take the carriage Lord Milton left behind. I will see you all later," she said to Royce and Della as Desmond followed her.

Della and Royce watched them leave as Aden stormed toward his horse, not saying a single word. He gathered up the reins and swung himself into the saddle. Della wondered what could have possibly happened between Aden and Maggie to have caused such a divide between them.

"Royce."

"Leave it for another day," Royce said to her. "For now, let us just celebrate the fact we are here, we are safe, and that this one—" he placed his hand on Della's stomach—"is too."

"I love you." Della smiled.

"If I ever take those three words for granted again, you have my permission to kick me out of our bed."

"You are a fool." Della laughed.

"I am, but I am *your* fool," Royce said, touching his forehead to hers. "Your Foolish Duke."

Epilogue

Derrington Chase
February 1813

The Green Room

"Royce is already a wreck. Could you two cease your petty squabbling until after the baby is born?" Grayson looked at Maggie and Aden as Royce paced in front of the bedroom door.

"I need to be in there with her," Royce said in a panicked voice as another moan came from the other side of the door. "Or perhaps not." He sat in the vacant chair next to the door and raked his hands through his hair.

"I think it will be a girl," Desmond said, breaking a moment of quiet.

"Boy," Maggie and Aden said simultaneously as they glared at each other.

"Girl," Grayson added, breaking the tension.

"Well, that is two for a boy and two for a girl. Brother, you are the tiebreaker." Desmond clapped Royce on the back.

"I do not care either way as long as Della and the baby are healthy." Royce's comment was interrupted when he heard a tiny wail.

After what felt like an eternity, the door opened, and a nurse smiled at Royce. "You can come in now, Your Grace."

In his eagerness to get into the room, Royce tripped over his chair, causing him to stumble into the room. He would have been embarrassed, but it quickly faded when he saw Della sitting on the bed, her tired but content smile putting him at ease.

"Will you come to say hello to your daughter?" she asked, cradling the newborn infant.

"Daughter?" Royce nervously made his way to Della's side. With a mix of excitement and fear, he reached down and felt the weight of the babe as Della placed her in his arms.

"Hello, little one. We have been waiting for you." Royce met Della's loving gaze, and he felt a warmth spread through his chest, as if he had finally unlocked the secret of what it meant to love and be loved in return. "What shall we name her?"

"I was thinking Nell, after my mother, and Wilhelmina after yours."

"Nell Wilhelmina Derrington it is," he said, as he gazed down at his daughter with more love than he thought he could ever feel.

Royce placed his finger into his daughter's hand, marveling at the perfect tiny creature they had made when Della's breath hitched, and he saw her hands clutching at her stomach.

The doctor rushed to her side as she let out a quick scream, and the nurse guided Royce and their newborn daughter out of the way, giving the doctor more room to work.

"What is it? What is going on?" Royce demanded, as Della let out another a cry of pain. With his daughter in his arms, he stood there, a sense of helplessness washing over him, as the doctor attended to his beloved wife, who he loved more and more with each passing day.

"What is happening, Your Grace—"the doctor finally said, between Della's moans—"is that you are now the proud father of twins. One girl and...one boy."

The doctor smiled at Royce as he handed the babe to the nurse and turned to take care of Della. After cleaning the babe up and swaddling him in a small blanket, the nurse placed him in Royce's other arm.

"You and your mother gave us quite the scare. Please refrain from doing so in the future. My heart cannot handle it." Royce heard a laugh and looked up to see Della smiling, looking more beautiful than ever.

"Well, what shall we name our little surprise?" Della asked as the nurse helped her to sit up.

"What about Reginald after my father and Ezra after yours?" Royce suggested, letting Della lift their son from his arms.

"Reginald Ezra Derrington," Della said lovingly.

"May we come in?" Maggie asked, nearly jumping out of her skin with excitement.

"Yes, of course." Della smiled brightly.

"Everyone else will visit later. They thought it best not to overwhelm you all at once," Maggie said as she, Aden, Desmond, and Grayson all piled into the room.

"May I present Nell Wilhelmina Derrington," Royce said, holding the babe so everyone could see her. "And her brother, Reginald Ezra Derrington," he added, looking at Della.

"There are two?!" Maggie exclaimed.

"Trust me, we are just as surprised as you are!" Royce laughed.

"My goodness, two more Derringtons. Mother will be elated!" Desmond smiled.

"Maggie and Aden, we have a question for both of you. We were hoping—" Della paused and looked at Royce.

"That you would do us the great honor of being godparents to these two." Royce continued. "With uncles like Grayson and Desmond they will need all the help they can get." Royce's eyes twinkled with laughter.

"What did we ever do to you?" Desmond asked in pretend outrage.

"I do not think you want Royce to answer that." Grayson clapped his brother on the shoulder and laughed.

"You want me to be a godmother?" Tears formed in Maggie's eyes.

Aden cleared his throat.

"What?" Maggie asked, planting her hands on her hips.

"Are you sure you are the right person for such a job?" Aden asked, taking a jab at her.

"And you are worthy of such a title yourself?"

Aden hesitated for a moment, as if he was about to argue, but then he put on a smile and turned to Della and Royce.

"I congratulate you both, and I will, of course, gladly accept. I could think of no greater honor. We better let the new family get some rest," he said, ushering everyone out of the room. "Beauty before smarts." He bowed to Maggie, waving her through the door.

"Then you should go first," Maggie said with a false smile.

Aden simply nodded and left without saying another word.

"Congratulations again. I love you both...well now the four of you." Maggie smiled before closing the door softly behind her.

Della sighed. "Royce?"

"Hmm?" Royce responded, smiling down at his daughter.

"Maggie and Aden—"

"What about them?"

"Do you think they truly believe in their dislike of one another?"

Royce sat gently on the bed and kissed Della soundly on the lips. "Who can say, What Fools Believe?"

A Little Bit of Pastry

Food played a crucial role in the daily lives of individuals during the regency era, just as it had for centuries leading up to the 19th century and continues to do so today. And as a culinary graduate, I could talk endlessly about the profound impact of food, not just as sustenance, but also as a key element of our social interactions.

Coming together around the dinner table with my dear friends and cherished family members has always held great significance for us, as it allows us to foster deep and lasting connections.

Through countless meals, we have deepened our bond in the exchanging of stories, laughter, and tears. That is why many scenes in my current and upcoming novels have so many moments revolving around food.

There is a heartwarming moment in the park where Royce and Della have a sweet interaction, which occurs when Della takes her first bite of a certain pastry. The pastry I am referring to is a petite duchesse, more commonly known today as an éclair.

According to food historians, Marie-Antoine Carême, a 19th century French chef, is believed to have created this wonderful little pastry. During that time, he was seen as being on par with the celebrity chefs of today.

In the novel, there are multiple instances where Royce and Della enjoy the company of each other while indulging in the deliciousness of a petite duchesse. This sweet treat also served as a secret code word between them.

The term petite duchesse, or 'little duchess', was used in France and England alike, until about 1850, when the use of éclair became more prominent. The term éclair means 'flash of lightning' because it is eaten quickly or in a flash.

Della mentions that, "the pastry was light with a soft crunch, the custard rich and sweet, and the chocolate..."

The process begins by blending butter, water, flour, and eggs together to form a smooth dough known as Choux, which is then piped into small straight lines. The pastry is carefully baked until it reaches a perfect golden brown, offering a delightful crunch on the outside and a hollow interior.

Once cooled, it is usually filled with luscious custard or fluffy whipped cream, though a plethora of other delicious fillings can be used, and is often adorned with a delectable flavored icing or rich chocolate.

One of my favorite aspects of culinary school was the days spent baking, where the kitchen would come alive with the sounds of whirring mixers and sizzling pans. The enticing scents of freshly baked pastries and sweets permeated the hallways, attracting students from other parts of the building who would stop by to observe us.

Our teacher, a chef of great acclaim from England, brought a wealth of culinary expertise to our class. Queen Elizabeth even recognized his exceptional talent in baking and presented him with a prestigious award for his service to the Royal household.

To say that I learned from the best would be a massive understatement!

I invite you to visit my website, www.ebfeatherston.com, and check out my cookbook nook for recipes and a little bit of history behind the foods and drinks mentioned in my novels!

About the Author

E.B. Featherston is just a girl from Kentucky, with a love of reading and writing, and a culinary degree. You can usually find her chasing her three kids around or with her head buried so far into a book, she forgets the outside world exists.

She loves hanging out with family and friends, playing board games or cards, and sewing/cosplay. Halloween is her favorite holiday, and she is constantly coming up with new themes every year to decorate. Her themes range from pirate and viking, to fairytales, and beyond. She even dresses as a zombie and takes part in her city's annual thriller parade!

Her love of reading and writing, though she has always enjoyed it, really blossomed when she was in the 8th grade. And unlike her first-grade writing teacher—who was disparaging and said she would never make it as a writer—her 8th grade English teacher was the exact opposite.

He was an amazing person, who inspired and promoted her love of reading and writing. He showed his students that just because you cannot travel physically to a new world or place does not mean you cannot travel there in your mind.

E.B. will never be able to thank him enough for the inspiration he instilled in her at such a young age.

She truly hopes you have enjoyed reading Royce and Della's story as much as she loved writing it.